HER FROZEN MEMORIES
A ROCKY POINT WEDDING BOOK THREE

VANIA RHEAULT

 Created with Vellum

ABOUT THE BOOK

Logan Draper hates Rocky Point.

He never intended to come back, but when his best friend asks him to be a groomsman in a wedding being held in their hometown, he has to accept.

His father's fists aren't the only thing he left behind.

When he escaped to go to college, he barely said goodbye to his high school sweetheart, and in eighteen years, they never contacted each other.

But after an accidental encounter, he admits that even after all this time he still loves her.

What can he do to make her give him another chance?

A chance he doesn't deserve.

Ivy Graves hates Logan Draper with all her heart.

Abandoned by her high school love and best friend, she's dealt with her own tragedies since he left.

Now he's back, asking for forgiveness and another chance.

She knows how to take care of herself. She doesn't need Logan.

But does she love him enough to learn to trust him again, or should she tell him to go to hell . . . a place she's been living for the past eighteen years?

CHAPTER ONE

"Hey, I'm glad you're still here! I need you to do something for me."

Ivy Graves slid her prepaid phone out of the pocket of her black uniform slacks. Midnight. She still had two hours left of her shift. Where else would she be?

She'd do the same tomorrow. Hilary had given her another shift. She didn't know how long she'd be able to get away with the overtime. She swore to God that whenever Desiree walked by the lounge and saw her working, the resort's manager did a quick mental calculation of her hours. So far Stacy, their payroll and HR girl, hadn't said anything, but she'd approve her overtime for only so long. The holidays helped. The resort was always short-staffed because everyone wanted to spend time with their families.

She didn't have anything to celebrate.

"What do you need?" she asked, drawing another draft for a man sitting near the window overlooking the slopes.

Karen, one of the cooks in the kitchen, held out an insulated to-go bag. "Logan Draper in Cabin A ordered a midnight snack just before we stopped taking orders for the night. I thought I was safe and let Cherry go home. I'm closing down. Can you run it over?"

She served the man his beer and glared at Karen on her way back to the bar. Dammit. The resort operated on a skeleton crew past midnight. "Can't you ask whoever's at the front desk to do it?"

"Drew's having a computer problem and needs to figure it out before the morning checkouts. Please?" Karen asked, shaking the bag.

She scowled. She didn't want to go out into the cold. She didn't want to deliver food. Not for a jerk like Logan Draper.

She'd been lucky so far. Avoiding him. It helped he stayed in one of the cabins and not in the resort.

"This is your fault," she said, wringing a rag in her hands. "I shouldn't leave the bar."

"It will only take a second. He already put the tip on a credit card. Shove the box in his hands and hurry back. Hilary's done it for me a couple of times. What's the big deal?"

It wasn't a big deal and had it been anyone but Logan, her ex-boyfriend from high school, she would've been halfway down the trail already, enjoying the unexpected break.

"Fine," she muttered.

"I owe you one," Karen said, dropping the insulated bag on the bar. "Cabin A."

"I heard you."

Karen hurried through the side door and into the hallway to finish cleaning the kitchen. The day cook would come in at four to prep breakfast for the guests who liked to get an early start.

She dried her hands and grabbed her jacket out of the stockroom.

Despite giving Karen a hard time, she didn't rush down the snowy path, the bag holding Logan's meal bumping against her hip. Occasionally a hint of garlic caught her nose and her stomach rumbled. It'd been too many hours since she ate dinner.

Snow crunched under her cheap tennis shoes, and her breath blew white in the frozen air. The sub-zero temperatures cleared her head, and the stars were pretty when she took a moment to appreciate them. Which wasn't often. Most days she was too tired to bother.

Through large windows that looked over the path and trees, Cabin A's lights blazed. Cabin B was dark, as was Cabin C, but Mitch said that cabin's wiring was messed up and no one could stay there until an electrician looked at it.

She envied Mitch. He met Callie when he thought he'd never find anyone to love him. A firefighter, Callie understood what hell Mitch went through trying to save those little girls. She was just what he needed to put the past in the past.

A relationship with Mitch would have been easy and safe, but she could see how much happier Callie made him, and deep down, she knew she never would've been able to do that for him.

Or he for her.

Only one man had ever made her feel loved.

And she stood outside his cabin.

She hadn't seen Logan since the day after high school graduation. He'd taken off with James Fox and never looked back. Not even once.

Forcing herself up the porch, she tried to calm the ball of nerves rolling around in her stomach.

She didn't still love him. No one could love a man she hadn't seen in eighteen years.

That's too much time gone.

Still, the could-have-beens haunted her, and that was her fault because she hadn't moved on. Found someone else. Unlike Mitch, her past would always be her future, and she faced it with steely resignation.

Treat him like any other guest and get your ass back to the bar, she told herself. Even at this late hour, the lounge shouldn't go unattended very too long.

She knocked on the wooden door, and footfalls sounded on the other side. The door creaked open, and Logan stood there in a University of Decatur sweatshirt and a pair of worn jeans.

His eyes were the same, though the frames of his glasses were different than the kind he wore in high school.

He smiled, and the years fell away.

Logan Draper pushed a smile to his mouth. He'd known, on some level, he'd see Ivy up close and personal, but he hadn't anticipated how much it would hurt.

"Come in," he said, widening the door.

She kicked the snow off her shoes and stepped inside.

Just one step.

Like he was a serial killer.

Or an artist asking her to look at his etchings. He already knew what was under her clothes.

"You can come in farther," he said, "so I can shut the door?"

She moved to the side instead, and he bit the inside of his cheek to keep from swearing.

They used to be friends.

Apparently, they weren't anymore. Not that he expected they would be. Enemies now, more like, but it's better he knew what he was dealing with.

"Karen said you tipped already, charged it to your room or whatever," she said, digging into the bag at her side.

She shoved the takeout box at him that held the spaghetti and garlic sticks he suddenly had the urge to order. The person taking his room service request hadn't been pleased, either, though she tried not to let it show, and it had made him feel like a huge inconvenience. So did Ivy's scowl.

"Anything else?" she asked, securing the Velcro on the bag and straightening.

He gripped the takeout box, the plastic container giving beneath his fingertips, his appetite dwindling with every second she wouldn't meet his eyes.

"Do you really hate me, Ivy?"

She met his gaze for the first time since she stepped into the cabin.

The hard look took him aback, but it shouldn't have. He hadn't completely shut himself off from Rocky Point, and he'd heard about the things that happened.

"I don't feel anything for you. Enjoy your stay." She slammed out of the cabin and into the darkness.

Stupidly, he worried about her walking back to the resort alone.

And more stupid, he wished she would have torn into him. Made him pay for the misery he put on her face.

He wanted her hate.

Hate would be better than nothing at all.

Ivy counted out her register.

Nothing had been amiss when she came back. No one was waiting to order a drink, no one needed a refill. Dollar bills were shoved into the tip jar near the register, and she didn't have to share them with anyone. Besides the time and a half, that was another reason she liked working the longer shifts. There were evenings she'd walk away with a hundred dollars or more. She stashed that money into her emergency account.

She was saving for more than a rainy day.

There weren't many cars in the staff parking lot, and because she'd worked at the resort for so long, she knew what everyone drove.

Mitch's truck and the bright pink rectangles was easy to pick out. Drew's old Jeep. Karen's station wagon.

Her little Toyota Camry sat under a parking lot light discreetly plugged into an outlet used for God knew what, but in the winter months, the forgotten outlet had saved her quite a few times from being stranded. The Toyota's engine did not like the cold.

Even plugging it in sometimes didn't help, and she said a quick prayer every time she started her car.

Mitch would give her a ride if she ever needed it, but now that he and Callie were together, she always ran the risk of interrupting them. He told her Marnie's parents were letting Callie sleep at their house while Mitch's mom and dad stayed in her room at the resort, but she knew Callie slept in Mitch's room more often than not. So far, Desiree hadn't said anything, but since he'd given his notice, Ivy wasn't sure she would.

She didn't want to feel like a pesky little sister always hanging around. Besides, he was moving to Decatur with his parents after the new year. The sooner she stopped thinking she could depend on him, the better.

She unplugged her car, struggling to separate the extension cord from the block heater, and threw the cord into the backseat. "Please, God, I'll keep doing my best to be a good person if You see me home safely."

Not an overly religious person, she didn't go to church, but it didn't stop her from throwing up the little prayer every time she started her car and tonight He came through for her one more time.

She rested her forehead against the cold steering wheel and willed her muscles to relax. After fourteen hours on her feet, her legs ached something terrible, and even as exhausted as her long shifts made her, sometimes her restless leg syndrome kept her awake.

He looked good though. She hadn't expected him not to. Expensive haircut, designer glasses. Even his casual clothes looked expensive.

Nothing from a crappy little department store for Logan Draper. Not anymore.

And that cabin didn't come cheap. For two weeks!

She wouldn't bother to add up how much that would come to after taxes and fees, but it'd pay her rent for a few months. She was certain of that.

She drove through Rocky Point to the outskirts of town, away from the lake and the pretty houses along the shore.

Instead, she guided her car farther inland, past Main Street and the smaller hotels. Past the fast food joints and the Country Kitchen to a small, rundown residential section where apartments in the low-income program were located.

After the paper mill closed, a few of the employees had chosen to move into the building or its sister complex next door. Rather than leave the area, they made do with what the mill threw at them in severance pay and the government benefits they were suddenly qualified for.

She parked in an empty spot away from the front door and snaked the extension cord from her car's block heater to an outlet in the side of the building. So far she hadn't been told she couldn't, and she'd use the building's electricity until she had to figure out something else. No one plugged their cars in besides her. Most of the tenants didn't have a job, or if they did, they rode the bus. Because Rocky Point was so small, only one bus ran, and the hours were limited. If she rode the bus to work, she had to ask Mitch to drive her home or call a taxi.

She and her mom lived in a corner unit on the second floor, and she did her best to make the apartment as cheerful as she could.

Her mother sat on the sofa, booze glazing her eyes over, clutching a framed photo of her brother.

She clicked the TV off, an infomercial playing on one of the fuzzy local channels. She didn't pay for cable. They owned a secondhand DVD player, and sometimes in the summer her mother sobered up enough to search rummage sales for cheap movies. These days, everybody streamed what they wanted to watch, but she couldn't afford internet.

Watching TV didn't interest her anyway. Usually too exhausted to focus on anything, she went to bed. On her days off she did laundry and cleaned and wished she was at work.

She covered her mother with a blanket and kissed her forehead.

"Ivy," her mother mumbled.

"I'm home, Mom. Go to sleep."

They were lucky and had been assigned a two-bedroom unit, but most nights her mother slept on the couch she'd scrimped to buy. The kind man at the furniture store had thrown in a forty-inch flat-screen TV they'd used as a sales floor display and free delivery.

She remembered people who were kind in case she could ever return the favor.

She remembered people who had not been kind, like Logan, who had barely taken five minutes to say goodbye.

By the light of the stove bulb, she heated up a bowl of soup in the microwave. Exhausted, she sipped her soup and groaned as she heaved herself up off the chair. Her shift had made her more tired than usual.

Or had that been seeing Logan? What had he asked her? Did she hate him?

She rinsed her bowl out and loaded it into the dishwasher, laughing bitterly. She'd been civil at least, and she'd enjoyed the hurt that shot through his eyes.

She crawled into bed and set her alarm to go off at ten the next morning. That gave her time to shower, make breakfast, and drive to the resort. Her shift started at noon.

This was her life.

Wash. Rinse. Repeat.

Logan didn't eat the spaghetti after Ivy stumbled off the cabin's porch and into the snow. He stored the meal in the fridge instead and took off his jeans and sweatshirt.

In a pair of boxers, he flopped onto the bed and bunched a feather pillow under his head.

Stared at the ceiling.

They'd always been friends. In kindergarten, she walked with him to the bathroom because he was too scared to go alone. In first grade, she shared her crayons and glue because he was one of the few kids who didn't bring school supplies to class.

In second and third, she read Choose Your Own Adventure books to him on the playground, urging him to make the choices of what the character should do next.

In fourth and fifth, she helped him do his math homework.

She'd always been smarter than him. Proved it in sixth, seventh, and eighth grades when they were paired up to do projects.

Someone, somewhere, had smiled on him and kept his guardian angel by his side through school.

Ninth and tenth grades they shared the same classes, and one afternoon, toward the end of their sophomore year, hiding from his father, they sat in their secret place near the water, a rocky beach hidden by lush evergreens, writing their English papers in longhand in beat-up notebooks.

She stood to stretch and waded into the water. Cold in May, but she didn't seem to mind.

And with the sun shining above her like a halo and a joy on her face she only showed when they were together, his heart dipped.

Jean shorts and a tank top, the strap falling down her shoulder, blue eyes laughing, her hair a wild mess like it had been tonight, and suddenly Ivy was more than a childhood friend.

The birds chirped in the trees, the leaves rustling in the breeze that blew her hair into her face.

He drank her in, all five feet one inch of her, and her smile faded as the atmosphere changed.

Their friendship disappeared and something else replaced it, and he'd never regretted anything more in his life.

No, that wasn't true. He didn't regret that afternoon he kissed her, water lapping at their feet, a boat's motor drowning out the slamming of his heart.

He didn't regret how sweet she tasted, or how she clutched at his old t-shirt when he prodded her lips with his tongue.

He regretted everything else that came afterward, and that was a lot of regret.

It didn't stop his cock from hardening when he thought about her slim, tanned thighs or the delicate gold ankle bracelet she used to wear.

Groaning, he shifted on the bed and resisted the urge to get himself off. He'd betrayed her enough without using her teenage vision to assuage his guilt.

There wasn't any way to make what he'd done to her go away.

There wasn't any way he could make it up to her.

He'd done what he'd done, and no amount of apology could fix it.

But God, he could still taste her kisses, the last one salty with tears when he told her goodbye.

He decided to eat breakfast in the dining room. Maybe James and Marnie would be there. But besides one of James's cousins, he didn't see anyone he knew, and he sat alone at a small table near a window that looked over the lake.

"You've been avoiding me," Autumn Bennett said, sliding into the seat across from him and hanging her jacket and bag off the back of her chair. She raised a white coffee mug at a waitress, and the waitress waved at her in return.

He stifled a sigh. "No, I haven't."

She laughed. "Yes, you have." She ticked the list off on her fingers. "You managed to not talk to me at Marnie's meet and greet. I didn't see you ice fishing. Did you hear Leah fell through the ice? You didn't talk to me at the pool party, conveniently playing water volleyball with James the whole night. You didn't show up at Marnie's fancy dinner, and you missed all the excitement seeing Rita back in town."

He didn't give a shit about Rita. In high school, Rita had been a goddess, and Logan, a bug under a rock. A spoiled woman who threw everything away because she wanted more than the good life Jared Hollister gave her. Jared leveled up, as far as he was concerned. Marnie told him about Leah helping Helen at the Supply Company. There weren't many people like that around anymore. Who cared simply because they did. "Rita's a bitch. Always has been."

Autumn's eyes widened. "Someone got up on the wrong side of the bed this morning."

He hadn't gotten any sleep. Dreams, no, nightmares,

about Ivy kept him up all night. The feel of her hair wound around his fingers. The scent of sunshine and lake water on her skin.

And something else.

A feeling.

Loss. It left him hollow inside, and he'd woken with tears in his eyes.

"I didn't sleep well last night."

The waitress came by their table and filled their mugs. "Are you going to order something, Autumn?" she asked.

Autumn paused. She didn't have a menu. "Could I have . . . never mind. I'll have the breakfast buffet."

"Sure thing. Go up when you're ready," the waitress said.

He wanted to hide in his cabin, but Autumn had a point. He'd managed to dodge her for the past week, and he wouldn't be able to do that much longer.

"I'll be right back," she said, and she hurried to the buffet like she thought he'd disappear while she loaded eggs onto her plate.

It was tempting to slip out now, but then Marnie would be after him. So far Autumn hadn't complained, but she would.

Fucking blog. He didn't want anyone to know he was in Rocky Point, though it really didn't matter. There wasn't anyone in town who would care. Not even his old man. He'd been keeping to himself, hoping these two weeks would go by without a hitch, and it had worked, until Ivy showed up on his cabin's porch.

That risk was what he signed up for when he agreed to be James's groomsman. He hadn't wanted to, either, but James had done so much for him he would have been a downright prick to refuse.

So here he was, sitting in the middle of a town he didn't want to be in, yet should have come back to long ago.

Autumn walked back to the table, a pile of scrambled eggs and a stack of bacon on her plate.

"Going low-carb?" he asked.

"What? Oh, no. I probably should though. If I keep partying like I have been, I'll be twenty pounds heavier when Marnie and James go back to Decatur."

He sipped his coffee and asked, "How have you been?"

She pulled an iPad that had a detachable keyboard out of her bag and moved the salt and pepper shakers aside to make space. "I'm okay. Same thing, you know? I'm glad wedding stuff is going on. It gives me something to blog about."

"You've done a good job. I *did* hear about Leah, by the way. Is she okay?"

"She seems to be. Got bad news, and she's back in New York for a few days."

He narrowed his eyes. "Was the bad news Rita's back in town? I don't suppose she particularly cared to see her hanging all over Jared."

She stared, her lips parted, holding a piece of bacon halfway to her mouth.

That was one of the things that scared him about coming back to Rocky Point. He had his sources, but sources could be wrong. He couldn't stand the thought of Ivy with someone. He hadn't heard she was dating anyone, though rumors swirled around her and Mitch Sinclair. He did a little sniffing around when he checked in, but all anyone said was that Mitch had gotten hung up on one of Marnie's bridesmaids.

Nothing more about Ivy except she worked herself to death.

"Her grandma had a stroke," she said. "What's your problem?"

"Nothing. Sorry."

"Are you okay?" She touched his hand.

Needing the connection, he flipped his hand over and laced their fingers together. He hadn't been particularly close to Autumn, though back then she'd been one of those rare students who could talk to anyone and not get any flack for it.

"Yes. No. I haven't been back to Rocky Point for eighteen years. I feel . . ."

"Out of place?"

"Maybe." How could he explain that it was more than feeling out of place? Like, more than not belonging.

He didn't want to be here.

But then he saw Ivy last night and wished he'd come back sooner.

She tugged her hand away and started typing.

Apparently, the interview started, but he had to give her credit. She kept the questions light and never asked about his parents.

Or Ivy.

When she took those two things out of the equation, he was surprised she had anything left to ask him.

"That wasn't so bad, was it?" she asked, shoving her iPad into her bag. "I won't do anything that bothers you."

"It was fine. Thanks."

"I'll leave you alone now, but if you ever want to talk . . . let me know."

The words were out before he could stop them. "How's Ivy been?"

She stood, tugged on her jacket, and hung her massive bag from her shoulder. She circled the table and kissed his cheek. "About the same as the rest of us." She weaved her way around the tables and walked out of the dining room.

About the same as the rest of us.

So, in other words, not very good at all.

He needed air, and after breakfast, he bundled up in his jacket and gloves. Working with James and seeing him and Marnie on a regular basis, he'd been on the ground floor of Marnie's wedding plans and had known to pack everything he needed for all her ridiculous outdoor activities.

He stood on one of the resort's docks, the wind whipping him in the face. The sky sparkled bright blue, not a cloud in the sky.

Fuck, it was cold out here. He should've worn a hat.

"Hey, I was looking for you," James said, walking over the snow-covered planks.

He flicked a glance over his shoulder. "What's up?"

James jammed his hands into the pockets of his coat. "Nothing. Marnie bumped into Autumn and Autumn said she pissed you off. Are you good? It takes a lot to piss you off."

"Yeah, I'm okay. I'll apologize to her later. Her stupid blog interview put me on edge, that's all."

"All right. If you're sure. I'll probably run into town later and hang out with Mom and Dad if you want to come along."

"No. I'm fine, thanks."

"Okay. Catch you later, then." James turned to go.

"Do you have any regrets?" he asked.

James lifted his shoulders and let them drop. "Do you

mean in school? Yeah. Like that one party we went to the night before we took our mid-terms. I could have aced those tests if I wouldn't have been hungover. Or when I took that history class thinking learning about World War Two would be awesome when I should have taken another English class."

"Just little things then."

"I guess. How about you?"

"I saw Ivy last night. I ordered room service, and she delivered it."

"You knew she worked here, that you'd bump into her sooner or later."

"Yeah. I saw her, and it was like these eighteen years never happened. It's so stupid, I wanted . . ." He swallowed and focused on the people ice fishing, black specks moving in the distance.

"What?"

"I should have married her. After graduation. We would've figured it out."

"That would've been a bad move. You know it now, and you knew it then. It's why you didn't. There might be a lot of things you regret in the past eighteen years, but that's not one of them. You were just a kid," James said.

"I know. But I could have helped her, somehow. Maybe Joey would still be alive."

"That's the stupidest thing I ever heard, and I've heard some dumb shit with all this wedding crap going on."

"I guess you're right."

"I *know* I am. Marrying Ivy then wouldn't have done anything for either of you. Ask Jared." James squinted against the sun. "Look, I know you missed her, and if you think she needs help, help her. You can do it better now than when you were an eighteen-year old moron. Besides, be honest with yourself. She wasn't the one who needed help back then. You did, and you helped yourself." James slapped him on the arm, but he didn't feel it. He didn't feel a thing. Help Ivy now? Why didn't he think of that?

"I'm going inside. It's cold out here. Make sure you're free later this week. We have tux fittings, and I want a bachelor party, man. Don't forget."

"Yeah, I got it," he said as James walked away, but his mind was on other things.

He wanted to help Ivy. Try to make up for the last eighteen years.

And for the next eighteen, when, after Marnie and James's wedding, he would say goodbye.

For the last time.

Ivy kicked the tire of her POS car. She knew this would happen, but she hadn't expected it at two o'clock in the morning after a double shift. The *click click click* when she turned the key in the ignition because her alternator finally died. She needed a tow. But before she worried about a tow, she wanted to go home. Get a bite to eat and fall into bed.

She trudged into the resort. There wasn't Uber in Rocky Point. The trend hadn't caught on in the little town, and no one drove for the app. She could call a taxi, but they charged twenty bucks just to pick you up, plus mileage. She would if she had to, but that was Plan Z.

"Hey, Drew." The night auditor, who doubled as the overnight front desk reservationist, looked over from his computer and cup of coffee. The night auditor did paperwork and checked out anyone who wanted or needed to get on the road between four and seven when the day front desk agent took over. "Is Blaine around by chance?"

"Sorry, he went home around ten. No one scheduled a shuttle pickup or drop off. Why?"

"My car won't start."

"Too cold?"

"No." She couldn't tell Drew she plugged her car in and didn't elaborate. "Maybe the battery. Alternator."

"Sorry, kiddo."

"Yeah, thanks. Do you know if Mitch is . . . alone?"

She could ask him to drive her home if Callie wasn't in his room. She still could, he wouldn't mind, but she didn't want to interrupt them. Mitch had early mornings anyway, and while being up at two in the morning was natural for her, for other people it was the middle of the night.

"Can't say. I haven't seen him, and there haven't been any maintenance emergencies. Quiet night, tonight."

"Thanks." She swallowed back tears. She'd have to eat the cost of a taxi ride. "Can you look up RP Taxi for me? I need their number."

"Hang on."

She didn't like using the internet on her prepaid cell phone. It charged her for every minute she was online.

She dialed the number Drew rattled off and requested a pickup.

"We're forty-five minutes out. The bars downtown are letting out."

"I'll wait, thanks."

She pushed her phone into her purse and sank into one of the lobby chairs. The electric fireplace was turned on, and she tried to relax. It wasn't the end of the world. She could afford to have her car repaired, it's why she saved, but feeding the lemon she drove would have to stop one day.

Why keep paying to fix her piece of crap car when she could make payments on one that hopefully wouldn't need so much work.

The automatic doors slid open and a gust of cold air blew into the lobby along with Logan and James. Ivy turned away and squished into her chair, trying to make herself as small as possible. If she couldn't see Logan, maybe Logan couldn't see her. She didn't want to talk to him, didn't want to see him. *Please, just let him go to his cabin.*

"Ivy."

She sighed. No such luck.

Reluctantly, she turned her head and met his eyes.

The cold made his cheeks pink, and the heat fogged his glasses. His blond hair stood up in a disarray, and she wanted to smooth her fingers through it.

She focused her attention on the fake flames flickering in the fireplace.

"What are you doing?"

"Sitting," she muttered. Couldn't he take the hint?

"I'll see you later," James said, his gaze going back and forth between her and Logan, an amused smile on his lips. Or maybe that was the booze. It was obvious they were coming in after a night of drinking.

"Yeah," Logan said, not taking his eyes off her.

Annoyed and tired, she asked, "What do you want?"

He cleared his throat. "Nothing, I guess."

"Good." She unzipped her jacket. She'd be waiting a while, and sweat slid down her back.

He shifted on his feet. "Is there something I can help you with?"

"What are you? Customer service? No, there's nothing you can help me with. Go back to your cabin."

"She's waiting for a taxi. Her car won't start," Drew volunteered.

She shot him a look that could have killed from fifty paces. He shrank back into the office.

Logan brightened. "I can take you home. My car's in the lot."

She wanted to scream. She had no choice but to take Logan up on his offer. She still had half an hour to wait, and his ride would be free.

No, not free. How much would she have to pay to sit next to him, breathe in his cologne and the scent of beer? To sit a foot away from him and pretend she didn't want to launch herself into his lap, wrap her arms around his neck, and tell him how much she missed him.

He didn't deserve that. He didn't deserve one ounce of her forgiveness.

"No. I'm fine on my own."

"I'm sorry, Ivy. For everything."

She would not let his puppy-dog eyes get to her. She would not.

With his shoulders hunched, he turned away.

"Oh, fine!" she huffed. She gave in to help herself, not for him. Never for him. *Take care of yourself, girl, and don't worry about anyone else.*

He whipped around, a smile lighting his face. "Great!"

She zipped her jacket and grabbed her purse off the floor. She couldn't resist giving Drew another glare on her way out the door and he grimaced.

"Which car's yours?" Logan asked.

"I don't park in this lot. Staff parking is behind the building." Thank God. She didn't want him to see what she drove.

"Oh. Right. You'll have to have it towed, I guess," he said, leading her to an SUV.

"No kidding," she mumbled under her breath.

She wanted to sneer at the Mercedes-Benz logo on the front grill, but surprisingly, she was proud of him, too. Logan's childhood had been so crappy, but he escaped and made something of himself.

He opened the door for her. Climbing into the luxurious vehicle, she ignored him, though it went against all her manners not to say thank you. He shut the door, a quiet *thump* in the still night.

"The seat has warmers, if your . . . ah . . . butt's cold," he said, settling behind the wheel.

"No, thanks. It's a short drive."

"Where're we headed?"

"South, toward Country Kitchen." Heat flamed her cheeks, and she was thankful he couldn't see it in the dark. He'd know where she'd been living for the past twelve years. Since . . . since, well, a lot of things.

And she didn't want him to know what she drove. God. So stupid. This was worse. So much worse.

Fatigue weighed on her. She was grateful she worked a regular shift tomorrow, but she wished she could've picked up more hours. On the other hand, she would have the evening to herself, and she'd need to deal with her car while the mechanic's shop was still open.

No rest for the wicked.

Or was that "No rest for the weary?" She never thought of herself as particularly wicked. Unless she counted wanting things she couldn't have.

"Ivy?" he asked, stopping the truck at a red light.

"Oh, turn right. In a few miles, turn left after Country Kitchen. Don't remember much of town, huh?"

Why should he? Nothing good had happened to him here. She wouldn't be so arrogant as to include herself.

"It's changed a lot since high school. When did the shoe store close?"

"A couple years after you left."

"Oh. And the bar on the highway . . ."

"Last year."

"That's too bad."

"When the paper mill closed, everyone's spending money dried up."

"The Country Kitchen's still going strong," he commented, driving past the restaurant.

"Truck stop, college kid hangout. That place will probably always stay open."

She waitressed there, briefly, but she broke too many dishes and quit before they fired her. Bartending wasn't waitressing, fortunately. She'd never waitress again. "Turn left at the light, then right at the next stop sign."

She toyed with the idea of telling him to drop her off somewhere else. Let him go another two miles to the residential section that bordered the cemetery. But she couldn't do that. She told herself a million times there was no shame in being poor and she wouldn't hide where she lived. Not from Logan, not from anyone. The dumpy little house he'd grown up in wasn't any better than the complex she lived in now.

"You can pull over here," she said, pointing to an empty space on the street.

"This is where you live? Ivy."

The pity in his voice made her turn on him. "What the hell am I supposed to do, Logan? You know what happened. I'm doing my best, so leave me the fuck alone like I asked. Stay out of my way, and I'll gladly stay out of yours."

She flew out of the truck and slammed the heavy door shut. Tears blurring her vision, she ran over the snowy lawn and stopped on the crumbling stoop where she fumbled with her key.

Quickly, she looked over her shoulder. He was still parked at the curb but she couldn't tell if he was staring at her or not.

Keeping her sobs tucked tightly in her chest, she ran up the stairs as fast as her tired legs could carry her.

Logan wasted no time the next morning. He'd wanted to help her, and like a gift from God, he knew exactly what he could do.

"What's Ivy's phone number?" he asked the perky redhead who was working the front desk the next morning. Her name tag read Sophia. He vaguely remembered her from when he checked in, but being in Rocky Point agitated him and James and Marnie had given her his information. Hidden in one of the cabins at the back of the resort he'd calmed down . . . at least enough he didn't feel like he was going to have an anxiety attack.

Sophia frowned. "Ivy who?"

Ivy couldn't be that invisible. "The bartender in the lounge."

Her expression cleared. "Oh. Ivy Graves. Sorry, I thought you were talking about a guest. I'm sorry Mr. Draper, but we don't give out information like that."

He leaned against the counter and said, "*Come on,* Sophia. Did you know Ivy and I used to be high school sweethearts?"

"Awww!" Sophia said, slapping her hand over her heart. "What happened?"

"I broke up with her to go to school in Decatur. It was a big mistake. I still love her, you know," he said, leaning closer to the young girl. "You never forget your first love. Are you dating anyone?"

Sophia beamed. "Yeah. Chad and I have been seeing each other for two years!"

"That's great. So you can understand my plight, can't you? I want to do something nice for her."

She worried her bottom lip between her teeth. "Okay, if you promise not to say where you got her number. I love this job. I had to call Stacy, she's the HR lady here, every day for two weeks." She rose on her tiptoes and whispered, "I think she gave it to me so I would quit calling."

"I won't tell a soul."

Her nails clicked against the keyboard. "Her number is 218-555-5489. Sometimes you have to leave a message because she's out of minutes."

"Out of minutes?" What the hell did that mean?

She shrugged. "I think she uses a pay-as-you-go phone. She doesn't seem like the type to have a lot of people calling her anyway, huh? She always seems so sad and lonely."

"Right." He looked up at her from the piece of scrap paper he scrawled Ivy's number on. "Let's change that."

"Good luck, Mr. Draper."

"I'll put in a good word for you with Desiree the next time I see her."

"Thanks! Just don't say anything."

"I won't." He winked. "You can count on me."

Ivy told him to never talk to her again, but he would conveniently forget she said that. He dialed her number and it rang twenty times. He counted. He checked the time. It was ten o'clock. Not early by anyone's standards, and he assumed she had to work today. He didn't know when, and maybe he should have asked Sophia that too, but it was too late now because he was already sitting in his truck letting it warm up before he drove out to her apartment.

He didn't remember that part of town. Had no reason to since he didn't know anyone who lived in the area. Even Ivy and her mom, dad, and brother had lived in a house in a decent neighborhood . . . before all that happened.

It shamed him he read about it in the paper. A small little square near the bottom of page five.

He parked in front of her building and called her again. Maybe the summer months made the outside look more cheerful, flowers blooming and trees a happy green.

"Hello?" Ivy answered, her voice suspicious.

"Hey, this is Logan."

She inhaled sharply, and he waited for her to hang up on him. "What do you want?"

"I thought you'd need help with your car."

"What kind of help? I already called and had it towed to the mechanic's."

"I don't know then. A ride?"

"I don't work until noon."

He deserved this. He deserved everything and more. But it still tried his patience. "How about . . ." How could he get her out of her apartment? "Breakfast?"

"No."

"Jesus Christ, Ivy!" He wanted to slam his hand against his steering wheel, but he didn't in case she heard it. "For old times' sake."

"We don't have old times, Logan. We don't have any times."

But . . . she hadn't hung up on him. That was something. "That's not true, and you know it. Please?"

She paused, and he thought he would suffocate, holding his breath.

"Fine. To thank you for giving me a ride, but that's it. When I told you to leave me alone, I meant it. This is it. Got it? What time are you picking me up?"

"I'm outside your apartment building."

The shriek of fury threatened to deafen him. He flung the phone away from his ear and it hit the window and clattered under his seat. "Christ."

He'd wait her out.

A half an hour later, she stepped out of the dingy building.

He had no intention of buying her breakfast—he could just imagine the conversation they'd have over pancakes—but he said nothing as she bustled into his truck wearing a worn jacket over her work uniform. "Where are we going?" she asked, annoyed. "The diner's still open downtown."

"You'll see."

"I don't want to eat at the Country Kitchen. The resort has better food. Let's just go there."

"Stop it. That's not where we're going."

She sighed.

He drove them to a Hyundai/Subaru dealership not far from the restaurant, and he parked in a space near the front entrance.

"What are we doing here?"

"I have an errand. Calm down and give me a minute, will you? Come inside out of the cold."

Last night he'd done some research on cars. What worked well in the snow, what would give him the most bang for his buck. Writing out a check to buy a used car wouldn't cost him much, and Ivy would have a vehicle she could depend on for the next ten years. He searched used cars in the area and crossed his fingers. It had paid off. A Subaru Outback sat at the dealership here in town. He'd get a better deal in Decatur, or even Marengo, but he had to make do with what he had.

He held the door open and pushed her inside.

"What kind of errand do you have here?" she asked, her eyes wide.

New cars sparkled in the watery light wavering in through the showroom's floor-to-ceiling windows.

"It'll be quick," he said instead of answering her question.

A young salesman wearing a shirt, tie, and jeans bounced across the showroom floor. "Mr. Draper? Rich Stuart. I received your online inquiry this morning. You're looking at the 2014 Outback, is that right?" He held out his hand.

"That's right," he said, shaking the man's hand. He liked the look of him. Nothing smarmy.

"Good car. Came in last week. I'm surprised it's still available. You're lucky."

"I am." He couldn't disagree. He'd known it when he saw it online last night.

"Are you purchasing for yourself?"

He tilted his head toward Ivy who was wandering around the showroom looking at the new cars, a wistful expression on her face. He cleared his throat. "For Miss Graves. She needs a dependable car."

"I see. Will you be needing financing?"

He met his eyes. He transferred money out of his savings this morning and had his checkbook inside his jacket pocket. "No."

Nodding, Rich said, "With cash up front, I can take

eight percent off the top. Not much, but it will save you taxes and plates. Wanna go take a look at it? You'll want to let her drive it, make sure it's what she wants."

He stepped closer to the salesman and lowered his voice. "Ivy hates me, Mr. Stuart. We dated in high school, but I moved to Decatur after graduation to go to college. I can't say I'm proud of how I broke things off, and well, she's not going to want this car. If you can be straight with me and tell me there's nothing wrong with it, if I can write you a check and let her drive it off the lot . . ."

"A Christmas present she doesn't want because she hates your guts. Got it." Looking at the floor, Rich hid a smile. "Believe it or not, I can work with that." He turned to Ivy. "Miss? If you can help yourself to a cup of coffee over there in the corner, I just need Mr. Draper to fill out some paperwork."

She fluttered her fingers in the air. She didn't care.

He followed Rich into a tiny cubicle.

"Car's in good shape. No bullshitting you. It was owned by a part-time pharmaceutical salesman. Most of the miles on it are highway, and not many at that. You saw the mileage on the website? The seats are a little worn, but it cleaned up nice. He wasn't a smoker, so there's that." Rich woke up his computer. "I don't suppose you know anything about her? Social security number, address, who she has auto insurance with? I'm assuming she has a car now?"

He used to know a lot about Ivy Graves. Her favorite color. Her favorite food. Her favorite subject in school. When they became intimate, where she liked to be kissed. That she loved it when he played with her hair. That she would cry every time she touched a fresh bruise on his skin.

Now he didn't know anything about her. She lived in low-income housing and worked herself to death. That's all he knew. That's all he'd know because Ivy would never let him get close to her again.

"No. Sorry."

"She'll be filling out some paperwork then. Can't be helped." Rich typed into his computer, and several minutes went by before he rattled off a total. He hoped they weren't taking too long. It would be like Ivy to get sick of waiting and try walking to the resort. Never mind they were on the opposite side of town.

He wrote out the check and Rich called his bank to verify funds. "Everything's good. Let's go out to the lot."

He followed Rich onto the sales floor. Ivy sat sullen, sipping on a disposable cup of coffee, watching a local morning talk show program on the TV mounted above the coffee cart. "We're almost done," Logan told her.

"Good. I'm hungry and you promised me breakfast. It's the least you can do."

Rich chuckled.

She walked beside him across the car lot, the winter wind doing its best to freeze them solid, and they stopped at a pretty forest green Subaru Outback. New tires. Full tank of gas. For sentimental reasons, Rich tossed in a two-year extended warranty, not that she'd need it, but at least her oil changes would be free for a while.

Rich pressed the autostart button. Another bonus that pleased him, and the car growled to life.

"What's going on?" Ivy asked, frowning. "You already have a truck."

He pulled off his mitten. He couldn't resist touching her. Just a light brush to her cheek. "This isn't my car. It's yours." He took the key fob from Rich and pushed it into her hands.

Then he turned and walked away.

CHAPTER TWO

Tears blinded Ivy for the third time that afternoon. She couldn't accept the car, but she wanted to, so badly. After Logan left, his head down, his hands in his pockets, Rich hadn't given her time to run after him, to tell him to go to hell. It was as if Rich had known she wanted to tear Logan to shreds, and he'd distracted her long enough to allow Logan to escape.

He'd taken her on a test drive and asked if she had any questions. She had many, but none he could answer. She'd filled out paperwork, tense, waiting for him to ask her to pay, but he never did. She kept looking over her shoulder as she drove out of the lot, thinking this was a big, fat joke and that Rich would run out of the building, yelling it had been a huge mistake and the car didn't belong to her after all.

But nothing happened. She'd driven to the resort, an hour before her shift started, and parked in her usual spot, stunned.

Autostart.

CD player.

Smartphone charger.

Then she went to plug it in, and she stopped dead.

She wouldn't need to plug it in. Rich said the engine had a block heater but it could handle the cold.

She'd leaned against the car and cursed Logan Draper all the way to hell and back.

She couldn't keep it. But, oh, did she want to.

Her vision blurry, she cut lemons into wedges.

She shoved a piece into her mouth, tore the fruit off the rind and threw it in the garbage. The bitter taste anchored her to the lounge, and she closed her eyes and wiped tears off her cheeks. When she opened them, Callie was sitting on one of the stools.

"Are you okay?"

She wanted to hate Callie, she really did. After the new year, she'd take her only friend away. But she made Mitch so happy, how could she blame the woman who sat in front of her, her head tilted in concern.

She jerked a shoulder. She could let resentment turn Callie into an enemy, or she could admit Callie wasn't the only reason Mitch was leaving Rocky Point. Decatur wasn't that far away. She'd still see him. Maybe. "Yeah. Just tired, I guess. Can I get you something?"

"Isn't it a little early to be drinking?"

She would be if she wasn't at work. No, that wasn't true. She enjoyed a drink here and there, but a glass of wine wasn't the first thing she thought of. "Lounge is open," she said as if it was a logical excuse.

Callie laughed. "What the hell. Do you have any Prosecco? Marnie stopped drinking. She thinks she's pregnant."

She dug into the cooler, pulled out a single-serve bottle of Prosecco, and poured it into a spotless glass flute.

"Is she happy?"

"Very."

"That's good, I guess."

One of the perks of bartending the early shift was the few people who came in wanting a drink. If Callie wouldn't have sat down to chat, she could have read the book she hid under the bar. She bought them by the bagful at the thrift shop in town. She gravitated toward the bright red covers, couples locked in a steamy embrace. Titles like *One Night with the Billionaire* and *Daddy Cowboy*, she devoured them as she leaned against the bar, waiting for resort guests who wanted to get their buzz on.

During the holidays, they offered specials, reminding people in town they didn't have to stay at the resort to drink there. A lot of the time it worked, and after Marnie's wedding, she'd have a couple weeks of busy evenings centered around Christmas and New Year's.

Then everyone would be gone, and she'd be alone.

Callie sipped the bubbles and asked, "Have you thought about kids?"

"I've thought about them." She thought about not having them.

"You don't sound happy about it."

"I don't want kids." It was that simple. But it wasn't Callie's business why she didn't. "Do you?" She asked to draw the attention off her. "Mitch will be a good dad." She often thought it, but she blushed. Mitch's procreation plans with a woman he'd known for only a week wasn't her business, either.

"Yes, he will," Callie said, unruffled. "But we're going to wait a while. There's a lot to work out with his parents' house, and moving . . ." She reached across the bar and touched her arm. "I'm sorry how that happened. I know you and Mitch are close."

"He deserves more than being a maintenance man at a

resort," she said. She believed that with all her heart. "You're giving him something he wanted, something he needed. He never admitted it, but he wanted it. And now he has you. I can't feel bad about that. Just, treat him well, will you?"

"I will. You deserve more too, don't you, Ivy? You work in this lounge day and after day . . . do you date? Do you go out and have fun? You ice fish."

She smiled faintly, remembering the morning she caught Callie wandering around on the lake. "And I got a good show out of it, too. Are you okay? I haven't had a chance . . ."

"Yeah, I'm okay. They didn't hurt me. I was lucky Mitch was there or they would have done a lot worse. Listen, Marnie, Leah, Autumn, and I are going to have a spa day pretty soon, here at the resort. Would you like to go?"

She opened her mouth to decline. She couldn't afford a spa day, even if she used her employee discount. Several of the female employees had a standing reservation to get their nails done or a massage, their hair cut and colored. The employee discount was very generous, but it still didn't make any of the treatments cheap enough for her.

"Don't say no because you can't afford it. It's all paid for."

"By who?"

"By . . ."

"Don't lie, Callie. I don't take charity." Only, there was a 2014 Subaru Outback parked in the staff parking lot calling her a liar.

Callie sighed. "It's part of the wedding package. I asked Marnie, and she doesn't care. I mean," she fumbled, "she doesn't mind if you come along. You'll be included, and all you'll have to worry about is if you want to tip your technicians."

It still didn't sound right. "Can I think about it?"

"Sure. We don't have the date set . . . Leah's in New York. Her grandma had a stroke. When she comes back and we book our appointments, I'll let you know. Hopefully, you can get the afternoon off."

She'd done enough favors over the years she could ask someone to cover her hours, but she wasn't used to spending money when she could be making it. Still. The thought of a couple hours being pampered, well. Her hair needed a cut whether she wanted to pay for it or not. Ratty and halfway down her back, she didn't think about it much, except to pull it out of her face. If she was feeling fancy, she'd wind it into a bun. Woo-hoo.

Callie drained what was left of her Prosecco and slid off the stool. She pushed a twenty toward her. "You can keep the change. Talk to you later. Oh, and Ivy? I'm glad you didn't bite my head off." Grinning, she hurried out of the bar, maybe to go hunt Mitch down who'd be around here fixing something, or maybe to his parents' room where Ruby spent most of her time resting.

A few days ago she had a nice talk with Leah before Rita the hag interrupted their conversation. She didn't like Rita, or the way she treated people. Jared had stumbled through Rocky Point in a grief-stricken haze when Rita up and left. She supposed a lot like she had when Logan ran off with James. Not that they were lovers eloping, high on love. No, they'd been high on the acceptance letters the University of Decatur mailed them. Logan's with a full scholarship.

She'd admired Leah's dignity and grace when Rita pummeled her with sickening politeness. It wouldn't be a bad thing to make friends. Leah. Maybe Callie. Autumn. She defended Mitch writing that article for the newspaper. God knew she was tired of being alone.

But she'd never have Logan, not the way she had him before high school graduation.

She'd tell him she couldn't keep the car.

There was only one thing she wanted from him. She thought she had it once, but that had been a lie.

She'd given up wanting his heart and focused on keeping hers safe instead.

Her mechanic called her cell, and on her break, she listened to the voicemail. Her alternator was shot, but she'd known that. So was her battery, if she wanted to be honest, but plugging her car in had coaxed a few extra months out of it. About six hundred dollars to fix it all, about what she expected. She called him back and told him to go ahead and fought off a wave of panic as she did so.

Six hundred dollars was a good chunk of her savings, but there wasn't anything she could do about it. She needed a working vehicle, and fuck Logan for thinking he could just ride in like a knight in shining armor on his trusty steed, make everything okay, and then leave, believing he'd done a good deed when all he'd really done was break her heart all over again.

Hilary took over at eight, and after punching out, she debated long and hard. It wouldn't be that big of a deal if she kept the Outback overnight. Just one more drive. Two if she counted driving it back to the resort in the morning to give the key fob to Logan. She didn't have to work and could spend an hour or so bitching him out and telling him what had been on her mind for the past eighteen years.

After that, she'd ask the resort's shuttle to drop her off at the mechanic's to pick up her Camry. No more rides from Logan. Then she'd do what she always did on her day off. The cleaning, the laundry. A trip to the grocery store. A hot bath and a long nap.

Encouraged by her plan, she said goodnight to Hilary.

She sank behind the wheel and started the engine.

So sleek, so smooth.

And she damned Logan Draper with every beat of her heart.

The next morning, she stomped her way to Logan's cabin, the Subaru's key fob clutched in her fist. She'd already become attached to the soft seats, the purr of the engine, the glide of the wheels over the snow. It was a good car, reliable, and probably why Logan chose it.

Give him the key fob, say thanks but no thanks, and get out.

Sunlight glinted against the windows, and she paused, her foot on the first step of his porch. Maybe he wasn't here. She'd overheard some of the wedding guests who were staying at the resort talking about an afternoon playing board games at the Fox house. It sounded like James's parents hosted something every day.

She'd met James's parents once or twice. They were nice people, though not on the top of the social ladder in Rocky Point. Marnie's parents did a little better, financially, but no one would accuse Marnie of marrying down.

Her family had been middle class for a long time. Until the ladder was kicked out from under them. It hadn't hurt her, and by then she already knew who her true friends were.

She pounded on his door. If he didn't answer, maybe she could leave the key fob on the porch in a place where he wouldn't miss it.

But his footfalls sounded behind the door, and she stood straight and didn't flinch when he met her eyes.

"Ivy. Good morning. Do you wanna come in?"

What she wanted was to throw the key fob over his shoulder and run the hell away as fast as she could, but she could do better. "Yes. Thank you."

He looked good. Khaki pants and a light blue dress shirt open at the neck, sleeves rolled up to his elbows. No one knew, she had no one to tell, but it was her favorite look on a man. Bundled up in a winter jacket, she hadn't gotten to appreciate his body yesterday. But she did now, her gaze roaming from his feet to his glasses that were slightly askew giving him an adorable, flustered look.

A laptop sat open on a small table in the kitchenette, the scent of coffee permeating the air.

"Were you working?"

"Just going over some notes. Would you like some coffee?"

She stood by the door, her boots dripping water on his floor. "Ah, no. Thanks. I gave it a lot of thought, and well, I can't keep that car, Logan."

A gust of wind blew against the cabin. The sky turned a dark grey, and snowflakes whipped past the window.

"But—"

"No. Eighteen years ago you left to go to school. Completely cut me off. I never heard from you again.

Then you come back like eighteen years was eighteen hours, thinking what? I don't hate you? That you didn't break my heart? That I was a naïve little girl, crying over her high school crush. Well, fuck you. I don't need your pity, and I don't need your charity. I take care of Mom, by myself, and I've been doing it since—" She dashed tears off her cheeks. "And I'll keep on doing it. Without your stupid help. I don't know what you were thinking. Trying to make up for how shitty you treated me, or trying to buy me off so you could stop feeling guilty, whatever. I don't need the car. I don't need you." Thrusting the key fob at him she said straight to his face, "I never had you anyway."

"That's not true. You were the only person I ever *did* belong to. Do you remember the first day of Kindergarten? In the lunchroom? I was crying because I didn't have anything to eat." His mother had barely gotten him to the bus stop that day. Too sore to do much else than help him get dressed, his mother hadn't packed him a lunch. It didn't matter because he didn't have a lunchbox to keep it in.

Her face softened. "Yeah."

"You sat next to me and asked me why I was crying. Hell, Ivy, even at five years old I was too ashamed to tell you I didn't have any food, but you shared your lunch with me. Peanut butter and jelly sandwich, homemade chocolate chip cookies. You even gave me half your apple." He remembered the meal like he'd eaten it only hours ago, but it had been more than the lunch that warmed his heart and soul that day. It had been a little girl who had long brown hair that curled down her back, her big blue eyes, and how she'd held his hand on the way back to class.

After that day, she always came to school with an extra sandwich, and he didn't miss lunch the entire year.

He stepped closer, and she stiffened.

"Just take the key," she said.

He ignored her and trapped her between his body and the door. "I've always belonged to you." He leaned closer, held her chin in his hand, and made her look at him. Slowly, he lowered his head and brushed his lips over hers.

She didn't taste how she had before he left Rocky Point. Before she knew he was leaving. Then she'd tasted sweet, the promise of a bright future flavoring her skin. A future she thought he would share with her. She'd tasted of love and innocence.

He didn't taste that now. He tasted hurt, betrayal, and loss. Her kiss tasted bitter on his tongue, and she tried to move, to turn her head, but he wouldn't let her. Her hands fluttered in front of his chest, not touching him. She wanted to push him away, but she couldn't, wouldn't, let herself. It humbled him that after all these years apart, it was still instinct for her to protect him from physical harm.

Pinning her hands above her head, he kissed her again, hugging her closer.

She struggled until all of a sudden she wasn't, and he released her wrists.

She wrapped her arms around his neck and poured herself into the kiss, opening her mouth.

This was what he wanted. This was what he'd missed.

Yes, the years fell away like she accused him of, and they were back to being teens, full of a love they didn't know what to do with.

"I've always been yours," he mumbled against her lips.

Tears ran down her cheeks. "Then where have you been?" she cried, crumpling to the floor. "Where have you been? What have you been doing?"

He crouched next to her and smoothed her hair out of her face.

She met his eyes, hers so full of pain he could barely look at her.

"Waiting."

He picked her up and carried her to the king-sized bed.

His cock throbbed so hard it hurt. If she didn't let him make love to her right this instant, he was going to explode.

She watched him, her eyes wary, as he slid the zipper down of the old, tattered winter coat she wore. Beneath it, a men's dark green V-neck sweater hugged her breasts, and she didn't need to tell him who the sweater belonged to.

He slid the sleeves off her arms and tossed the coat onto a chair. Kneeling in front of her, he brushed his thumbs over her cheeks. "You are still so beautiful."

She blushed and looked at the floor. "No, I'm not."

"I don't want to fight, Ivy. Let me love you. It's been so long, and I've missed you so much."

"Have you, though?"

"More than I can explain."

Maybe it was the truth in his words, maybe it was the pleading look in his eyes, whatever it was, she nodded, and he let out a relieved sigh.

He wasn't stupid. A bout of sex wasn't going to erase the past eighteen years, or the betrayal, or the hurt, or the hate. In fact, making love right now would probably make things worse before they got better, but he couldn't help himself and he pushed his hands under her sweater and reveled in her skin's heat.

"I didn't hurt you, did I?" she asked, brushing her fingers across his cheek. "No matter what's happened between us, I would never—"

"No, no, you didn't." Her thoughtfulness brought tears to his eyes. "God, Ivy . . ." He kissed her again, raking his fingers through her hair, gently tugging on a snarl.

She moaned.

"Let's get you out of these clothes." He pulled the baggy sweater over her head and threw it onto the floor. He revealed a plain white lace bra, and dipping his head, he licked at the edge of the lace.

"I haven't been with anyone . . . mean, I'm sorry it's not fancy . . ." she muttered.

"It's okay, sweetheart. It's not the bra, it's what's inside." He unclasped it, drew the straps along her arms, and he threw the lace scraps next to her sweater. "And trust me, darlin' you're good enough. More than good enough."

He nuzzled one breast and then the other. He couldn't decide which one to focus on. Like a kid in a candy store, he wanted all of it . . . now.

He pressed a kiss to her belly and nudged her to stand. Tentatively, he unbuttoned her jeans. "Please don't change your mind."

"I won't."

"Thank you." He lifted her feet, one at a time, and took off her boots so he could tug the denim down her legs. All the standing she did behind the bar gave her firm thighs, and her butt was perky in a pair of plain pink panties.

"This won't fix anything," she said.

"I know that." He peeled them off her body too, and

tossed them on top of the rest of her clothes. He inhaled her scent, his nose grazing the soft hair between her legs. Unable to resist, he skimmed his fingers along her seam, barely touching her. She shuddered.

"Logan."

"Yeah?" he asked, his voice scratchy.

"Will you get undressed now?"

"Yeah." He stood and reached for the top button of his shirt, but she stopped him.

"Let me."

"Okay."

She slowly unbuttoned his shirt, one excruciating button at a time, and he said, "Do you remember the first time we did this?"

Ivy's hands stilled.

Shit. Maybe he shouldn't bring up the past. There wasn't anything good that could come out of reminiscing. He'd thrown all their memories away the minute he left Rocky Point and didn't look back.

"Yeah. My parents announced a spur-of-the-moment trip to go shopping in Marengo. Joey—" She stopped and swallowed. "Joey was outside playing baseball, and we had the house to ourselves."

"I was so nervous."

"You were? I never knew that." She finished unbuttoning his shirt, and he flung it onto the floor. He wore a white tank top under it, and that quickly followed.

"I didn't know if it was the right thing to do."

Peering up at him, she asked, "What do you mean?"

She pushed his pants down his legs, and he stepped out of them. His tighty-whities wouldn't win him any sexy prizes, but she didn't say anything, just trailed her fingers over the hard ridge straining the cotton. It seemed surreal to be talking about their first time when right at this moment, it felt like they were doing it for the first time all over again.

Yeah, he'd had women since her, hell, in eighteen years he would've questioned his sanity if he hadn't, but being with Ivy right now, the snow blowing outside, the fake flames wavering in the fireplace, and her skin sparkling in the white light coming in through the window behind the bed, he was as nervous as he'd been as a teenager, sitting on her pink bedspread, harder than a rock. And wondering if he was craving something he didn't have the right to take.

"We'd been friends all our lives. Literally, for most of my life, you had been by my side. I didn't want anything to destroy that. I didn't want to ruin the best thing that ever happened to be because we had sex."

It wasn't the sex that destroyed their friendship, they both knew it, and she didn't have to say it.

And she didn't. "It turned out okay." Kneeling at his feet, she slid his briefs over his legs, letting his erection spring free.

Impatiently, he kicked them aside, but he stood in front of her and let her look.

He was bigger than he was at eighteen, thank God, and she brushed her fingers over his cock, getting used to the feel of him. Lightly, she played with the thatch of hair beneath his balls, and they tightened.

"Yeah. It did."

The sex had been okay for two teens fumbling around having only the basic idea of what needed to go where. He hadn't said it then, but he'd loved her. Had loved her kind heart, her generous nature. Her willingness to protect him no matter what. Despite his young age, it had been more than losing his virginity, more than a quick romp. Even then he'd wanted to show her that he cared about her, that he appreciated her.

She smoothed her tongue up his cock and lapped at the pre-come welling at the tip. "Ivy, I think . . ." But he couldn't keep going because she took all of him into her mouth, adding a slight pressure, and his words were lost.

When they were kids she'd confessed she didn't know what to do. Just being with her had been enough, and he told her it didn't matter. Now she was giving him a blowjob, a very good blowjob, and jealousy flared. Who the fuck taught her how to do this? What schmuck had she been with? Did he know the asshole?

He had to stop thinking or he was going to lose his erection, and God, their relationship was tenuous at best. He might not ever get her here again. Especially when in a week from now he was going back to Decatur.

He wrapped his hand around her arm and asked her to stand. He was determined to put everything out of his mind except making love to the one person who'd ever meant anything to him.

"We didn't use anything that afternoon," he said, turning down the bedspread. He asked housekeeping to come only when he was gone, and the pillow and sheets smelled like him, like sweat. His nightmares had started coming back. They would go away after he left.

"We were stupid, and lucky." Resting her hands on his hips, she brushed a kiss to the middle of his back.

"Yeah." Now was the time to have the talk. "I'm healthy. I just had a physical, and I'm going to wear a condom because I don't want kids. *Still* don't."

After they were done, they'd had a quick, tense conversation about her last period, and they crossed their fingers that her getting over it five days prior would be enough.

It had been, and he'd never felt so grateful.

The scare didn't stop them from doing it again, but he'd swallowed his pride and bought a box of condoms at the drugstore, ignoring the giggling freshman who rang him up.

She stiffened, and he knew it though she was standing behind him. "Is that what you think I'm doing? Trying to get knocked up to trap you in a relationship?"

He spun around, appalled. "Of course not. That's not what I was getting at. I was just saying . . . I don't want kids. Warning you, I guess . . ."

She slid into bed, indignation burning in her eyes. "The last thing I need is someone else to take care of. I figured you packed condoms. Maybe you thought you'd hook up with a bridesmaid or one of the housekeeping staff. Congratulations, you got the bartender. Are we gonna do this or not?"

He'd need more foreplay now. Her accusation sucked the mood right out of the room.

She noticed too, and slapped an arm over her eyes.

Her reaction made him laugh, and he crawled into bed. He nuzzled the corner of her mouth with his lips. "I'm sorry. I found a few in the drawer of the nightstand, that's the only reason why I have some. I didn't bring any because I didn't have any intention of having sex while I was here. You taught me sex should mean something. The first time we did it, all I wanted was to show you much I cared about you. You set the bar high, and yeah, I've had sex, I've been in relationships, but I've *never* had a fling, sex just for sex."

He kissed her and let his fingers explore. That's all it took. She was wet and hot, and she lifted her hips wanting more.

Carefully, she took his glasses off and set them on the table near her side of the bed.

"I've always cared about you too, you know," she said softly.

"I do know. And since you shared your lunch with me on the first day of Kindergarten, I have never taken you for granted."

Doubt shadowed her eyes.

She didn't believe him, but that was okay. How could she when he'd shown her the complete opposite?

"Make love to me, Logan," she whispered, holding his head in her hands and licking at his lips.

"I will, sweetheart. Give me a second." He leaned away just long enough to grab one of the stray condoms in the drawer and kissed her, long lazy kisses that hid how close to the brink he was.

She helped him put the condom on, his fingers shaking so badly he couldn't rip the package open. Again, his heart tugged. Who taught her to roll a condom onto a guy's dick? Who stole precious seconds with her in the dark, telling her he loved her, making promises he evidently didn't keep?

He gripped her ass, his fingertips sinking into her soft skin, and anchored himself over her. She wiggled, and seconds later he found home.

While living in Rocky Point, that's what Ivy had been. His home.

Living under his father's roof had been wrought with tension, anger, and violence, but whenever he was with Ivy, he'd been able to breathe. She'd been his safe haven, a place where he could let his guard down.

Escaping Rocky Point, he'd thrown it away.

And he'd do it again.

She nibbled at his neck, and he came in a burst of contentment and pleasure. Having her in his arms was a dream come true.

This dream would turn into a nightmare, but he'd take what he could for now.

"Help a girl out," she panted, and he pulled out to give himself room to lick one of her nipples. He still remembered her body, still remembered what made her come, and his fingers rubbed her clit as his teeth delicately nipped at her breast. Love bites, he would tease.

Whimpering, she came under his hand.

"There you go, baby," he mumbled, kissing up to her mouth. He took her lips tenderly, the last quivers of orgasm leaving her sweaty and breathless, and he cradled her to him, burying his face in her hair.

She burrowed into the pillow.

"Do you work later?" he asked, tugging the bedspread up to her chin.

"No, not today."

"Then why don't you doze?"

"What are you going to do?"

"Wipe off and get dressed, have some coffee. Do you want some?"

"Sure. Thanks."

"Still just cream?"

"Yeah."

Her eyes drifted closed, and he pressed a kiss to her forehead.

He put on his glasses and cleaned up in the bathroom.

When he pissed her off, it could have gone either way. He was lucky they were both already naked. The chance she would have stormed out of his cabin had she still had her clothes on was high. She wasn't the type of girl to get knocked up to trap a man, but he wanted her to remember his vow from so long ago. He'd never have kids. He wanted to get a vasectomy, but he couldn't find a doctor who would give him one. Thirty-six years old, never married, they said he would change his mind.

He never would.

He pulled his pants on and left his dress shirt hanging open.

Leaning against the counter, he poured a cup of stale coffee. The wind beat against the cabin and the snow made visibility almost nothing. The blizzard had come out of nowhere, and he was glad he had a few odds and ends in his fridge. But enough for two?

He could order delivery, but the resort's delivery person was sleeping in his bed and he didn't want to let her go.

He cleared his throat. That would be something to deal with later.

His cell buzzed, and James's number flashed on the screen.

"What's up?"

"Are you okay in this storm?" James asked, his voice tight with worry.

"Yeah, why? Are you guys?"

"We're okay, but Jared took his plane out and got caught up in it. Someone at the airport called Briar. He had to make an emergency landing."

"Shit, is he okay?"

"If you can call being stranded in a field south of here okay, then yeah. He's not hurt, but it's cold, and the blizzard's bad. No one can go out to look for him."

"My SUV has—"

"No. Don't try. You can't see an inch in front of your face and all you'd do is end up in the ditch. He's good right now, and that's something. We're in for a lot of snow in the next few hours, and everything's shut down. Marnie and I are in our room. Did you want to try to walk over and wait out the blizzard with us? Or the resort has a few ATVs. I could try to pick you up."

"No, I'll stay. I have enough food to last a little while. I was looking over the Johnson's estate notes when Ivy stopped by."

"Ivy's with you?"

He paused. "Yeah."

James laughed. "No wonder why you don't want to leave. Okay. I'll keep you in the loop."

"Thanks." He disconnected the call.

He carried his mug to the table and woke up his laptop. His iPhone flipped over to data instead of connecting to the cabin's modem, but he didn't need an internet connection to look over notes. At least the electricity held so far.

He resisted the urge to crawl back in bed with Ivy, curl his body around hers, and sleep forever.

He had to take this slow. He didn't even know what "this" was. What did he want from her? To assuage his guilty conscience like she accused him of? Something more?

Christ, he hadn't come back to town for her, but when she'd shown up at his cabin to deliver his order, seeing her had taken his breath away.

She'd be pissed when she woke up, and he better be prepared to do damage control. Pissed at him, pissed at herself, and pissed she was stuck here until the storm passed.

She opened her eyes to the blinding white and the scent of coffee.

Feeling more rested than she had in a long time, she

stretched, but she shot up in bed, her heart slamming against her ribs, clutching the sheet to her breasts. She shouldn't have fallen asleep. She had too much to do.

"Easy," Logan said, the mattress dipping under his weight. "You were out pretty good there."

"What time is it?"

"Three-thirty. You said you have the day off?"

She relaxed but didn't loosen her grip on the sheet. "Yeah, kind of. I have stuff to do at home. Sorry. I didn't sleep well last night. I was going to nap later."

"It's okay."

She wanted to put her clothes on. She wanted to get out of there as fast as she could. She couldn't believe all it had taken was a smile and a kiss to get her naked. She was so pathetic. "I need to go." And not come back.

"It's storming. We're not going anywhere."

"The resort isn't far. I can handle it," she said, but she bit her lip. The snow was so thick she couldn't see anything out the window, and the wind beat against the cabin. It'd be difficult to walk back.

He rested his hand on her knee. "Are you hungry? Or thirsty?"

"No. Well, a cup of coffee?" she asked. It did smell good, and it would help her shake off the fuzz in her brain. She needed a clear head to fight through the snow to the resort. She'd need to stay on course or she'd find herself frozen in the middle of the lake.

While he poured her coffee, she quickly put her clothes on. It was stupid to be embarrassed, but it mortified her how fast he'd talked her out of them.

He turned holding a coffee mug and his face fell, but he quickly hid his disappointment, smiling faintly. Walking toward her, he said, "I guess it was too much to hope we could wait out the storm in bed."

She gripped the mug's handle and gulped the strong brew. "We don't need a next time. *This* time was a mistake. You know it, and I know it. You came back to Rocky Point for James and Marnie. Not for me. If they had gotten married in Decatur, you wouldn't have given me a thought. I'm not a fool. I got caught up in seeing you again, that's all."

"You're right," he said, sitting on the bed next to her.

His prompt agreement set her teeth on edge. Not even a denial.

"At least we're on the same page." She hopped off the bed and carried her mug to the kitchen. She poured out the remains and ran water into it, leaving it in the sink.

When she turned around, he was right there, crowding her. He trailed his finger over the frayed V-neck of her sweater. "I'm sorry about Joey."

She knocked his hand away. "I don't need your sympathy." All she'd wanted was his love, but he hadn't wanted to give her that, either.

"I'm still sorry."

Tears clogged her throat. Everyone left her. Logan. Joey. Her dad. The men in her life didn't love her enough to stay. Well, what happened wasn't Joey's fault.

She'd stopped being angry at him a long time ago.

"We can agree to keep out of each other's way while you're here, right?" she asked, shoving her feet into her snow boots.

"Yeah, sure."

"Good. And I'm not keeping the car."

"Okay."

She narrowed her eyes. "What's going on? You're being too agreeable."

"I don't want to fight. You can have whatever you want."

She clenched her teeth together to hold in a sob, and she brushed her trembling fingers over his unbuttoned shirt. Swallowing, she tried to find control. She had just enough to say, "That's not true. I've wanted a lot of things, and I haven't gotten a single one."

He grabbed her hand, but she yanked away and put on her jacket. A quarter of a mile. Not far. She could make it. She'd do anything to get away from him.

From his sad eyes, his hurt puppy-dog expression.

The words came by rote. "Enjoy your stay."

She opened the door and stepped into the screeching wind and pelting snow, pausing on the porch to rally her courage. She wished he'd ask her to stay, tell her she was being stupid for trying to walk to the resort in this, but he let her go and shut the door behind her.

Well, fuck him.

Not literally. She'd already done that, much to her shame and regret.

She tightened her hood and pulled her hands into her jacket's sleeves. She didn't think she needed mittens and left them at home.

She had to admit, this wasn't one of her finest moments, but on the bright side, maybe she could work. The resort was surely short-staffed. No one would be able to drive in this.

Taking a deep breath, she stepped off the porch.

Without the cabin blocking the wind, the punch of it knocked her sideways, and she stumbled. She couldn't spare a moment to glare at the cabin, Logan warm inside, sipping hot coffee.

Her only satisfaction was her scent lingering on his pillow. She hoped to God he missed her.

Yeah, right. Eighteen years passed like they were nothing.

Bent in half, trying to protect her face from the biting snow, she slogged through drifts that went up to her knees.

It felt like she'd been trudging forever, but when she looked behind her, she could still see the silhouette of Logan's cabin through the blowing ice.

Frozen to the bone, she'd only made it a few feet.

She tried not to cry.

The tears would only freeze on her cheeks.

He gave her a few minutes before going after her.

He was wrong. Ivy hadn't been pissed. She was sad and embarrassed. Humiliated.

She was right when she said their making love had been a mistake. Well, half. He didn't think it was a mistake, but he should have waited.

He'd made love with a stranger, but there was nothing he wanted more than to change that. He couldn't let his impatience get the better of him again.

Or he'd keep running her off. Like now.

When he thought enough time had gone by, he dressed in his boots, jacket, hat, and choppers. He hoped she would come easily. He didn't want to fight in the middle of a blizzard.

The wind slammed him in the face the second he stepped off the porch, and he fought to breathe. He thought of Jared alone in this and muttered a quick prayer that his friend was okay. Jared's plane wouldn't offer much protection, but some was better than nothing.

He searched for Ivy through the blowing ice, and squinting, saw a faint figure moving away from him. She hadn't gotten far.

Trudging through the snowdrifts, he told himself he deserved this. He'd deserve dying of hypothermia. When it came to Ivy, he acted like he didn't have a brain in his head, when, in actuality, he'd graduated with top honors from the University of Decatur.

He didn't know if Ivy had gone to school.

"Ivy," he called, but the wind tore the words from his lips and whipped them into the trees. At least that's the direction the wind seemed to be blowing.

"Ivy!" he shouted, trying again.

He'd need to catch up with her.

It took him only a few minutes, but he was frozen to the bone by the time he did.

He could afford the best winter gear. She couldn't. He'd seen it when she put on her crappy winter jacket. She'd be a block of ice by the time they made it back to the cabin.

He grabbed her arm and she turned, tears streaming down her face, snot running over her upper lip.

Her eyelashes were frosted white, and her cheeks were so red he wanted to kiss her all over, snot and all.

She loathed him so much she would rather face a storm than spend any time with him.

"We need to go back," he shouted.

She paused, debating on whether or not to fight him, but she finally nodded and flung herself against his chest.

He tucked her under his arm and tried to shield her from the wind the best he could. He hustled her inside, and she fell to the floor in a pile of snow and blubbering tears.

Crouching, he held her in his arms, his chin resting on the top of her head.

They sat like that for a while, trying to warm up, the snow melting off their clothes and dripping on the hardwood floor.

She looked at him, tears trailing down her still-pink cheeks. "You came for me."

He hugged her. He could say something witty, or serious, or romantic, but he said nothing.

He couldn't anyway, around the ball of humiliation in his throat.

She said that like she thought him going after her was the very last thing he'd do.

And it very much shamed him that she had any reason to think it at all.

CHAPTER THREE

Logan insisted she shower, and she gratefully accepted, stealing a moment to smell his shampoo and body wash.

She used the bottles the resort supplied, but they were enough to get the job done.

Clean and warm, she wrapped herself in one of the thick terry cloth robes hanging on the back of the door and walked out of the bathroom in a puff of steam.

The kitchenette smelled of spicy tomato.

"I made some soup, but we have to be careful with the food. I don't know how long the storm's supposed to last, and I don't have much here." He turned and his jaw dropped. "You look . . . warm."

"I feel better. Thank you."

"You're welcome."

She sat at the small table.

He'd moved his laptop and he sat with her, tomato soup steaming in two bowls.

She spooned up a bite and blew on it. "Thank you for

coming after me," she murmured. "It was a stupid thing to do."

He covered her hand with his, and she needed every bit of her willpower not to look for comfort in it. "I'm sorry you felt like you couldn't be here, or that you didn't want to be here. I guess it's the same thing, but it doesn't have to be like that. We could be friends."

"We used to be friends," she said, swirling her soup in the ceramic bowl the resort supplied in the rooms that had kitchenettes.

"I know. Until I fucked it up. But we could be friends again. We used to like each other."

"You left and didn't look back."

"You know why I did what I did. You know how hard it is for me to be here."

"That's why being friends is worthless. You *wouldn't* be here if Marnie hadn't wanted to get married in her hometown, for the tradition of it. You're here for James, not for me."

He opened his mouth, his cheeks an angry red.

"Don't bother to deny it," she said before he could try to defend himself again. "How long would it have taken you to look for me? On your own?"

He stared at his soup.

"*That's* why we can't be friends," she muttered, her appetite gone.

She forced herself to eat. She didn't want to get sick. There wouldn't be any help until the blizzard cleared.

Quietly, he said, "Phones work both ways, Ivy."

She dropped her spoon and it clattered to the table spraying Campbell's Tomato Soup everywhere. "What?"

Abruptly, Logan stood, the chair screeching across the floor.

The idea had come to him, just now, just as it felt like she was going to win.

He shouldn't have to take all the blame.

"You heard me. After I left, you never called. You never asked how I settled into the dorms, you never wrote me a letter, or sent me a care package. Why didn't you?"

Enraged, she stood up too, clutching the lapels of the robe. "You were the one who said goodbye. You were the one who left."

"So? Kids go to college all the time and they stay in touch. Decatur's only three hours away. You had your driver's license and a car. Joey—" He stopped. Ivy's life wasn't shit then. Joey had still been alive, but it was best not to bring that up. Her brother didn't have anything to do with it. "Not once did you visit me."

"You said goodbye!"

"How long are you going to hold on to that? How long is it going to stay my fault? Did you go to college?"

God, wouldn't it be a kicker if she'd gone to the U of D? No, the campus was huge but he would have bumped into her.

"Yeah, I did," she said, blinking at the sudden change of topic. "I got my associate degree from the community college."

"I'm glad," he mumbled. "Sit down and finish your soup."

Silently, she sat and wiped the drips off the table.

He ate a spoonful of the lukewarm soup.

A thick tree branch flew into the picture window behind the bed, the loud *bang* breaking the silence.

She jerked as the branch dropped to the ground.

He inhaled a calming breath through his nose. The window didn't break. They were all right.

"I need to call my mom," she said, pushing her bowl away.

"Hopefully there's service. While you were sleeping, James called me. Jared was flying and got caught in this. He had to land his plane."

"Is he okay?"

"He's not hurt, but he's stranded out there somewhere. I offered to help look—"

"You can't go out in this."

"I know."

"I met Leah, and she seems nice. They would make a nice couple if they got together."

"She's not from here," he said tersely, clearing their bowls from the table. He didn't know much about Leah and Jared's relationship, though he knew enough people couldn't control who they fell in love with. Jared had a long, hard road ahead of him if he fell for Marnie's bridesmaid.

"No, she's not, but people can always make it work if they want it bad enough."

He narrowed his eyes at the jab.

They couldn't compare their relationship with Jared and Leah's. They were adults. When he left Rocky Point, he'd been a kid who had only one plan, one escape route, and he hadn't let anything hold him back.

He washed the bowls, scrubbing harder than he needed to.

Ivy's murmuring carried to him from where she perched on the side of the hot tub.

He'd buy her a new phone next. If the device was paid for, the service contract wouldn't be much more than what she prepaid every month.

Fuck it.

He'd add her to his plan and she wouldn't have to worry about a cell phone bill at all.

He looked forward to that fight.

Her low voice sent shivers up and down his spine.

They were on even footing now.

He hoped the storm lasted a good long time.

Ivy pretended to talk to her mom for longer than she really did. Well, she hadn't spoken to her mom at all. Her mother wouldn't surface until she got hungry and couldn't find food.

Today should have been her shopping day.

She left a message but didn't hang up. When their landline answering machine disconnected, she stayed on, giving herself time to think.

To think back to the day Logan told her goodbye.

James had leaned against his car parked in front of her house waiting for Logan, arms crossed over his chest. They were leaving early to settle into the dorms. James's parents fixed it so they could share a room.

"You'll be okay," Logan said, wiping the tears off her cheeks. "You'll be just fine." He sounded as if he was trying to convince himself as well as her.

"Good luck. I'll miss you."

"I'll miss you, too. You know I love you, right?"

She sniffled. "Yeah. You know I love you too, right?"

"Yeah, I do. Don't be a stranger, okay?"

"Yeah."

"Promise."

"I promise. Now go. James is waiting, and you're making it harder."

He kissed her, knowing his choice to break up with her was ending a precious time in their lives they would never be able to get back. He'd done it to give them freedom to pursue different things, even if those different things involved other people. She hadn't asked him to, hadn't told him she thought it best they broke up, but she hadn't tried to stop it, either, because she knew he wouldn't listen.

Don't be a stranger.

She'd forgotten he said it. Lost in the heartbreak and misery, and as the years went on, bitterness and resentment, she forgot the simple invitation he whispered before he bounded down the steps and climbed into James's car, never to see Rocky Point again.

The invitation to at least keep their friendship going.

She hadn't.

As time went on, neither had he.

What would a "thinking of you" card have done for their relationship? A box of his favorite peanut butter cookies?

They wouldn't have kept a friendship alive for eighteen years, but she wouldn't be in the situation she was in now.

Logan blaming her just as equally for the end of them.

This wasn't her fault. She knew the reality. Studying law was no small thing. Even if they had stayed in touch, their friendship would have faded to nothing. Clerking, cramming to take the bar, not to mention the classes themselves and a part-time job, her little life in her little town would have been forgotten in all Logan had to do to become the success he was.

Maybe it wouldn't have hurt so much.

Maybe it would have hurt more.

"Bye, Mom," she said, raising her voice and flipping her phone shut.

"Is she okay?" he asked, standing in the kitchenette and drying his hands with a towel. His pants were still wet.

She didn't know if he knew. He was surprised enough about her living situation when he brought her home the other night. Maybe he didn't know about her mom.

It would suit her just fine if he never found out.

"Great," she said with fake cheerfulness, padding barefoot to the window. "God, it's horrible out there."

"Yeah. We might be stuck for a while."

His voice came from right behind her, and she jumped.

"I hope not too long. I have to work tomorrow."

"No one's going to be out drinking in the storm," he said, wrapping his arms around her.

"People staying at the resort will be, dummy," she said, amused. She didn't want him to think she meant the insult. "What else do people do when there's nothing else to do?"

"Is that what you want to do? I have a couple of bottles of something around here."

She leaned her head against Logan's chest. "I don't drink much. Being around booze all the time made me lose my taste for it."

That and seeing how her mother self-medicated with it. She was afraid she'd like how she felt burying her sadness under a bottle of gin.

She worked instead, and their bills thanked her for it.

"Then we should do something else to pass the time,"

he said, bending closer to whisper in her ear. "It's still early yet."

She shivered. "What did you have in mind?"

"How about . . ."

Her heart thudded against her ribs. She wanted him to take her to bed. Right here, right now. She didn't even need the bed. Against the window would work just fine.

"A game of Scrabble?"

She whipped around. "Scrabble? You did that on purpose!"

He blinked. "Did what?"

"Nothing." She smothered a huff. It wasn't his fault she was sex-starved. Touch-starved. Love-starved. "Scrabble it is."

She wanted him, but instead of feeling smug, Logan was relieved. Come hell or high water, they'd be friends when he left after James and Marnie's wedding.

He laid out the game on the kitchen table. If he set it up on the bed, they wouldn't be playing Scrabble.

The game didn't interest him. He liked watching documentaries, reading nonfiction. Taking a pro bono case here and there. He always tried to better himself and expected nothing less of the people he surrounded himself with.

Scrabble was to put Ivy at ease. He wanted to spend the rest of the evening getting to know her. She'd changed as the years went by without him.

She sat at the table, and he poured the dregs of the coffee he made that afternoon into their mugs. If she didn't want a drink, the only other thing he could offer her was tap water.

He let her go first.

"How long have you worked at the resort?" he asked, studying the tiles.

"About twelve years."

"So right after . . ."

"Yeah. Dad left, Mom was grieving, and it didn't take me long to realize there was no money coming in."

"Do you like it?" he asked, skimming over the other parts. He'd get to her mother later, and what happened after Joey's death.

She set her tiles on the board.

EXILED

"Nice," he said, noting her score on the tiny pad.

"I suppose," she said, picking up a wooden square and turning it over and over. "The tips are nice, and the people are decent to work with. So far, Desiree, the resort's manager, lets me work as many hours as I want."

"What do you do when you're not at work?"

She frowned. "What do you mean?"

"You still have hobbies, don't you? You used to like to read."

"I don't have time to do other stuff, Logan. I don't go out with friends. Yes, I still like to read and I buy books at the thrift store or go to the library, but mostly I do chores and worry about my stupid car. I try to relax in the tub every now and then, and I sleep. I'd rather not die from a stress heart attack before I turn forty."

He played his word.

LILT

It's all he could think of and he didn't care about the outcome of the game. He wrote down his tiny score.

She chose more tiles, her lips pressed into a thin line.

"Where does your mom work?" Rosie had to work somewhere, even part-time at the grocery store, to help Ivy pay the rent.

"She's between jobs right now."

She played her word.

ALONE

"What about you?" she asked.

"What?" He scratched Ivy's score onto the pad and chose more tiles.

"What do you do for fun? Golf? Schmoozing clients at expensive restaurants?"

"I'm not that kind of attorney." He gritted his teeth. She cared so little about him she hadn't bothered to find out what kind of law he practiced. "I'm an estate attorney. All my clients are dead."

The word hung over the table.

He played his word.

HELP

"And I play squash," he added, to poke at her.

"Of course you do."

"What's that supposed to mean?"

She chose replacement tiles. "Nothing."

He wrote his low score on the pad.

They played in silence, Ivy adding LONELY onto his L in HELP.

He played YELLOW off her Y, and she played STRANDED off the E.

"I don't have any good letters," he said, glaring at the tiles as if that would turn them into something useful.

"That's okay," she said, hopping off her chair. "We don't have to play anymore." She stood in front of the window, her hands deep in the pockets of the robe, her hair tumbling down her back.

He bit back a sigh. He'd been able to get a few things out of her, at least. Rosie not working must put a huge strain on their finances.

Dammit.

He studied the board before sliding the wooden squares into the box.

ALONE

LONELY

EXILED

STRANDED

He'd learned more than the fact she still liked to read.

She felt alone and abandoned. Stranded in her crappy life.

He had to help her fix it. There had to be a way.

He just didn't know how.

The rest of the evening drifted by as the snow flew past the window. The cabins didn't have a TV and the internet was down. Streaming a movie on Logan's laptop wasn't possible, but Ivy didn't mind. She liked the quiet, listening to the wind whistle past the cabin.

For a late dinner, he grilled them ham and cheese sandwiches and opened a bag of Cool Ranch Doritos. The meal was similar to what she would have made herself at home.

Afterward, he settled in to go over notes, and she paged through a true crime book he packed. They sat in comfortable silence on the bed, the huge down pillows propping them up.

She had a flash of a lifetime of evenings like this, if they were married. If they could somehow move past what they'd done to each other.

"This is nice," she said.

"Hmmm?" he hummed, a pencil hanging between his lips as he read something on his laptop's screen, a legal pad beside him.

"It reminds me of when we used to do our homework together."

He pulled the pencil out of his mouth and smiled. "Or not do our homework."

"That, too." She paused. "I'm sorry."

He closed his laptop and set his things on the night-stand. "For what?"

She closed the book on her hand to her hold place. "You were right. I could have at least sent a card. I have no excuse except on the porch, when you said goodbye, it sounded so final. Like you didn't want me to bother you."

"You have never been a bother."

"I know, but you had all this stuff going on, and I wanted to give you space. I thought that if you wanted to talk to me you would, and as the months went by, you didn't."

"I was pretty busy," he said, scooting down the mattress.

She dropped the book on the floor and did the same. "I know, and in all fairness, I was, too. Life was good back then, besides you being gone. Joey seemed okay, Mom and Dad got along. School was fine, and I worked here and there to pay my tuition. I tried to enjoy life the best I could without you in it."

He slid an arm under her pillow and wiggled closer.

She bit her lip. She had something to tell him, but he didn't need to know. Nothing would change between them, and there wasn't anything he could do with the information once he had it.

She should keep it to herself, but she opened her mouth anyway, and the words tumbled out. "I helped her get away."

He leaned back to look at her.

There wasn't anything to be gained by telling him except that even though they hadn't been speaking, she wanted him to know she hadn't hated him or taken her hurt out on his mother.

"What?" he asked, his voice hoarse over the storm.

"I helped her get away. I drove her to the airport."

He swallowed. "I sent her money."

"I know. She told me on the way to Marengo. But he took it, and she couldn't leave. You wanted her to get away from him so badly . . ."

But you didn't come home to help her.

The unspoken words hung between them.

"What happened?"

"He found the bus fare you sent her, and she called our house and asked for me. She didn't have anyone else. In the middle of the night, while he was passed out, I picked her up and drove her to the airport in Marengo. I watched her board and stayed until her plane took off. I stayed until the departure screen said it landed in Denver. I stayed until I knew she wouldn't have to come back."

Tears shimmered in his eyes. "I never knew. She didn't tell me."

"I told her not to say anything. I didn't want you to think I helped her so you would start talking to me again. I did it because she needed help and even though by then we hadn't spoken in four years, I still loved you."

He didn't say anything, only stared at the ceiling.

"I didn't tell you to make you feel bad. She told me all she wanted was for you to get out, and you did."

"How did she pay for her plane ticket?"

She cuddled into his side. "I paid. I had a job and a credit card. She called and told me she landed safely, and I never heard anything else after that."

"She's doing okay. Still lives with Aunt Paula and works full-time at a café."

"Have you gone to visit her?" she asked.

"No. I've been busy helping James get our firm off the ground."

"Yeah."

"I'll pay you back for the ticket."

"That's not why I told you."

He turned on her. "Then why *did* you tell me? To rub it in my face? Make sure I knew what a shitty son I was back then? What a shitty son I am now because I don't visit her? To accuse me of thinking only about myself for the past eighteen years? I did want she wanted me to do. I got out."

"Telling you was a mistake. I'm sorry. Forget I said anything." She *had* wanted to jab him with the sharp point of a knife. Maybe not shove it in his back, but . . . "I told you because I wanted you to realize that when you left Rocky Point behind, you left people who cared about you behind. You didn't look back."

"And this is exactly why I didn't look back. This town is full of unhappiness and bitterness."

Like her. She was unhappy and bitter. Got it.

She rolled over but didn't pick the book up off the floor. If the snow stopped, she had to work tomorrow, and if it didn't, she'd walk to the resort anyway, no matter how bad it was, even if Logan came after her again.

After this, she had a suspicion he wouldn't bother.

"Ivy," he said.

"It's fine. I know why you left, I know why Elora wanted you to get out. You were doing what was best for you. No one can fault you for that."

"But you do."

She squeezed her eyes shut. The sun had set a long time ago, leaving the cabin dark except for the reading light on Logan's side of the bed. Always bone-tired, she could sleep through anything and the glow while he studied his notes wouldn't bother her, but he put his laptop on the kitchen table and shut the light off.

He pounded his pillow and adjusted the bedspread, and lying still, he stayed close to the edge of the bed.

The mattress was a million times better than what she slept on, the old bed she was able to keep from her child-hood bedroom. Most of the other things had been sold when the bank repossessed their house.

She woke up at four to use the bathroom and Logan's arm was tightly wrapped around her stomach, his face pressed into her neck.

Carefully, she disentangled herself without disturbing him.

The wind stopped, but she couldn't see how much snow accumulated because of the storm.

Relieved she wouldn't have to fight her way through the blizzard, she fell back asleep, smiling a little when Logan cuddled her close to him again.

Ivy dressed before the sun came up, tiptoeing around the cabin and holding her breath when Logan rolled onto his back, mumbling something she didn't understand. He settled into a deep sleep as she stood frozen, her jacket gripped in her hands.

A snowblower growled outside. Thank God the resort was so quick about stuff like that. It would be a lot easier to walk back if the trail was cleared.

She debated taking the key to the Outback, her hand hovering over the fob sitting on the kitchen counter, and despite her reluctance, she put it in her pocket. It would be days before all of Rocky Point's streets were cleared, and if she wanted to check on her mother, the Outback was the smarter choice.

Even after all this time, Logan knew exactly where to hit her.

Damn him.

Mitch was clearing the cul-de-sac using the resort's riding snowblower, and when he saw her, he cut the engine and jumped off the seat. "You spent the night with Logan?"

He only asked because he cared and didn't want her hurt, but the question still got her back up.

"I had to. He bought me a car—" Mitch raised his eyebrows— "and I came to return the key. It started snowing while we were arguing. That was one of the fastest storms to blow in I've ever seen."

"I heard Jared was out in it," Mitch said.

"Yeah. James told Logan. Any word if he's okay?"

"No news, but then, people aren't too quick to tell me things. Callie will know something sooner than I will, but I'll let you know when I find out."

"That's okay," she said. "Don't go out of your way if you're busy."

"It's no problem, especially if you'll be in the lounge. Going back to the resort?"

"Yep. I need to check on my mom and get ready for my shift."

"I heard the main roads are cleared, but I don't know how easy it will be to get to your apartment. Be careful."

"I will. Thanks for plowing."

"It's what I get paid for."

"How are your parents doing?"

He adjusted his hat, tugging it lower over his ears. "Good, but the snow's going to slow the house stuff down. They were supposed to go out and see what they could salvage, but they can't now. Dad was able to pick Luna up from the vet though, and she's been sleeping in their room."

"That's good. He must have missed her."

"Yeah. Callie, ah, did a nice thing. Anyway, I need to keep going. There's more to plow, but I already did the parking lots. You should be able to get out. See you later. Be careful."

"I will. Thanks."

He climbed onto the snowplow and the engine roared to life. He still had plenty of snow to move in front of the cabins, and she left him to it.

The staff parking lot was clear, like Mitch said, but she had to brush the packed snow off the Outback. She started right up, something her old POS car never would have done after a blizzard. The vents blew warm air, and the windows were defrosted in a matter of minutes.

She'd forgotten what money could buy.

After she checked on Rosie, she'd take a shower and find something to eat for breakfast. The grocery store wasn't open yet, but chances were good Rosie's vodka supply and a bag of chips would keep her going until she could make a food run.

Just because Logan was in town didn't mean her life wasn't going to change. She had to remember that.

If she could handle it, she could take what he offered, use him for what she could, and then after the wedding, after he left, at least she could say she'd gotten something out of it.

Cautiously, she drove through a snowdrift on her street. The building's parking lot was buried under several feet of snow and she wouldn't be able to park in a parking spot, but that was okay. She wouldn't be here long.

Her thoughts heavy, she parked on the road and climbed out of the car.

She couldn't use Logan. She wanted more out of life, but not like that.

No matter how hard she wished it, he wouldn't be the one to give it to her.

Half asleep, Logan reached for her but came up empty. Her pillow was cold, her side of the bed nothing but a tangle of bedspread and sheets.

He sighed.

He was good, kept his hands to himself all night. He'd woken briefly with her in his arms, and he'd fallen back to sleep, more content than he'd been in a long time. He wasn't a monk and he'd had women stay over at his place, but Ivy was different.

She'd always be different.

His phone buzzed, and he hefted himself out of bed to answer it. After the blizzard, anyone could need help. Even

Ivy, since she was probably halfway across town by now. Damn her stubborn ass.

James's name glowed on the screen. "Hey, what's up?"

"We just came back from Jared's place. I tried to get a hold of you, but all I got was voicemail. He's okay," James jumped in, without saying good morning. "He spent the night in a barn, and some old coot gave him a ride into town. He's exhausted and kicked us out to get some sleep. Marnie wants us all in the dining room to have breakfast. Did you want to meet us there? How'd you and Ivy make it through the storm?"

He found his glasses on the nightstand and put them on. "Thank God Jared's okay." His stomach rumbled. "I could eat. Sorry I didn't hear my phone. Ivy had to spend the night, but she was gone when I woke up. Someone at the resort must have cleared the trail already."

"Road crews have been out since the snow stopped, and the roads were plowed when we drove to Jared's to wait. Marnie freaked out when she heard he was flying in the storm. Leah's not back from New York, either. No one's heard from her. If she was trying to get back during the blizzard, she might be stranded in an airport or something."

"She's not texting?"

"Marnie doesn't want to bother her."

"Yeah, true. If she needs help, she'll let us know."

"Maybe. She's used to being on her own."

Just like Ivy.

"I need a shower. I'll see you in the dining room in half an hour."

"We'll have the coffee waiting."

He hung up and stood under a hot shower, rinsing Ivy's scent off him, much to his regret. He'd see her later. He'd make sure of it.

He dressed in jeans and a sweater, shrugged into his jacket and pushed his boots onto his feet.

Ivy took the Outback's key.

He grinned.

Maybe she'd keep the car after all.

CHAPTER FOUR

His friends weren't hard to find. The large group sat in the dining room, the tables pushed together, silver coffee carafes shining. Some people were eating, famished after hearing the good news Jared was okay, but most were ignoring their meals, cradling coffee mugs, too tired to do anything else. Cole was unobtrusively taking pictures and Autumn was pulling off her coat, a determined look on her face.

Uh oh. More blog interviews.

At least this time she wouldn't zero in on him. He didn't have anything new to say.

"Hey," James greeted him, pushing out an empty chair with his foot. "I saved you a spot."

The words came out of James's mouth, but the voice belonged to Ivy. Every day in elementary school they had to sit with their class in the cafeteria. "Saved you a spot," she'd say, grinning, an extra sandwich and bag of chips her mother packed sitting on the table next to her, waiting for him.

James frowned. "Are you okay?"

He cleared this throat. "Yeah. Sorry. The wind beat against the cabin for a good long time. Didn't get much sleep."

"Neither did I. Marnie and I stayed up all night waiting to hear news about Jared. Let's grab some food," James said, jerking his thumb toward the buffet, "and I'll fill you in."

They stood in line and Logan loaded eggs, sausage, and hashbrowns onto his plate. Sitting at the table with his friends, he poked at the pile of scrambled eggs and sipped on a cup of coffee flavored with hazelnut and chocolate creamer.

James shot him a look and shoveled breakfast potatoes into his mouth. "How'd it go with Ivy?"

He huffed. "Not very well. She resents me."

"She'll come around."

"Doubtful."

"You were gone for eighteen years, it's not like you can pick up where you left off. She pissed you didn't go to Joey's funeral?"

"She hasn't said anything about it. We didn't talk about Joey much, but his death tore her family apart. Her mom doesn't work, her dad's gone. Her life's pretty fucked up."

"You said you were gonna help her fix that, right?"

James chewed on a piece of bacon, and he poured more coffee. Conversation hummed around them.

"I bought her a car. Did a little research and bought her something decent that will get her through the next few winters. That's why she was at the cabin yesterday, to give the key back. I can help her, but she's going to think I'm trying to pay her off because I was a dick for the past eighteen years."

"You weren't being a dick. You were doing what you had to do. Could you have gone about it differently? Sure, but we can all say that. Even Ivy." He paused. "You were in love with her in high school. Do you still feel that way?"

"'Yes' is on the tip of my tongue, but she's different. She's changed. I don't know her anymore."

"But you want to."

"Yeah."

"What's the problem, then?"

"She doesn't want to get to know *me*. Her opinion of me isn't very high." He wanted to tell James about how she helped his mother, but that would be best left for another day when they didn't have fifteen people sitting around them buzzing from caffeine, lack of sleep, and relief.

"All you can do is try," James said, slapping him on the back. "I've always liked Ivy. You could do worse."

"Gee, thanks."

"No, I mean it. She's a sweet girl, and you know she'd have your back. Invite her out. There's a sleigh ride tonight. All this fresh snow, it'll be a good time. Ask her to go."

"She's working."

"No, she's not."

"What do you mean, 'no, she's not?' She told me she was. Probably pulling another double. She works. All. The. Time."

"Not tonight."

He narrowed his eyes. "What are you going to do?"

"Leave everything to me."

"I don't like the sound of that."

"Marnie isn't the only one who wants to see her friends happy. I know after the way you grew up you don't want kids, but that doesn't mean you have to spend the rest of your life alone, either."

"I guess not."

"You know it's true or you wouldn't have dated."

"I wasn't looking for anything permanent. I missed Ivy, that's all."

"You don't have to miss her anymore, do you?"

He opened his mouth to reply, but Marnie, Cole, and Autumn included James in their conversation, something about Leah driving from Marengo to Rocky Point and how she was sleeping at Autumn's right now.

Leah had balls driving in the dark on the slippery roads, and in all that snow, too. She'd be good for Jared if they could figure it out, but they'd have a tougher time making a go of it than he and Ivy would if he could convince her not to hate him for leaving.

He envied James and Marnie their easy relationship. She rested her head on his shoulder, and he had his arm wrapped around her. Every so often he'd press a kiss to the top of her head and she would look at him, her heart in her eyes.

He wanted that.

More than distance stood in his way, and he'd have to do some heavy soul searching to decide if Ivy was worth it.

Scratch that.

She was worth it.

Fuck yeah, she was. But he'd been running for a long time and coming back to Rocky Point was only the first of many things he'd need to do if he wanted to keep her in his life.

First, the sleigh ride.

He'd let James do his magic, and then see if, under the twinkling stars, he couldn't make a little magic of his own.

The car looked out of place on the worn-out street.

If Social Services found out about the new...er car, she'd be screwed. Social Security sent her mother a small disability check every month because of her doctor-diagnosed depression which led to her inability to work, and Ivy had to declare any changes to their household income. They needed her checks, every little bit helped. Thankfully, insuring the Outback wouldn't cost much more than her Camry, so that wasn't a worry, but why did driving a dependable car feel like a punishment?

She checked on her mom. The blinds in the living room were closed, the air musty. Rosie needed a shower. Sometimes she was good about it, sometimes she wasn't, and before Ivy went to work, she'd have to rouse her and remind her that even drunk, she was still alive and needed to take care of herself.

She took a shower first, her body sore in ways that were pleasant yet so old they were unfamiliar, and she washed Logan's and the resort's body wash scents off her skin. Then she cleaned the kitchen. While she was trapped with Logan, her mother made toast, and crumbs covered the counter. There were dishes in the sink and the trash needed to go out.

Rosie hadn't noticed she wasn't around. Sleeping, drifting in and out of a reality where Joey still lived, her mother didn't surface often. She almost preferred it. Because when Rosie *was* sober, she promised her things she knew would never happen. A job. Sobriety. A better place to live.

Despite everything, she still loved her mom, and it broke her heart over and over again to watch her struggle with Joey's death.

"You have to shower," she said, opening the curtains to let the sparkling white light into the living room.

Rosie squinted against the sudden brightness. "What time is it?"

"Too late for you to be doing what you're doing," she said, dragging the blanket off her mother's lap and setting aside the framed picture of Joey her mother always held on to like a lifeline.

"Just a little longer," Rosie mumbled.

"You can go back to sleep after a shower and a meal. I work later." She finished under her breath, "And I can't stop you."

"You're a good girl," Rosie said, reaching for the vodka bottle on the floor near her feet.

"That's empty, Mom. Let me help you."

Rosie swiped her frizzy blonde hair out of her eyes.

She used to be pretty, her mother.

In brief, unexpected glances, she saw why her father had fallen in love with her. But now booze and dehydration had destroyed her hair and her skin was sallow due to poor nutrition and lack of sunlight. She carried extra weight in her midsection and hips, and her boobs sagged. Rosie didn't care about wearing a bra anymore.

"Logan's back in town," she said, holding her mother's hand and urging her to her feet.

"That little boy . . . his daddy beats him up."

"He used to," she said, "but his daddy hasn't beaten him up in a long time."

"Still lives across town," Rosie said, letting her guide her to the bathroom.

"Logan's dad? Yes, he does."

She helped Rosie get undressed, ran the water a little on the cool side to help her wake up, and pushed the shower curtain aside. "Be careful in there. Don't fall. And don't forget to wash your hair."

While her mom showered, she finished straightening the apartment and ran the vacuum. She shoved all the empty liquor bottles into the recyclables to be dumped with the trash on her way out.

She tried her best to keep the apartment looking nice. For low-income housing, the insides were better than she'd expected when she signed the lease, tears streaming down her cheeks after the bank repossessed their house.

Her parents had had five years left of their thirty-year mortgage when Joey died.

Apartment living was difficult to get used to. She'd taken for granted a yard to sunbathe in, a garage to store her bike.

A house didn't mean family.

Logan and his mom and dad had lived in a house. A little house, kind of like Mitch's parents' house, older.

That could have been a home. Logan could have had a family.

He would have happily lived in a small apartment like this had it meant he had two parents who loved him instead of one who used her body as a shield and the other who thought himself a man every time he laid a hand on the people he claimed to love.

She had the apartment set to rights when Rosie came out of the bathroom wearing clean sweatpants and a t-shirt, her hair a tangle of wet knots she wasn't trying to comb out.

"I made you a cup of coffee," she said, nudging her mother onto a chair. She grabbed a hairbrush and went to work on her mother's damp strands. It would be easier if her mother remembered to use conditioner. "I need to go to work, but I promise I'll go to the grocery store later."

Her mother sighed and sipped her coffee. "How's the resort?"

"The wedding stuff is keeping everyone busy."

"Who's getting married? Do I know them?"

"Maybe. Marnie Zimmerman and James Fox? They moved to Decatur after graduation."

"Logan went with James."

"Yeah, he did," she said, tugging the brush through Rosie's damaged hair.

"You were crushed."

"It was a long time ago."

"Not so long."

"No, I guess not."

She finished brushing her mother's hair. "There you go. I better get to work. Some of the roads are still bad because of the storm. Don't try to go out," she said, though her mother wouldn't bother. "The apartment people haven't cleared the sidewalks, and God knows when they will."

Her mother settled in her place on the couch and turned the TV on. Judge Judy rolled her eyes at the defendant. Rosie held Joey's picture against her chest, and everything in her life slid right back into place.

"Bye, Mom," she said, opening the door.

Rosie ignored her, her fuzzy attention focused on a Tide commercial. She couldn't remember the last time Rosie had done laundry.

She drove to the resort, the seat warming her butt, the tires gliding under her.

She reached the turn that would either bring her out of town or deeper into it, and for one split second, one crazy second, she wondered what it would be like if she just turned left instead of right.

The only problem was, everyone she loved, everything she held dear, was in Rocky Point.

And that, unfortunately, included Logan Draper.

Ivy hung her jacket and purse up in the back with the boxes of booze and went through what she needed to do during her shift: count the cash in the register, refresh lemon and lime slices, make a note of the liquor bottles that were running low, and put in an order for more cocktail napkins.

"Desiree wants to see you," Karen said, peeking into the lounge. The bar wasn't open yet, and she stood outside the stockroom adjusting her vest and tie.

She froze, and dread pooled in her belly. This was it. This was when Desiree would tell her she couldn't keep approving her overtime.

Frantically, she began thinking of places in town where she could get a second job.

She swallowed against the bitter taste of panic in her throat.

"It's probably not that bad," Karen said, noticing the pinched look on her face.

She tried to breathe. "Right. I'm sure it's nothing."

Her heart hammered the entire way to Desiree's office. Across the lobby, Mitch gestured at her, wanting to talk, but she waved him off and he scowled. She wanted this meeting over with as quickly as possible.

Leaning into Desiree's office, she asked, "You wanted to see me?"

Piles of paper were scattered on Desiree's desk, and faint frown lines hugged her mouth.

Crap.

"Yes. Come in and have a seat. I know the lounge is about to open, so I won't keep you long."

Tentatively, she stepped farther into Desiree's large office and perched on a seat in front of her desk, trapping her hands between her knees. She didn't want Desiree to see them shaking.

Desiree tapped a pen on top of a piece of paper. "I'm giving you the evening off."

Apprehension and sweat prickled her skin. "Why?"

"The resort's sponsoring sleigh rides tonight, and I need you to participate on our behalf. Similar to when you were fishing at one of the resort's ice houses. We received positive feedback about your presence there. Only, I hope this time you won't be a party to assault."

"Callie—"

"I know what Callie Carter did wasn't assault, at least, the young man she dumped on his ass isn't pressing charges, though after he and his friends ambushed her outside the hospital, he has no right to do so. But this is proof violence, in any form, isn't the answer, nor a message the Rocky Point Resort owners want to convey. Nonetheless, we do have two sleigh rides scheduled this evening, and I would appreciate it if you would be there."

"But my hours . . ." She wouldn't be paid to go on a sleigh ride, no matter how much the idea appealed to her. She counted on the overtime and took whatever shifts came her way.

"I'm sorry I can't let you stay punched in, but I'll compensate you for the lost time." Desiree handed her a sealed envelope. "Think of it as a non-taxable gift."

Reluctantly, she took it. She had no choice. A crappy

twenty bucks wouldn't replace the six hours of overtime she would have earned otherwise.

"I can see you're not happy about it," Desiree said, sitting back in her chair.

"No, it's fine," she said, forcing a smile. "I want to be a team player."

"Thank you. Try to have a good time. Marnie Zimmerman's wedding party booked the first ride at seven tonight. They'll be meeting in the back, near the staff parking lot, and the ride will go through the woods beyond the cabins. They paid for two hours."

"Do I need to go on more than one?"

"No. The second ride will have two front desk representatives in attendance. You're free to do what you like after the horses return to the resort."

She fingered the white envelope, her name written on the front in Desiree's own handwriting.

"Ms. Arnold—"

"Desiree, Ivy. I keep telling you that."

"Desiree," Ivy corrected, though it didn't sound right. "This all sounds . . ."

Desiree lifted her eyebrows.

"I mean, I've worked at the resort for twelve years, and I've never been asked to do something like this."

"That's not entirely true. You've been asked to bartend at various events."

She tilted her head, unable to disagree. There had been times she'd manned an open bar at a convention in the ball-room or a dinner like Marnie's meet and greet. "Will there be booze at the sleigh ride?"

"Peppermint schnapps and hot chocolate will be provided."

"I don't know . . ." She wanted to work her shift at the

bar. She'd already calculated how much her next check would be.

"Ivy," Desiree said, nudging her chair forward, "go and have a good time. I know you picked up for Hilary again, and those hours have been covered. You're being compensated generously for missing that shift. Take a couple hours to yourself tonight after the ride. Go home and get some sleep."

There wasn't anything more she could say. She mumbled, "Thank you. Have a good day," and shuffled out of Desiree's office, the envelope dangling from her fingers. It felt heavy. There wasn't a check or cash in it. A gift card then.

Desiree hadn't paid her. She'd given her a worthless gift card that would end up in the back of her kitchen's junk drawer.

Fabulous.

This wouldn't be the first time her paycheck ended up short. Sometimes, rarely, but sometimes, everyone worked their shifts, and there weren't any extra hours available.

She leaned against the wall and fought back tears. Her hands shaking, she opened the crisp, white envelope.

Get it over with and see how much money she was shafted.

She pulled out the VISA gift card and blinked.

Five hundred dollars.

She blinked again.

The second zero didn't disappear.

Five hundred dollars. Not fifty. She made more than minimum wage and fifty bucks wouldn't have covered what she'd lose, but five hundred was about what she made in a week after taxes. It was too much.

Wait a minute.

What had Desiree said? Her presence was only required at the first sleigh ride of the evening, and who reserved the first ride?

Marnie and her friends.

Logan would be there tonight.

Desiree hadn't ordered her to be there to represent the resort but because Logan decided he wanted her there.

Dammit.

She straightened. She'd give him a piece of her mind.

But that would have to wait.

She still had to work her shift.

There would be plenty of time to tell Logan she didn't need him or his money.

She'd give him the key back to his stupid car, too.

She would really miss those butt warmers.

"What are you doing here?" she asked Lola. A fill-in for various positions at the resort, Lola waitressed if a server called in sick and cleaned rooms if housekeeping was short-staffed. She often bartended, pouring and mixing drinks at the cash and open bars if the meeting rooms were full, which they usually were, especially this time of year.

That was the main reason she had wanted this job so badly. Booze meant job security and plenty of hours, either as a party bartender or in the lounge.

"I'm supposed to tell you to take an extra hour."

"To do what?" she asked, annoyed. It seemed like it was her day to be bossed around.

"Have dinner with me."

She twirled at the sound of Logan's voice.

"You're going on the sleigh ride with us, aren't you? I don't want you to be hungry while we're gone, and you don't have time to go home first. Come on, we're meeting in the dining room."

He looked good in jeans and a dark blue sweater, his blond hair shimmering gold in the fire's light. He'd always hated his glasses, but she liked them. They made him look smart and handsome.

That hadn't changed.

"I can eat something in the kitchen. It's where I take my breaks anyway," she said, crossing her arms in front of her chest.

He scowled.

She enjoyed it.

He'd paid for her time. She didn't have to make it easy on him.

He sighed. "Please?"

"Honey, don't turn down the pleasure of this hunk's company," Lola said, her long nail poking her shoulder.

"You don't even like men." She frowned and jerked away.

"Doesn't mean I can't appreciate the finer of the species," Lola said, winking a heavily made-up eye.

She glared at Logan. "Fine, but that doesn't mean I'm happy about it."

She went to the stockroom for her jacket and heard Lola say, "She'll come around, honey. She doesn't date much."

"Much?" Logan asked, and he sounded way more interested than he should have.

"Okay, none. She needs a little fun, and a little *fun*."

She pictured Lola leering.

"Oh, I've got that covered," he said.

Dammit. He could charm an Eskimo into buying ice.

"Knock it off," she snapped, stomping out of the stockroom.

Lola whistled. "Honey, you ain't got that covered *enough*."

"I'll keep working on it," he said, laughing. He grabbed her arm in a strong grip, and she let him lead her out of the lounge.

"I know what you're doing," she said, yanking away from him the minute they were out of Lola's sight. She didn't want to give Lola anything else to tease her about.

That's why she pulled away. Not because she liked the feel of his hand on her arm.

"And what's that?"

She stopped in the middle of the hallway, her jacket clenched in her fists.

"You paid for me!" And that way, the way that sounded, brought tears to her eyes. "You paid to have me on this stupid sleigh ride. You're fucking with my *job*, Logan. This is where I *work*. My paychecks pay my bills. When you leave, I'll still work here, and I can't afford for you to be fucking around with my hours or my reputation as a dependable worker."

"Desiree said it was okay. She wouldn't have let you go if she needed you."

"You don't get it. I *want* to be needed. Living wage jobs around here are slim to none. I want to be needed here because I need this job. You will *never* do this to me again."

"Did Desiree give you—"

She lifted her chin. "Yeah. She did. Do you think that makes it better? That you can afford to buy my time like I'm a whore?"

"That's not what this is about."

He stepped forward.

She stepped back.

They danced until she was pressed against the wall, and he crowded her with muscle and Obsession.

"Then what is it about?"

"I told James I wanted to spend time with you. He spoke to Desiree, not me."

"James paid me off?" Rage boiled in Ivy's blood. "I don't want his fucking money."

Logan cupped her face in his hands, his palms warm. "Calm down. James didn't give her money to give you. He might have said you were worried about lost wages, but if Desiree reimbursed you for missing your shift, James didn't have anything to do with it, and neither did I. I promise."

She tried to free her face from his grasp, but he gave her no room to move. "I don't believe you."

He leaned an arm against the wall over her head. "When have I lied?" he murmured, his breath whispering across her cheek. "When have I ever lied to you?"

"You haven't," she murmured, closing her eyes. He had never, as far as she knew. She'd always trusted him. With everything. Until the day he left.

"I haven't, and I wouldn't start now. Ivy, last night, sleeping with you in my arms . . . I told James I wanted to spend time with you. It was his idea you come tonight, but I knew you'd be working. He said he would fix it, and he did, but if you don't want to go . . . take the night off and go home. I'm not going to force you to do something you don't want to do."

Silence filled the hallway and the narrow space between them. His blue eyes searched hers, his face close enough it would take nothing but the smallest movement for their lips to touch.

In this moment, she would make or break their relationship.

Not their friendship because they would always have
that, as fragile as it was, but the love they shared in high
school and the love they could share now, as adults, would
disappear if she walked away.

He would stop pursuing her, and that made her want
to cry.

She'd missed him. God, she'd missed him, but did she
want to give him another chance? The odds were good the
only chance she was giving him was another chance to
break her heart.

"Will you kiss me?" she whispered.

He groaned. "You *never* have to ask." He wrapped his
arm around her waist, brought her body flush with his, and
claimed her mouth, hungrily, possessively.

She couldn't catch her breath.

Didn't want to.

His fingers grazed her breast, and heat flooded her
panties.

Even after all this time, the slightest touch could make
her want. Make her need.

"Let's go eat dinner," he whispered against her mouth.

"Okay."

He set her on her feet, and she stumbled against the
wall, trying to find her bearings.

His kisses had always been like that.

A hard tumble.

He smoothed his thumb over her jaw. "Are you okay?"

She huffed a laughed. "Yeah. You've always been able
to sweep me off my feet."

"You mean like this?"

He lifted her up and cradled her against his chest. He

kissed her again, long and hard, there in the hallway like he didn't have a care in the world.

She dropped her jacket and wrapped her arms around his neck.

"Thank you for coming tonight."

She wanted to be angry, but he kissed the fury out of her. "Thanks for wanting me along bad enough you talked to Desiree."

"I'm not going to walk away, Ivy. From us. I'm not that teenager anymore, and I want this."

She skimmed her fingertips over his scruff, a delicious scrape against her skin. "You don't know what you're asking. A lot has changed."

He brushed a kiss over her lips. "I know, baby."

The endearment melted her heart.

She was such a sucker.

He carried her all the way to the dining room, and embarrassed, she wanted to tell him to put her down, but she didn't. He stepped past the hostess's podium and all his friends catcalled to them.

Her cheeks flamed, but he laughed and kissed her, there in the middle of the dining room.

God help her, she enjoyed every second.

Eating out was a luxury, and when she did, she drove through the McDonald's drive-through and ordered off the dollar menu.

No five dollar coffees for her.

Everyone was thrilled when Starbucks came to Rocky Point.

She hadn't cared.

She skimmed her finger down the menu, the prices leaping out at her, mocking her.

The five-hundred dollar gift card was in her pocket, already spent on the car repairs she authorized. She still hadn't decided if she was going to keep the car Logan bought her.

The weight of his arm around her shoulders made her heart hum, but he'd been away too long, too many things had happened, and he'd have to do more than fling money at her to turn her head.

"What are you going to have?" he asked, his lips close to her ear.

She hesitated, searching for the cheapest thing on the menu.

"Order what you want," he said. "Please."

"Okay." Against her better judgment, she ordered a steak.

A luxury she'd never be able to afford on her own.

After everyone put in their orders, Mitch dragged his chair to sit next to her. "This is different, huh?" He straddled the chair, his arms resting on the back.

"Yeah." She didn't have to ask what he meant. Being part of a group. Friends.

She and Mitch weren't the only ones experiencing it for the first time. Anytime someone asked Leah a question, she would turn to them, her eyes wide and glazed over, like she couldn't believe they would bother to talk to her.

"Is everyone being nice to you?" she asked. Mitch hadn't had it easy, not with the way people treated him since the accident.

"Yeah. This is a good group. You and Logan back together?"

"I don't know. He said he wants to spend time with me." She lowered her voice, but Logan was talking to Jared and only squeezed her knee under the table when Mitch pulled a chair over to talk. "I guess it's a start."

"If that's what you want, then it's a good start," Mitch said, nodding.

"There's a lot we don't know about each other, that's all."

"I hear you. I haven't met Callie's family, and moving will be hard. I don't know if a big city is going to be the answer."

She brushed her hand over his. "You and Callie will have a good life no matter where you are. She loves you, and she's kick-ass."

He looked down the table at Callie who was laughing with Marnie. "Yeah. She is. She won't let me hide anymore."

"That scares you."

"Yeah. Logan isn't going to let you hide anymore, either. If you stay together, your life will be different, too."

"I don't hide."

He stared at her. "Yes, you do. You hide behind all the hours you work. If Logan wants a serious relationship, he's not going to let you work sixty hours a week, and you won't have to. You'll have his help."

"I know. He talked to Desiree and she gave me the night off. I'm supposed to be in the lounge now."

"See? It's already happening, but don't run from it, Ivy, not if you want it. Sometimes change can be good, even if it doesn't feel that way. Meeting Callie was scarier than hell, but she's the best thing that's ever happened to me."

"I'm happy for you." She tried to smile.

After the wedding when Logan went back to Decatur

and Mitch moved after Christmas, she'd be all alone. Maybe not *alone* alone. Logan would still call her, maybe visit her on the weekends, but she couldn't push away the knot of dread when she thought about it.

He had such an easy time walking away eighteen years ago. What would stop him from doing it again? Not her. He hated Rocky Point and he was here because of the wedding and nothing else. He had no reason to feel guilty for taking care of himself, but her heart was collateral damage and she hadn't been able to repair it.

Mitch looked around the table. "This friend stuff, huh?"

Ivy shrugged. It didn't matter if she had friends or not. She'd been without friends for so long she'd forgotten how to be one.

Sitting in her place next to Jared, Leah met her eyes and smiled.

She could try to get to know Leah. Earlier, she announced she bought the Supply Company from Helen. That was nice. Leah would always be around. And Autumn. She was in love with Cole McClure, but that didn't mean she'd be here forever. Cole would never leave his little boy, though, so if he and Autumn did more than avoid each other, she'd be making Rocky Point her home, too.

Maybe she could try to be friends. With people who wouldn't leave.

It wouldn't hurt so bad then, when Logan went back to Decatur and forgot about her. She wasn't stupid. It's what would happen.

No one was saying she couldn't move too, but Rosie would always need her and she didn't expect Logan to understand that.

The waitress set a hot plate in front of her, the steak

sizzling. "Thanks, Marilyn," she said to the plump waitress who'd worked in the dining room for the past three years.

"You're welcome, doll. It's good to see you doing something besides slinging drinks."

Mitch squeezed her shoulder. "We'll talk later."

She nodded, but she looked down at her plate to hide the tears in her eyes. Losing Mitch's friendship was one change the new year would bring that she wasn't looking forward to.

She didn't want to know what else was coming.

Mitch was right. She was hiding.

She needed the lounge. The comfort of pouring beer and mixing drinks.

There was safety behind her walls, and whoever tried would have to work like hell to knock them down.

Logan didn't like how quiet Ivy turned after her conversation with Mitch. The first time Logan saw him, he was ashamed to admit he'd flinched. He hadn't read much of the story when the accident happened and barely remembered it. He and James had been in Decatur putting every second they could into their fledgling law firm.

He knew Ivy and Mitch were good friends, and him meeting Callie shoved a wedge between them.

"Are you okay?" he asked.

She sat next to him, stiff, cutting her steak into little bites. "Yeah."

"Good. We'll be heading outside soon."

"Okay."

He let her be and picked at his chicken, listening with

half an ear to James talk about his parents' new furnace. He should have known Ivy wouldn't be all giggles and dreams because he came back to town, but convincing her he wanted to keep her in his life would take more work than he realized. Quite honestly, he wasn't sure if he was up to the task.

She left half her food on her plate, but she perked up outside under the stars. He blew out a breath, relieved.

The fresh snow the blizzard dumped on them would give the horses plenty of the white fluff to play in. She petted them, a gentle hand to their noses. He'd been on the receiving end of those touches, and his throat burned.

The group climbed into the sleigh, the coachman handing out blankets to anyone who wanted one. Logan took one and motioned for Ivy to sit next to him, and he covered their legs with the red and black plaid wool. He put his arm around her, hugging her close, and she burrowed into his side.

Cole McClure showed up as they settled onto the benches, a camera bag hanging from his shoulder.

Logan liked Autumn, and he hated she always looked sad whenever Cole was around. As couples, it made them even in number. He wondered if Marnie invited Rita and if she felt left out. Jared had it rough. An ex-wife at home and a fiancée in his arms.

He and Leah hadn't announced anything, but Logan could see it when he looked at them. They'd be together for the rest of their lives.

They huddled under a blanket, Jared whispering in Leah's ear, and in the light of the moon, tears glistened in her eyes, but she laughed, happy. No, not happy, goddamned relieved Jared made it home safely after his emergency landing and overnight stay in a barn.

"They look good together," Ivy said, following his gaze.

"Yeah, they do. I guess love does that to people."

He tilted her head and kissed her, her lips soft and warm under his. The horses set out, and lurching, he broke the kiss sooner than he wanted.

Marnie started singing "Jingle Bell Rock," and amidst groans and laughter, everyone sang along except Ivy.

As Marnie led the carols, she passed around spiked hot chocolate.

Ivy finally joined in when the carol switched to "Winter Wonderland."

"That one's my favorite," she said, holding a Styrofoam cup of hot chocolate, her cheeks pink.

Logan pulled off his hat and tugged it over her head to cover her ears. She hadn't any warning she'd be spending hours in the cold.

"Are you warm enough?" he asked during a lull between songs.

"Yeah, thanks." She cuddled into him, and he hugged her, grateful he'd been given a second chance. A chance he had absolutely no idea what to do with.

Autumn launched into a haunting rendition of "Silver Bells," and they listened to her sing the first verse before joining in on the chorus.

He didn't know Autumn could sing, but then, he'd spent as much time out of Rocky Point as he had in it. He'd been working his ass off to bury where he'd come from and hide from who he'd been.

James's wedding forced him back to Rocky Point.

Now he had to face the person he'd become, and he hoped that person was good enough for the woman he'd left behind.

CHAPTER FIVE

"Keep the car, Ivy."

They stood in the staff parking lot after the sleigh ride, and Logan shivered, cold and annoyed.

Everyone went inside the moment the last person set foot on the ground. Chilled to the bone, they chattered about sipping hot toddies and spiked hot apple cider in front of the fireplace in the lounge.

Maybe Ivy declined because in any other circumstance, she'd be the one serving the group.

Instead, she said she needed to go home but stopped abruptly near the Outback. She held the key fob in her hand and looked between him and the car.

He could imagine the tangled thoughts in her head, trying to figure out how to say she couldn't keep the car despite her obvious want to get in and drive away.

"I shouldn't." She still wore his hat on her head, pulled down around her ears. Her fingers were bright pink. She didn't have mittens.

"I know what you think," he said, trying not to lose his temper. Yelling would make her yell, and if he made her angry, this would be that much harder. "I know why you don't want to keep it. But if you would swallow your—" He stopped. Telling her to swallow her pride wouldn't work, either. All she had left was pride. "You need a good car. What if you broke down on your way home after work? You don't get done until the middle of the night and you'd be all alone. Rocky Point's small, but there are still creepers around here. What if you or Rosie get sick and need to go to the ER? People need reliable vehicles. There's no getting around it, especially in weather like this." He pointed at the resort. "You're always saying you need to work but how can you if you don't have a way to get here? Whatever you feel, or don't feel, for me, after all this time, can you . . . I don't know, say, 'Thank you, Logan' and keep the car?"

She wanted to keep it, he could see it in her eyes and how she inched toward it.

Finally, she sighed. "Okay. I'll keep it. Thank you, Logan."

"You're welcome. I'll see you later?" He wanted her to go back to his cabin, wanted her to spend the night in his arms, but he wouldn't push. He already overstepped arranging for her to go on the sleigh ride.

The next time they saw each other, it would be her call. He'd wait. None too patiently, but he'd wait.

"Yeah, sure. Goodnight. Thanks for tonight."

"Yeah, no problem."

He stood in the parking lot as she started the car and backed out of her space.

The bright red taillights disappeared down the hill.

He debated going to the lounge and ordering a hot apple cider to warm his insides, but in the end, he took his time walking to his cabin, enjoying the silence after singing so many gaudy Christmas carols.

He had a lot to make up for, and he had no idea how, or if Ivy even wanted him to.

She agreed to keep the car easier than he thought she would. He could take that as a sign she'd forgiven him for leaving, but he wouldn't be so arrogant, or so ignorant. She'd been living with a broken heart for eighteen years.

Just because he was suddenly around wouldn't fix that.

He didn't know what would.

Trudging over the snow, he stepped into his cabin a little after nine.

A heaviness weighed on him, and he undressed, emotionally exhausted. A full night's sleep would do him good, but he changed into sweats and a t-shirt, grabbed his cell phone out of his jacket pocket, and flopped onto the freshly laundered bed.

He brought up his mother's name in his contacts and bunched a pillow under his head. The line rang.

Elora Draper answered, her voice light and breathy. It had taken several years for the stress and tension to fade, and every day she sounded happy was one more day he thanked God. "Hi, baby," she said, and the softness and understanding brought tears to his eyes.

"Hi, Mom, how are you doing?"

"Good. Met a friend for tea after work. Your aunt's doing well. Adopted another scruff ball, but he likes me. She didn't appreciate that, but it looks like I have a dog now."

"How does Precious feel about that?" he asked, referring to his mother's snooty Siamese.

"She wasn't impressed, either, but Baxter, that's the mutt's name, is trying to win her over."

"I'm glad you're happy."

"But you're not. What's wrong? Is it work?"

He blinked back tears. He spoke to his mom maybe once a month, to avoid emotional outbursts like this. "I'm in Rocky Point."

"Oh, Logan, why?"

"James and Marnie are getting married. I've been at the resort for a couple days already, and I . . . it's hard."

He felt like an absolute asshole for dumping this on her.

"Have you . . . have you seen him?"

"No."

"Oh. Oh, Logan. But you've seen Ivy."

"Yeah." He wiped his eyes.

"How is she?"

"Not very well. Works a lot. When her brother died . . . I should have been there. Here."

"She loved you so much." Elora sighed.

"The other night . . ." He wouldn't get into Ivy spending the night with him, not now, not with his mother. "She told me you called her and asked for help. Why didn't you . . . why didn't you tell me he took the money I sent? Why didn't you tell me you needed me?"

"Logan, the only thing I wanted was for you to get out of Rocky Point. When James came to the house and helped you leave, that was the happiest day of my life. Besides the day you were born, of course. James . . . he had the courage to keep your father away from you. Eighteen and a spine of steel. He's been a good friend."

"Yeah, he has."

"I'd already let my weakness ruin your life. I let him put his hands on you, and it's my biggest regret. I didn't want you to go back to Rocky Point, for any reason. I took a chance Ivy would help me, and she did. I only wanted a ride to the bus station, but she did more and wouldn't let me say no. She drove me to the Marengo airport and bought me a one-way ticket. She stayed with me, and I was so grateful."

"She told me that. She said she stayed in Marengo until your plane landed in Denver."

Elora blew out a breath. "Bless her heart."

"You should have told me. I would have come back."

"At what cost? Your law degree? Your firm? I made sacrifices, and I asked you to sacrifice even more. I was done asking. I wanted to give, and I did. I gave you freedom."

He took his glasses off. Tears and misery fogged the lenses.

"Logan, are you still there?" Elora asked.

"Yeah."

"Please don't hold it against me. It all worked out in the end."

"Not for Ivy. She can barely look at me."

"She knows why you left, Logan. She can hardly hate you for that."

"It's not that. I never wrote, I never visited. I didn't go to Joey's funeral. She thinks that James's wedding is more important to me than Joey's death."

"She's been hurt. My poor baby, you must feel like you can't win."

That's exactly how he felt. Like all the choices he'd made had dire consequences on the ones he loved most.

"She doesn't trust me."

"You won't earn it back overnight. You know that."

"I know."

"You still love her, don't you?"

He thought of her tucked under his arm on the sleigh

ride, snuggled under the blanket, envy and loss bright in her eyes as Leah and Jared cuddled on the opposite bench, completely in love. How soft she'd been in his bed, how giving, returning his kisses like he hadn't shattered her heart then stomped all over the pieces. "Yeah."

"She took care of you all through school. That's supposed to be a mother's job. Guide her children through school, nurture them into caring, capable adults who can build successful lives after graduation. I couldn't, but Ivy did. Do you remember when we would play hide and seek?"

Elora's mention of the game brought a stab of fury to his heart, and his hand tightened on his cell phone. Hide and seek was what his mother called it when his dad was violent-drunk rather than happy-drunk, and they would hide in his closet until he sobered up or blacked out.

"How could I forget?" He couldn't keep the bitterness out of his voice.

"You'd talk about Ivy," she said, ignoring his tone. "Ivy shared her lunch. Ivy gave you a new box of crayons. Ivy gave you a piece of candy. Then when you were older. Ivy partnered with you in Art. Ivy helped you study for an Algebra test. And even later, when we still hid from your father because I was afraid you would retaliate, the stories grew more serious. Ivy went on a date and the guy was a jerk, what was she thinking? You kissed Ivy at the lake and you hoped it wasn't a mistake. You asked Ivy to prom, and she said yes. I knew you were in love with her before you did. She's been with you in a way that I wasn't, that I couldn't have been. At age five she was a little mother, making sure you had enough to eat, had all your school supplies."

She stifled a sob, and he waited for her to continue.

"When you're a parent, your main goal is to raise your

children to live without you. It's bittersweet, to know you've done your job. Ivy did her job. You felt secure enough in her love to fly away, and Logan, that's how it should be. Exactly how it should be."

He didn't understand. "Then what am I supposed to do now?"

"What do you want from her? She can only give you what you know you want. Do you want her to accept your apology? Do you want to date her? That might be difficult when you're in Decatur and she's in Rocky Point. Do you want to marry her?"

"I don't know what kind of husband I'd be."

"You're a kind, loving man, and you'd make any woman happy. You are *not* your father. You've proven that several times over."

His pulse raced with possibilities. With dread.

Ivy could give him only what he knew he wanted.

He didn't know what he wanted.

He dated because he missed Ivy. He hadn't dated with intent. He hadn't dated to find a lifelong mate.

Maybe he should start with what Ivy wanted.

Maybe they wanted the same things.

"Logan, I'm glad you called. I have something I need to tell you."

He sat up. "Are you okay?"

She laughed, a frothy, sweet sound that made him think of whipped milkshakes.

"The friend I saw for tea . . . is of the male persuasion."

His throat worked. "You're dating?"

"Yes. And I hope you're happy for me."

"Of course I am. All I want is for you to be happy."

"And that's my one wish for you. To be happy. Give Ivy my love when you see her, will you?"

"Yeah, sure."

"Maybe . . . this summer, will you visit me?"

"I will. I'm sorry, Mom."

"And bring Ivy with you?"

"I don't know. We're not in a good place. It's too soon to be thinking about something like that."

"I understand." She paused. "Logan, can I ask you a favor?"

"I'll do my best."

"I sent a letter to Rosie Graves a while ago, years ago now, and it came back. Can you thank her for me? Thank her for everything she did to help you?"

"Yeah. Ivy's dad left after Joey died, and they lost their house. If you used their home address, that's why."

"Oh, Logan."

"I'll tell Rosie, before I go back to Decatur."

"Thank you. Goodnight, baby."

"Sleep well, Mom."

He disconnected the call. He was glad he talked to her, and he promised himself he'd do it more often. When he left town, he cut himself off from everything.

That included everyone but James.

He'd been wrong, but back then, he'd been homesick and heartbroken, emotionally hurt and suffering from trauma the way most abused kids do. He didn't have the energy to do anything but try to heal and move on the best he could.

That's what he needed to know.

If leaving Ivy behind had been worth it. If he'd healed.

If he didn't know that, how would he move forward? Especially with Ivy since she was part of a past he was trying so desperately hard to escape.

He'd go see Rosie. He hadn't any idea Elora felt so

beholden to Ivy's mother, but he would extend thanks on his mom's behalf.

Then he'd go from there.

When James asked him to come back to Rocky Point for the wedding, he thought it would be a quick visit, spitting on the black smear that had been his childhood.

He should have known better.

He was such an idiot.

The next morning, he called the reservation desk. He wanted to know when Ivy worked. He doubted it would go over very well if he tried to visit Rosie while she was home.

A competent sounding young man he didn't recall meeting before. told him, albeit reluctantly, that Ivy would be in at noon to open the lounge.

That worked, and he settled in to have a quiet breakfast and maybe read a little, but James texted him and asked if he wanted to have coffee in the dining room.

He accepted and was crunching his way over the snow ten minutes later.

The temperature held steady at five degrees Fahrenheit, and the sky was a brilliant, crisp blue.

Maybe Marnie had more activities planned and James wanted to fill him in . . . or warn him. Though, he had to admit, the sleigh ride last night was fun, and he still hadn't tried skiing.

Pulling off his jacket, Logan dropped into a dining room chair opposite James who was sitting alone, reading the paper.

"Where is everyone?" he asked, tipping his cup right side up to indicate to the waitress he wanted coffee.

"Marnie's sleeping. We stayed up way too late last night. You were smart, going to bed. Marnie's going to be disappointed when I sleep through our honeymoon." James stifled a yawn. "Ivy go back to your cabin with you last night?"

He smiled thanks to the waitress who filled his coffee cup.

"Creamer?" she asked.

"Do you have the chocolate hazelnut?"

"You betcha." She pulled a handful of creamer pods out of her apron's deep pocket and dropped them on the table. "There you go, hon."

"Thanks." Logan stirred three of the pods into his coffee. "No. She went home. I talked to my mom last night, though."

"How's she doing?" James asked, folding the newspaper.

"Good. She's dating someone. She was afraid I'd be upset, but I'm glad Dad didn't beat out her spirit. She sounded happy. Asked about you, and I told her I was in Rocky Point for your wedding, so of course, we had to talk about Ivy. Our conversation brought back a lot of memories."

"You two looked cozy last night. Kiss and make up?"

"Hardly. We had a big fight. She accused me of buying her time like a whore. Desiree must have given her some kind of compensation to replace her work hours." He gulped half the coffee in his mug.

James shook his head. "No, I did. Desiree said Ivy wouldn't get paid to go on the sleigh ride, and I bought a

VISA card at the resort's gift shop. I take it the amount was enough?"

"Shit. I told her we didn't have anything to do with it."

"It doesn't matter."

"Yes, it does. Ivy doesn't like to owe people, and neither do I." He scowled. Five hundred dollars wasn't a big deal, James was right about that, but he always paid his own way whenever he could.

"You don't have to pay me back. Settle down. You worked your ass off to help me start our firm. You looked for the space, you hired our secretary and paralegal. Hell, you even arranged to have the office scrubbed down while we're here, which was a great idea, by the way. You can think of it as a Christmas bonus on me if you'd like, but don't insult me by insisting you'll pay me back. I said I like Ivy, and if I can help you two get back together, so much the better. Now, do you want to eat or what?"

He winced. He hated making James upset after all he'd done for him.

Silently, they went up to the buffet and loaded loaded their plates.

Sitting in his seat, he said, "I'm sorry. Talking to my mom brought back a lot of memories, and I don't think I thanked you, really thanked you, for helping me get out of here."

James stabbed at a sausage link. "I wasn't the one who pulled the grades I needed to earn a full scholarship. I wasn't the one who filled out the application or begged his teachers to write letters of recommendation. I wasn't the one who nailed that ten thousand word essay explaining why I deserved a full ride to one of the best schools in the state. You did that all on your own."

"Yeah, but you came to my house and physically got me

out of there. None of what you just said would've made a bit of difference if you hadn't confronted my dad, told him to fuck off, and drove me out of town." His hand unsteady, he poured syrup over his waffle.

"You're my friend, and you helped me out, too. I acted tough, but I was scared shitless. I was so homesick for this bumfuck town, and we were only three hours away. I needed you too, so stop feeling like you owe me. We leaned on each other."

"I had no idea, Mr. Confidence."

James scoffed. "I missed Mom and Dad. My room. Our dog. Marnie, even though we agreed to cool it like you and Ivy. To be honest, if we hadn't bunked together, I would have dropped out and come home. Who knows what that would have done to the rest of my life. Christ, I might not be an attorney now, and that would've screwed up bumping into Marnie again. Might not be getting married in a week, so if anything, I owe you. Forget the ride to Decatur, forget about your dad. Forget about the money I gave Ivy. We're friends, and friends don't keep score. Now shut up, you're ruining my appetite. Eat your waffle and drink your frou-frou coffee, you pussy."

He laughed. He didn't know James had been home-sick. Either it was a lie to ease his conscious, or James had been good at hiding his feelings. He hadn't seemed anything but self-assured and confident all through school.

He'd been worried about his mom, and he'd missed Ivy with a deep ache that hadn't entirely gone away. He'd only buried it under schoolwork and then, after graduation, setting up their office and hustling for clients.

"You ever think about going to see him?"

"Who? Do you mean Rosie? I'm going to stop by and

see her later. My mom has a message she wants me to pass along."

"How does Ivy feel about that?"

"She works today, but there's no reason why she wouldn't want me to visit. When I could sneak out of my house, I practically lived at hers."

"They weren't able to keep their house after Joey died. My mom told me that," James said.

"No, but I know where they live. I brought Ivy home that night she was sitting in the lobby. Her car wouldn't start. I haven't . . . looked around town much, at all that's changed."

"There's a Starbucks here now. Rocky Point's slowly crawling out of the Dark Ages. But I didn't mean Rosie. I meant your dad. Are you going to see him?"

His frou-frou coffee churned in his stomach. "Why would I do that?"

"To put the past behind you. You haven't been back for almost twenty years. If you want to say goodbye to this place once and for all, go see your dad. He can't hurt you anymore. He hasn't laid a hand on you since the summer you turned sixteen and went through that growth spurt. The old man knew you could take him."

"He still tried every once in a while, and I let him get in a shot or two so he'd leave Mom alone. I let him the day I left. Mom never told me what happened after we drove away."

"Your mom's safe and has been for a long time. Moving on in her own way if she's dating. Go see him. Show him he didn't beat you down. Hell, if you want, I'll go with you."

He hadn't planned on seeing his father. In fact, he'd planned to do the complete opposite. Stay as far away from Maple Lane as possible.

"I'll think about it," he said.

But he wouldn't.

They finished eating, and James brought Marnie breakfast, saying he might go back to bed and sleep off the Apple Pie he drank the night before.

Logan walked back to his cabin and wasted enough time to know Ivy would be in the lounge, and the Outback in the staff parking lot proved him right. He drove to her old house, a taupe two-story that had white shutters and a matching front porch. Eighteen years ago, that's where he stood and said goodbye.

He shouldn't have goaded her. The day he left, he said, "Don't be a stranger," and he poked her with it because he was tired of carrying the blame for their crumbled friendship, but he hadn't expected her to do anything. He'd been clear they were over and he hadn't given a thought what he would've done had she sent him a card or a gift.

Thrown it away?

Maybe.

He'd needed to build a new life in Decatur, far from the violence he grew up with.

Ivy wasn't a reminder of that violence, never had been, but she'd stayed in Rocky Point which, in his mind, amounted to practically the same thing.

He didn't know the family who moved into the Graves's house. Did they have a daughter who kept Ivy's pink, sparkly walls? Did they hear Joey's ghost, teasing them through her locked bedroom door?

Most of the time they were on her bed, and she'd sit in

his lap and hold him. He'd hide his face in her hair, trying to find comfort in the floral scent of her shampoo.

She'd been his safe place. For many, many years.

A young woman and a German shepherd puppy attached to a bright blue leash came out the garage door, and he took that as his cue to leave.

Yet, he lingered, reluctant to say goodbye for the last time.

He and Ivy shared a lot of good memories in that house.

Lost his virginity in that house.

Told the only woman he ever loved "I love you" in that house.

She'd been a girl then, and it made her cry.

He drove slowly over the snow-covered roads, through the main part of town, and to the residential section on the other side.

The street in front of Ivy's building wasn't cleared, and he parked down the block where he could find space. He didn't need his truck stuck in the snow. The city crew had yet to plow this far out, and the lazy property management hadn't done anything, either.

He followed a narrow walkway made by others coming and going to the street. He hit the buzzer for Ivy's apartment, GRAVES typed on a label next to a chipped white button.

Rosie didn't let him in, but he tried the security door anyway, staggering backward when it didn't resist.

The hallway smelled of burnt bacon, and mud and traces of road salt stained the brown utility carpet.

He trotted up the stairs to the second floor and knocked on the door of a corner unit.

A TV murmured through the thin walls, and the scent of stale coffee met his nose.

He knocked again and tried the doorknob, but it refused to turn. Ivy locked the door when she went to work.

Leaning against the wall, he thumped the heel of his hand against the wood in frustration. He knew Rosie was home.

The door swung open, and he jerked back in surprise.

"Who're you?" Rosie Graves muttered.

He stared in dismay.

People said vodka didn't have a scent, but it did, and she smelled like a Screwdriver factory, the sharp tang of citrus mingling with the alcohol.

"Mrs. Graves, it's me, Logan Draper."

Rosie stepped back dressed in a pair of navy sweats and a t-shirt so worn he couldn't read the letters stamped across her sagging breasts.

"Come in." She shuffled away, leaving the door hanging open, not caring if he and the rest of the town came in or not.

Tentatively, he walked into the tiny apartment and closed the door.

Ivy tried to turn the apartment into a home. Lace curtains hung in front of small windows that were frozen shut, and cheap prints added color against the plain cream-colored walls. Someone had recently vacuumed the carpet, tracks evident in the piling.

Rosie settled on the couch, a framed photo of a young boy in her lap.

He stood by the door, his hands shoved into his pockets, unsure. He hadn't expected Rosie to be a drunk. Ivy hadn't mentioned her mother was an alcoholic, only that she was unemployed.

Now he could see why.

He toed off his shoes and sat gingerly on an old chair next to the couch.

Rosie stared at the TV playing a soap opera.

He doubted she was with it enough to follow the plot lines.

"Mrs. Graves, do you remember me?" he asked. "I used to date Ivy."

She took the remote off the coffee table and muted the volume, silencing two women screaming at each other. Apparently, they'd married the same man.

"I remember you," she said, a little more clearly. "You broke her heart when you went to school."

He swallowed. There was a scratch in his throat. "Yes, ma'am, I did."

"She turned out okay."

"I've seen her at the resort. She's doing well," he said, but he couldn't extend his opinion to her mother. Rosie's blonde hair frizzed, her skin had a grey, ashy sheen, and she'd put on a lot of weight.

"She cried for a long time."

"I'm sorry."

It had been a bad idea to come, but it explained so much. No wonder Ivy worked herself to the bone. She had no financial help, no emotional support. How tired she must be.

"My mom asked me to stop by, Mrs. Graves."

"Rosie."

"What?"

"Call me Rosie, Logan. I'm not a Missus anymore."

She blinked and some of the mist faded from her eyes. Slowly, she was coming back to the present. Judging by the way she gripped that photo, he knew where she spent her time.

"I'm sorry about that, too."

"How's your mother?"

"She's good. Lives in Colorado with her sister, my aunt."

She smiled. "That's nice. Ivy told me you were back to go to a wedding. What do you think of town?"

"I haven't seen much of it. I've been mostly staying at the resort, keeping to myself."

"You don't want to see him."

He knew exactly who she meant. "No."

"But you came to visit me."

"Yes. My mom wanted me to tell you how sorry she is about Joey."

"He was so beautiful." Tears filled her eyes and she handed him the framed photo.

Joey sat in front of a grey and black background wearing a black dress shirt and a black, red, and grey tie. His adult teeth were too big in his mouth, and a cowlick stood his hair up. His blue eyes were bright with laughter, and a cheerful smattering of freckles dotted the bridge of his nose.

He couldn't pin down how old he was in the school picture. Seventh grade, maybe eighth. He didn't live to see his ninth.

Ten years younger than Ivy, Joey had been the apple of everyone's eyes.

Precocious and funny, he loved to tease him and his sister, making gagging noises when he caught them kissing. He played catch in the yard with his dad, learned how to ride his bike without training wheels, and one summer had a lemonade stand and made five bucks. Then he drove away and Joey stayed eight in his mind forever.

"He didn't suffer, Mrs. Graves . . . Rosie . . ." He held her hand. "Because of the lack of oxygen, he was unconscious and didn't know what was happening."

It was all he could give her. Joey was the only person he knew who died that way.

She burst into tears and flung herself at him, and he couldn't do anything but hug her and let her cry against his jacket.

Three more fights and two sets of commercials later, she lifted her head.

"I'm sorry," she said, wiping her eyes.

"It's okay. But . . . Joey's been gone for a long time. Ivy's been doing her best all these years, and maybe she doesn't want to tell you, but she could use some help."

"I can't help her, I can't," she cried, clutching Joey's photo, her knuckles white against the black frame. "My baby's gone."

"Ivy's your baby, too."

She narrowed her eyes and sniffed.

He leaned away, his senses on red alert. Alcohol mixed with anger would always be a trigger.

"I'm dealing with Joey's death the only way I know how. Your daddy liked to beat you up, and you did the only thing you could. You ran away. You didn't care about anyone else, did you? You left your mama behind and you broke my little girl's heart, but I bet all my booze no one told you that you were wrong. You were grieving, a lost childhood, a boy who never had a daddy, well, I'm grieving, too. My little boy drowned. No one told you that it was wrong not coming back for Joey's funeral. No one told you that you were an asshole, forcing my baby to look for you, hoping against some shit hope you'd show up and dry her tears. Don't you dare tell me how I'm grieving is wrong. *No one* is wrong for how they grieve. Do you understand me? Get out."

He stood, shaking, his heart beating so furiously he felt like he was going to have a heart attack.

Or was that his heart breaking at the image Rosie painted of Ivy searching the church hoping he'd walk in at the last second, hoping she could find comfort and love in his arms, and maybe, even hoping he'd take her away from it all.

"That's not true," he said, his hands trembling at his sides. "Our grieving *can* hurt people, and I *did* hurt Ivy the way I grieved for a family I wanted but never had. You grieve for your son, but you have a daughter who's tried to hold it together because she loves you. You're right, Mrs. Graves, nobody told me that running away was wrong, and just because Ivy doesn't tell you she needs help doesn't mean what you're doing is okay, either. We're both wrong, and Ivy has paid for it."

Rosie paled.

"I didn't come back for Ivy. I know it, and she knows it, too. Maybe it didn't start with her, but it will end with her because I love her. Even if I need the rest of my life to do it, I'll make it up to her. Somehow. What will you do? You're looking for Joey but anyone who has ever drank to forget can tell you one thing: the answer isn't at the bottom of an empty bottle." He pushed his feet into his shoes. "Ivy loved Joey, but you know what? Joey loved her, too. Would he like how you've been treating her because you're grieving? Look around this little apartment. Ivy does her best by you every day. What do you do for her?"

He let himself into the hallway, quietly closed the door, and sagged against the wall. He always respected his elders, but Rosie hit all the wrong buttons.

He *hadn't* been right avoiding Rocky Point.

He'd been wrong leaving his mother to fend for herself, he'd been wrong abandoning Ivy, never to look back.

He'd cut all ties because he was a victim of his father's violence, but that didn't make him right.

His actions still hurt people, and he couldn't bear to calculate just how much.

Ivy worked her shift and watched the skiers through the window, envying their speed and freedom.

She wouldn't mind a vacation. Somewhere warm where she could bake the cold out of her bones.

Since Logan left Rocky Point, she felt like she'd never feel warm again.

She ate a quick dinner in the kitchen, and Leah found her swapping places with the girl who covered her break.

"Hi," Leah said, sliding onto a stool.

"Hi." Ivy tried to unstick her tongue from the roof of her mouth. "What can I get you?"

"A glass of blush or something is fine."

She poured rosé in a wineglass and placed it on a cocktail napkin in front of Leah. "There you go."

"Thanks." Leah sipped and looked around the lounge. "I'm so bad at this."

Relieved she wasn't the only one who had a difficult time holding a conversation, she said, "Me too. You must be glad Jared's okay after the blizzard."

"I really am. It's hard though, staying at Autumn's when I know Rita's here. Jared's been great about it, always asking me how I'm handling things, if I'm okay, but I don't know what he'd do if I said I wasn't. Rita's Briar's mom. She has more of a right to sleep there than I do. They bought that house together."

"That's not true. Jared loves you, and he's not in a relationship with her anymore. She's the one who left, and I bet he already told you he wants to sell his house and buy something different. Did she skip the sleigh ride last night?"

Leah traced her finger around the wineglass's rim. "He mentioned selling his house, but he also said it might take a long time. All we can do is wait, but I have plenty to do and it won't be so difficult after she leaves." She paused. "I don't think Marnie invited her. Marnie wants all of us to get along, but Rita rubs everyone the wrong way."

"She's always been like that, even in high school. I was surprised Jared married her, or that Rita hung around long enough for him *to* marry her. She's always hated Rocky Point and acted like her classmates were her subjects and she was the evil queen."

Leah laughed. "It seems like you could hold your own."

"In high school, all I cared about was being with Logan. I wasn't popular, not like Marnie's group of friends, but when you're with the right person, none of that matters. You and Jared are together now, and you've taken over the Supply Company. You can be the new queen of Rocky Point."

"I won't forget the little people," Leah said, a smile quirking her mouth. "What are you doing tomorrow? Working?"

"Actually, tomorrow's my day off."

"That's great timing. Callie said she invited you to our spa day. We're meeting outside the spa doors at noon, and the schedule said we'll eat a late lunch while our toes dry. Are you still up for it?"

She hadn't let herself think the invitation was real.

Callie only invited her because she was Mitch's friend. No, that wasn't fair. She resented Callie for stealing him away from her, and she had to stop feeling like that. She was happy for him and would gladly sacrifice their friendship if it meant he wasn't alone anymore.

"Ivy?" Leah asked, frowning. "You still want to go, don't you?"

"Yeah, that sounds good. I can be there."

Leah's face smoothed out. "Great! Autumn will be there, and Cole's going to stop by and take some photos. Ask him to take your picture *before* the facial masks. Has Autumn interviewed you for the blog?"

She shook her head. "No. She's never interviewed me for anything."

On her breaks, she'd been reading the blog articles, and she'd read Logan's interview. He looked so sharp in the picture Autumn published with the post.

"She said she wanted to, and you should remind her. She's always looking for content, but she's afraid she's going to bother people. You'll be her new best friend. How are you and Logan? You guys looked cute at the sleigh ride last night. Did you have fun?"

"We did, but we haven't talked about anything. I mean, like what's going to happen after Marnie's wedding. I guess he'll go back to Decatur, and I'll . . ." *Stay here and freeze to death.*

"Go with him?"

"I can't. I have to take care of my mom."

"What does that have to do with anything?"

"Logan's not going to want to deal with that, and I would never ask him to. Besides, I don't think he wants anything like that. He wants me to forgive him for the way he left Rocky Point, and I have."

Leah sipped her wine. "What do you want?"

"If I could have anything?"

"Sure."

"I'd dry my mom out, marry Logan, and we'd move to Decatur. She needs to get away from where my brother died."

"I'm sorry. I didn't know about your brother."

She rubbed a rag at the bar though it was already spotless. "He drowned when he was a kid. It was a long time ago."

"I'm still sorry. Talk to Callie tomorrow. Her brother's in rehab, and maybe she can recommend some places where your mom could go if you and Logan work things out."

"Thanks, but the chances of us staying together after Marnie's wedding are slim. He didn't come back for me."

Leah held her hand. "Hey. When Rita came back to Rocky Point, Jared didn't talk to me, didn't text me. I had to go back to New York when my grandma had a stroke, and I was half a country away with no word from him. He said felt stupid talking to me while Rita was here and wanted to explain in person. I understand his reasons, but the distance made it worse. Things would've been so much easier if he would have just called and told me how he was feeling. He was in love with me, and I had no idea." She sighed. "If you want to know what he's thinking, you have to talk to him."

She blushed. "I'm sorry to hear about your grandma. I hope she's doing okay now." She'd made the conversation about herself. What a great way to start a friendship.

"It's okay. You and I haven't spoken much, and I'd like to change that. Even if you move to Decatur, I'd like us to be friends."

"Yeah. I was thinking that at dinner last night. Friends would be good."

"Here's what I think you should do—"

"Hold that thought." She served spiked hot chocolate to a couple sitting by the window. When she took her place behind the bar, she filled Leah's glass. "Okay."

"Well, we have a spa day tomorrow, and you have the evening free. Why don't you ask Logan if he wants to go out for dinner. Not here. Do you have a place you like to go to have a fancy meal?"

Immediately, a little lakeside restaurant popped into her head. "We could go where we ate dinner before prom."

"Oh, you went to prom? I'd love to see the pictures."

"Yeah. Sure. My mom took a million of them before we left the house."

"Great! Anyway, spa day tomorrow, so get your hair done, your nails, have a facial. Go out to dinner, then when he asks you to go back to his cabin, say yes."

"I don't have anything to wear." She hadn't needed a dress in forever. She'd kept her prom dress for sentimental reasons, but she shoved it into the back of her small closet and rarely looked at it.

"I'm taller than you are, but you and Callie are almost the same height. We'll see what she can do. She brought a ton of dresses because she knew Marnie wanted to party. Text Logan right now so he doesn't make plans with James. They're always going to the Viking."

"Are you sure?"

"Don't feel pushed into sex if that would complicate things, but dinner in a quiet place where you guys can talk? How is that bad?"

"That's true. We do have a lot to talk about."

"Keep it light, reminisce about prom if it won't hurt either of you, and pick his brain. You're a woman. You don't need to be blatant about it. You know subterfuge."

She stared. "Subterfuge? I know how to mix drinks."

Shrugging, Leah said, "You can be the female version of 007. All I'm saying is if you don't talk to him, he's going to think you don't care, and he'll go back to Decatur without either of you opening your mouths. When I was in New York, I could have texted Jared, too. I never did because I thought he and Rita were back together. We *both* went through hell for nothing."

"Okay. Just to talk, though. I don't expect him to get down on one knee or rescue me from my pathetic life. He has no idea my mom's an alcoholic. I try to keep that kind of thing to myself, and I'm not going to tell him, either."

"That's up to you, but at least dinner alone would be a start."

"Yeah, you're right. I'll text him."

She messaged Logan, and while she waited for a response, refilled the couple's hot chocolate and served two women sitting in front of the fireplace champagne spritzers. After she made her rounds, she checked her phone. Nothing.

Her heart sank. She couldn't expect him to answer so quickly. Or if he wanted to answer at all.

But then her phone chimed, and he responded, *Sure. I'll pick you up at 7.*

She groaned. "He wants to pick me up at home."

"You don't want him to?"

"Not really. It wouldn't be a very romantic start. Our crummy little apartment."

"If he loves you, he won't care, but I understand. My apartment in New York is crummy, too. If you're going to borrow a dress from Callie you can get dressed in her room . . . crap. She gave her room to Mitch's mom and dad, and she's been sleeping with Mitch. You can change there, right? You're friends and he won't care. After the spa, run home and check on your mom, then come back. Logan can meet you in the lobby."

"Are you sure Callie won't mind? I don't want to assume she'll do that for me."

Leah narrowed her eyes. "I'll talk to Callie, you tell Logan."

"Jeez, okay." She tapped out her message and he agreed the moment she sent the text.

"We're meeting in the resort's lobby at seven. He'll probably think I want to eat dinner here, but the other resort will be a surprise. A good one, I hope."

"Excellent! I need to get going. I have to check in at the Supply Company. Helen lets me come and go, but I think she'll be happy when I'm settled and I won't need her so often. I'll see you tomorrow at noon." She slid off the barstool.

"Leah?"

Putting her jacket on, she paused. "Yeah?"

"Thank you."

"It's no problem." She grinned. "This friend stuff is going to take some getting used to."

"That's what Mitch said last night."

"But it's a good thing."

"Yeah, it is. Talk to you later."

She floated through the rest of her shift. Friends, a free spa day, and a date with Logan.

She hoped she could talk to him, really talk to him, about a future. If they were only meant to be friends, then knowing would be better sooner rather than later.

Before she lost her heart all over again.

CHAPTER SIX

Ivy woke early the next morning to start on her chores. Since she wouldn't be home for most of the day, she needed to do laundry, clean, and run to the grocery store, something she hadn't been able to do because of work and the storm.

For the first time in a long while she resented taking care of her mother, and she felt terrible.

Rosie seemed even more down this morning, sulking into a mug of coffee.

She didn't have time to ask why, rushing through the cleaning and vacuuming. It would be such a weight off her shoulders if Rosie shared the chores. It wouldn't take much. Vacuuming now and then, cleaning up after herself in the kitchen, doing her own laundry. Her mother had laundry because she made sure Rosie changed her clothes on a daily basis. Before Logan came to town, she thought she'd take care of Rosie for the rest of her life, and talking with Leah yesterday made her realize not only was that unrealistic, it was unnecessary.

"Mom, I'm going to be out most of the day. Will you be

all right?" she asked, unloading groceries. At ten o'clock in the morning, the store hadn't been busy, and she was in and out in half an hour. She indulged a little, using some of the gift card Desiree had given her to go on the sleigh ride, and feeling guilty, she hid a few things in her bedroom. She didn't want Rosie to eat them while she was gone. It was her money that paid for the groceries and she was entitled to a few luxuries, as small as they were.

"What if I worked?" Rosie said suddenly, muting a diaper commercial on TV.

She frowned. "You haven't worked since Joey died. You have no résumé, no recent job experience." *And you're rarely sober.* "I think you need to take baby steps if you want to find work. Help around the apartment, do your laundry. Start going outside. Don't watch so much TV. I have plenty of books to read."

It wasn't fair Rosie was talking like this. It made her think change could be possible when she knew the truth. Her mother was living in a rut so deep she'd never be able to climb out of it.

Rosie shrugged. "Maybe."

A spark of anger flashed through her and she gritted her teeth. Where would her mother be if she up and left? Stopped paying the bills, stopped cleaning? Stopped buying food? How long would it take Social Services to come and see what was going on? A month after the rent stopped being paid? Maybe two if the property management over-looked the first forgotten payment?

She sagged against the kitchen counter. She'd never do that to her mother, no matter what happened. "I'm going out. There's plenty of food if you get hungry, but I'll be by to check on you later, okay?"

Rosie stared at the TV, the remote in one hand and Joey's picture clutched in the other.

Her mother would never clean herself up for her. Joey had been the love of her life, in every way. She'd let her husband leave, she let her work her fingers to the bone to keep a roof over their heads and food in the fridge. All Rosie could think about was having to live without her little boy.

How could Logan want her?

How could anyone want her?

When her own mother didn't?

Tears blurring her vision, she drove to the resort, parked in the staff parking lot, and sniffled her way to the spa.

Marnie stood by the door, the first to arrive, and Ivy's cheeks burned. Marnie hadn't issued the invitation, and she felt like an intruder. She wanted to turn around and walk right out of the resort.

"Hey," Marnie said, straightening. "What's wrong?"

"I feel stupid for being here," she said, blurting out her feelings. "Callie and Leah keep saying this is free, but I don't know how it could be and I can't afford it."

Marnie laughed. "Awww, sweetie, it's okay. I'm sorry I didn't talk to you during the sleigh ride, or at dinner before. James told me how Logan grew up, the kind of home life he had. You know more, since you were Logan's best friend in school. If you two can find something . . . I mean, James and Logan are tight. They'd have to be to get through law school and open their own firm, and I know that nothing would make James happier than if Logan could settle down with a woman who understands him.

You don't have to feel stupid for being here. I want you here. And no offense, but you look like you could use a good spa day."

"Sometimes life is fucking hard," she muttered, trying not to cry.

"Sometimes life is *really* fucking hard," Callie said, striding down the hallway.

She relaxed. It's not that she didn't like Marnie, but she didn't know the bride-to-be very well. Marnie's comment didn't offend her, but Marnie lived a charmed life and didn't know what it was like to struggle. Some people were blessed with good fortune, and Marnie, from the minute she popped out, was one of them.

She settled near the others, keeping to herself as they chatted about Marnie's bachelorette party, dresses, and setting aside an evening to put together centerpieces that would go on the tables at the reception.

When it was her turn to have her hair cut, she sat in the chair and studied herself in the gleaming mirror.

"What were we thinking?" the stylist asked, running her fingers through Ivy's hair, catching the snarls.

"Take it all off."

She grimaced. "Really? With your bone structure, that wouldn't look right."

"Well, maybe not all off," she said, backtracking. She didn't want all her hair cut off, she liked it long, but she needed a change, too.

"How about to here?" the stylist asked, tapping her shoulder, and she nodded.

Conversations murmured around her, and she sat through the cut, a conditioning treatment, and a style. She had a pedicure, her fingernails buffed to a shine, and her makeup expertly applied. She pushed away how much this would cost Marnie and promised herself that as a way to say thank you, she would buy Marnie and James a wedding gift.

She didn't want to check on her mom and didn't need to. Rosie had always been fine on the days she worked a double shift, and she'd be fine now, too, but she didn't have anything else to do until she needed to change.

To use up five minutes, she stopped in front of a large decorative mirror hanging on the wall outside the spa. Marnie ambled away talking her mother on the phone, waving vaguely in her direction, and Leah dashed off saying Helen needed her at the store. Autumn left with Leah to give her a ride, but also to stop at the newspaper's offices to write another blog post.

Callie smudged one of her toes and stayed behind, asking the nail technician to fix it, and she stood by herself, studying her reflection. Her hair felt so light. The stylist cut off over five inches, and now it shined under the hallway lights

She didn't bother wearing makeup very often, but the colors the woman chose made her blue eyes pop, and her lashes were curved, long, and very dark. The foundation matched her skin perfectly, and the dark bags under her eyes were gone. Mauve lipgloss glittered on her lips.

Callie slammed out of the spa and stopped. "You look fantastic. That haircut really brings out your cheekbones."

"Thanks. That was the first time I ever had my eyebrows waxed."

"She did a great job." Callie hiked her purse strap onto her shoulder. "Do you need to go home? Leah said something about you checking on your mom."

Her cheeks flamed. God. Did everyone know Rosie drank all day? "Not really. She's always fine when I'm at work."

"Good. Autumn asked if I would bring you by so she could interview you, and then we can stop at Marnie's parents' house. It makes more sense if you picked out a dress there than me bring everything to Mitch's room."

"Are you sure? Did Leah coerce you into this?"

Callie laughed. "Sure, she did, but I don't mind or I would have told her no. I want to help. It's what friends are for."

"Are we? Friends?"

Zipping up her jacket, Callie tilted her head in the direction of the lobby. "Come on, I'm parked out front. Of course we're friends. I admit I was a bit jealous of your friendship with Mitch, but I'm thankful, too. You guys needed each other, and there's nothing to be jealous about. In fact, I hope you don't think he's not your friend anymore. He's always going to consider you one of his closest."

That wasn't much of a consolation when Mitch would be living in Decatur after the holidays, but she shrugged it off. Life moved on. People moved on. Only she was stuck in Rocky Point. That didn't mean everyone else had to be. "It's fine."

"I can tell by your tone that it's not," Callie said, tugging on her arm to hurry her along. "Leah told me about your mom, but we weren't gossiping, I promise. My brother, Brandon, is in rehab. He was a firefighter, and during a job, he got trapped in a burning building and almost died. He started drinking and one afternoon went on shift drunk. His captain put him on leave. He checked himself into a rehab facility to dry out and think about what he wanted to do. I know what it's like to live a life you don't want to live," she said, pushing her through the lobby doors and into the cold. "My dad would shut down if we talked about not wanting to be firefighters anymore. It's hard living your life for someone else."

She followed Callie to a compact parked in the middle of the lot. Callie started the car and shut off the freezing air blowing out of the vents.

"My mom would never check herself in. She's happy where she's at," she said, fastening her seatbelt.

"Then tell her things need to change."

She scoffed. "Why? What would I do then? At least if she's with me I'm not alone."

"Mitch said you don't date and all you do is work. Is that really how you want to live? Keep living?"

"Sometimes you have no choice."

"No choice, or no motivation to change? Are you scared, Ivy?"

"Yeah, I am. Who isn't?"

"Touché," she said, her mouth twisting into a wry smile. "You got me there. I was scared, too, for a long time. Of what my dad would do if I told him I didn't want to be a firefighter anymore. Of what Mitch would do once he found out. I was scared he wouldn't want me or that he would decide he could live without me. What are you scared of?"

Callie drove the car out of the resort's parking lot, down the hill, and into town. She sorted through what she was most scared of and decided to be honest. Callie was trying to be her friend, and there was no reason to lie.

"I'm afraid Logan will decide he doesn't want me, and he'll go back to Decatur and not look back, just like last time."

"He was a kid, a boy who had lived through a lot and survived it the best he could. You were a little girl, and be honest. What would you have done if he would've stayed? What would you two have done?"

d. She'd been so full of resentment that
ought about what they would've done if
ky Point. "I don't know. He wouldn't have
at the paper mill. His dad worked there."
dded. "Okay, so he might have worked on a
uction crew or driven a school bus like Mitch.
What would you have done? Probably the same
ou're doing now. Go two years at the community
e because that's all there is and eke out a living. Didn't
want better for yourself? For Logan? What would this
y town have given you?"

"We might have moved anyway," she said defensively.

"Might have. But there's no way Logan would be an attorney now. No way. Careful or not, you probably would have gotten pregnant, and you'd have a kid you loved but couldn't afford."

"Logan doesn't want kids. Not after the way he grew up."

"Then he would have left you," Callie said, her voice firm, and she believed her. Logan didn't want to be a dad, couldn't be a dad, and he would have walked away, no matter how much he loved her. "And you'd be in the same spot you are now, except with a teenager who couldn't go to college. I'm not saying this to be mean or turn Logan into an asshole. If he got you pregnant, he might've stood by you, he's not a jerk like that, but that doesn't mean you guys would've been happy. Don't hate him because he left you. It was for the best."

"I don't hate him."

"You don't?"

"No. I just wish . . . I wish we could have stayed friends."

"He had to leave his dad behind, and that meant everything in Rocky Point. Including you."

"Then why would he want me back?"

"Everything and everyone comes around full circle he'd really wanted to avoid Rocky Point, James would ha understood, don't you think? James knew what Logan w running from. He knew Logan's father liked to beat on him and call it discipline." Callie turned into the newspaper's parking lot. "James would have said, 'No problem' and let things be, but Logan came back. He said he came back to be a groomsman, but that wasn't it at all." She twisted in her seat, rested her head on the steering wheel, and met her eyes. "The wedding was a convenient reason to come back for you."

She was tempted to tell Callie she was full of shit, that just because she was all ribbons and glitter since she met Mitch people weren't meant to be wrapped up in pretty bows. Logan had a reason to come back to Rocky Point. Joey's funeral was plenty of reason. *She* was a reason. Neither had been enough.

But she dressed in Mitch's room and kept her mouth shut. She'd spent a lot of time there, keeping him company or catching a nap between shifts. If she didn't feel like talking to the chef or his assistants, she'd grab a plate and bring it here to eat in silence, but she had to stop doing that when Callie started hanging around.

She didn't want to interrupt a little afternoon hanky-panky if Mitch didn't have anything to repair.

"You look beautiful," Callie said, smoothing her hair.

She didn't look terrible, she had to admit. The dress fit

her as well as anything she could have purchased off the rack. Think satin straps rested on her shoulders, the bodice hugged her breasts, and darting tucked in the waist. The hem of the black dress fell a couple of inches above her knee. Demure, but still sexy as hell.

Callie loaned her a pair of sheer black tights, but she wore her own black flats. She hated heels and didn't own any. Callie's feet were bigger than hers, giving her the excuse to beg off a pair of glittering stilettos.

Her makeup had faded a little, and Callie refreshed her lipstick and mascara using her own supply.

"Don't let him rip my dress off you. I need it later," Callie joked, flopping onto Mitch's bed.

The thought of Logan's touch sent shivers down her spine. His fingers gliding over her thighs as he pulled the tights over her legs . . .

"Cough, *cough*. Earth to Ivy." Callie laughed. "Dinner first, then sex."

"Who said anything about sex?"

"Who said anything about *no* sex? Leah? Don't let her fool you. She jumped into bed with Jared the minute he asked. It's okay to want to be wanted."

No, it wasn't. It wasn't okay because that was the one thing she'd miss more than anything. Being touched. Being held. Having his arms wrapped around her. Being needed, being wanted, was a dangerous thing to get used to.

"We've already . . . you know," she mumbled, tucking her hair behind her ears then changing her mind and tousling the strands. That made it worse. That made it look like she'd just been . . . Hmmm.

"Did he touch you like he loved you?" Callie asked, rising onto her elbow.

"Yeah, I guess so."

"That means a lot. Anyway, you should get going. It's almost seven, and he'll be early. Make him watch you walk across the lobby. Go slow, he's going to notice your new haircut and makeup. You look a-maz-ing. Use it."

Callie's advice made her palms sweat. She didn't know how to be a woman. She didn't know how to play the games. Subterfuge.

Crap.

"Use it to do what?"

"Use it to prove to him that he can't live without you."

Too late. She already knew he could. "You're too happy."

"Can anyone be too happy? I want to know the all details."

"Yeah, sure. Thanks for the dress."

"Have fun!"

She shut the door and walked down the hall, her jacket hanging over her arm. Mitch rounded the corner and whistled. "You're too good for him."

It should have made her smile, but it didn't. "No, I'm not." If anything, they were right for each other.

He understood immediately. "You're right. He's been through a lot. I hope you can talk and get some things straightened out."

"Maybe. At least I'll know what he's thinking."

"Good luck. You deserve to be happy."

"I think I've told you that a million times, too."

"Yeah. My happy's in my room, I think."

She tried to laugh. "She's still there."

"Call me if you need anything."

"Okay. Bye."

Logan stood looking out the lobby doors, frost creeping across the glass. He wore dress slacks and black dress shoes.

Black leather gloves dangled from one of his hands, and his soft black wool jacket stretched across his broad shoulders.

Her heart raced as he turned to look at her, and she forced herself to ease across the lobby, Sophia and Blaine gaping at her.

"You look lovely," Logan said.

"Thanks. Callie let me borrow the dress. She said not to ruin it."

A smile played with his mouth. "I'll do my best, but no promises. Are we eating here? Or did you have something else in mind?"

"I . . . made reservations at Evergreen Hill, do you mind?"

His smile faded, but he said, "No, not at all. I didn't know if we were staying here, so the car's cold."

"That's okay."

She followed him out of the resort and into the frozen air. The sun had set hours ago, and small dots of light raced across the frozen lake, the roar of snowmobile engines carrying to her from miles away through the brittle dark.

He unlocked the door of his truck, and with his hand to her waist, she slid in feeling like a princess. The Outback he'd given her was a great car, but nothing like the Mercedes-Benz he drove. She could close her eyes and pretend he was her bodyguard, that she needed him to keep her safe from harm.

Because she hadn't done it herself, he leaned over and latched her seatbelt. "What are you thinking about?"

"Nothing."

"You can tell me."

"I was just being silly. How was your day?"

They made small talk as he drove them through, then out, of town, and along the lake. Located at the uppermost part of the state, water hugged Rocky Point on almost all sides.

He turned into the resort's parking lot. Smaller than the Rocky Point Resort, Evergreen Hill still boasted five-star dining, rustic, but luxurious, sleeping rooms, and excellent fishing all year round. Near the entrance, white fairy lights sparkled on a huge evergreen.

"Being here brings back a lot of memories," Logan said, holding the door open and gesturing her into the restaurant's small lobby. The restaurant connected to the resort, but it had its own entrance for patrons who were not staying there.

She hoped that having dinner at the resort would encourage him to reminisce. She wanted him to remember the good times they had before he left. "It was a fun night."

"Yeah. Remember you had to drive us because I was too scared to work? I didn't want Mom alone with him for longer than she had to be."

She squeezed his hand.

"Do you have a reservation?" the hostess asked.

"Yes. Under Graves," she said, stepping closer to the podium.

"Right this way."

The hostess showed them to a small table that overlooked the lake, the winter's chill penetrating the glass. Gooseflesh covered her skin. Callie's dress didn't offer much in way of material.

"Cold?" he asked.

"Maybe a little, but I'll get used to it."

A waitress approached and offered them drinks, and Ivy ordered a spiked coffee. Logan ordered the same.

Five minutes later the waitress came back, her cheeks red. "The bartender doesn't know how to make that."

She laughed. "Do you have a pen and piece of paper? I can write down what's in it."

"Thanks. He wasn't sure what you wanted."

"No problem. There are a lot of different kinds."

He watched the waitress weave around the tables to the bar. "Looks like this place could use your help."

"Nah. I work enough. How were you and James able to take two weeks off?"

"We tried to clear our calendar the best we could, and our secretary has been fielding our calls. Can't stop people from dying."

She put her elbow on the table and rested her chin in her hand. He was so handsome, the candlelight sparking off this glasses. She'd missed so much in the past eighteen years. Years she was acutely aware they'd never get back. "How did you decide to go into that kind of law?"

He leaned back to give the waitress space to serve their coffees. "James and I thought long and hard about it. We wanted the security, but we didn't want to be tied up in court all day. Sometimes you get a family member wanting to contest a will or something, but most of that can be settled out of court. We enjoy helping families navigate the legal system when someone passes away. They need an attorney who's understanding and won't try to rip them off. Either because they inherited a shit-ton of money or because they have so little they can barely afford to pay us. A different attorney could cheat them and charge them for things that aren't necessary. We know most of the estate attorneys in the state, but there are always a few scammers sniffing around."

"That sounds nice." She wrapped her hands around the warm mug, breathing in the Irish cream and sugar. "Do you think about the future?"

He brushed his fingers over her wrist. "I didn't until James told me he and Marnie wanted to get married here. Ever since they started planning their wedding, you were all I could think about. I know you don't believe me and that it's not fair to say it, but it's true. I don't have any rights where you're concerned and you can tell me to fuck off any time, but I wanted to see you."

"But you never thought to before then."

It wasn't a question because she already knew the answer.

"No. Being afraid of my dad overpowered everything else. I couldn't think beyond staying away from him, and that alone should make you want to stay far away from me."

"Then what do you want?"

Holding a pad and pen, the waitress walked toward their table, and he glared. Taking the hint, she pivoted mid-step. He sighed, sagging in his seat. "This is why you wanted to talk."

"Kind of. Leah said I should play it cool, poke around for answers, but that's not who I am. If you came back as a favor to James and you had no plans to do anything more than say hey, then tell me. I can handle it. Don't lead me on, letting me think that we're going to have something when you have no intention of any such thing. It was a low blow inviting you here, but I wanted you to remember the good times." She huffed a laugh. "But the joke's on me because back then there were no good times. Not for you."

Logan wiped a smear of whipped cream off Ivy's nose. Rimmed with black, her eyes were huge, and they reflected a sadness he'd felt deep down in his soul since he said goodbye to her eighteen years ago.

She smiled faintly and rubbed her nose.

He picked up a spoon to give himself a moment. "That's not true. There were good times, many good times, and they all had to do with you. You helped me with homework, you gave me rides to football practice. I hated football, you know. I just wanted to get out of the house."

"I know."

"You weren't disgusted whenever I had a new ache, whenever I would wince when you touched me."

"I never would have been. I understood, and I loved you. I wanted to take care of you."

"And I left town to learn how to take care of myself."

She opened her menu. "You did a good job."

She was quiet, the leather hiding half her face.

He opened his, different from eighteen years ago. The dining room looked the same, though they'd replaced the carpet, the tables, and all the fixtures. But the wide windows still gave them a clear view of the frozen lake and car lights cutting through the dark on a road somewhere miles away.

The wary waitress approached their table to take their orders. She looked between him and Ivy and hurried away, scribbling as she went.

"I went to see Rosie yesterday."

She stiffened. "Why would you do that?"

"Because my mom had a message for her. She said she'd written to thank her helping me, but it came back. She didn't know you lost your house. Ivy, will you look at me?"

She stared out the window looking like she wanted to be anywhere but sitting there with him.

"Ivy."

Finally, she turned toward him, her eyes glistening.

"Why didn't you tell me?"

"Tell you what? That my mom's an alcoholic? That she hasn't had a job since Joey died? That my father never calls? That I don't know if he's dead or alive? *Tell you what?*"

"All of that. Why didn't you tell me when we were snowed in at the cabin?"

"What would you have done? Said, 'I'm sorry?' You haven't had to live with it. You haven't had to pick up the pieces."

"I've picked up pieces." He picked up pieces for eighteen years and had the scars to prove it.

"Oh, don't play the martyr with me, Logan. James helped you get away, and you left everything behind. You didn't give a shit about me."

"That's where you're wrong. You think just because I could leave without looking back that you weren't always in my thoughts? In my heart? Ivy, I loved you."

"That didn't keep me from having to work doubles all these years. That didn't keep me from having to clean up after Rosie when she had another bender. That didn't keep me from crying myself to sleep at night. This was a mistake." She dropped her black cloth napkin onto the table and shoved her chair back.

Panic pummeled him. He couldn't let her leave. He'd never see her again. He knew for certain if he brought her home, she'd avoid him until the wedding was over. "Please don't go. Don't go." He reached across the table and gripped her arm, his fingertips digging into her skin.

He released her, his hand shaking.

She paused, then slid her chair forward. "Will you tell me what you want?"

"Can we be honest with each other?"

She nodded.

"I don't know what I want. I want to see you. After the wedding, I mean. I don't want to live another eighteen years without you. I know what you think of me, but living in Decatur, it hasn't been easy. I missed you . . . well, we already decided you wouldn't believe me. You weren't the only one crying herself to sleep. Will you tell me the truth? Do you hate me for what I did to you?"

The waitress chose that moment to serve their meals. His steak sizzled, but the spices only churned his stomach.

"Can I get you anything else?" she asked, already inching away from the table.

"No," he growled.

"Enjoy." She rushed across the dining room.

Picking up her fork, Ivy stared at her plate and bit her bottom lip. "Do you want to know the real truth?"

He forced himself to smile and play it light. "Not if you're going to tell me you never missed me after all and you don't want to see me after the wedding."

"It's not that. I was happy you were getting away from your dad. What kind of girlfriend would I have been if I'd begged you to stay here? Begged you to marry me instead of going to school, figuring out who you were when you weren't being your dad's punching bag, or later, your mom's bodyguard? Life was okay while you were gone. I went to college, I dated. I went to hunting cabin parties and got drunk with my friends. I hung out with Joey. We'd go to Dairy Queen get ice cream and go to the beach. I was . . . *normal* after you left. Because you're right, kids break up to go to school and we weren't doing anything a million other high school couples haven't done."

He tensed and drank the rest of his coffee, hoping the alcohol would take the edge off her words.

"If Joey hadn't died . . . Logan . . . the honest truth is I might have been okay without you. But Joey *did* die, my dad left, and I was alone with a drunk woman who loved her dead son more than me. I needed you, God, I needed you, and were gone. You were gone and I didn't know what to do." She sprang to her feet and ran across the dining room, leaving her salmon filet behind.

He pushed his plate away and rested his head in his hands, his elbows braced on the table. She was honest, and that was what he wanted, wasn't it?

She would have been okay if Joey hadn't died.

He would have wanted that for her. He would have wanted to come back to Rocky Point knowing she was married and had a couple of kids. Joey playing the doting uncle while her mother and father spoiled their grandkids. If he could have chosen any life for her, he would have chosen that. And he would have kept the resentment she'd moved on to himself.

Because there would have been. Oh, yeah, there would have been a shit-ton of resentment.

Did he love her less because Joey's death made her realize how much she missed him? No, not missed him. Needed him. Which, of course, was worse.

Or did she feed him a line of bullshit to make him feel better? Maybe she *wanted* to believe she would have been okay, when she would have been anything but.

He shuddered a sigh. It didn't matter anymore. Joey was dead, her mother was a drunk, and she never told him if she hated him. She could, he knew that. Hate him, but that didn't mean she didn't still love him, too. They were the opposite side of the same coin. Heads, you win. Tails, you lose.

"Do you need some to-go boxes?" the waitress asked, a hand to his shoulder.

"That would be great, thank you."

He paid for their uneaten meals and put them in the truck.

Then he set out to find the love of his life. It's what she was, and all she'd ever be.

Ivy stood on the snow-covered dock. The cold had frozen all the feeling out of her, and she stood as still as a statue, her eyes fixed on a green light in the distance. She'd read once that the green light in *The Great Gatsby* signified hope, that one day Gatsby would have Daisy's love.

She didn't have much hope, and she stared down the green glow until whatever it was disappeared, and the horizon blanked black as far as her eyes could see.

Logan's boots crunched on the snow behind her.

"Do you want to know the thing that hurts the most?" she asked, her throat raw.

He stood behind her and drew her to him. "What?"

She turned in his arms and buried her face in the scratchy wool of his jacket. It smelled like him, and she took a deep breath. "I loved him, too. No one remembers that. I loved my brother, too, and I haven't had a chance to cry since he died."

"Cry now, baby, cry now."

He tangled in fingers into her hair as she keened into his jacket, gripping the lapels in her fists until her hands ached.

No one asked if she missed her brother, too. No one asked if she was okay. No one stayed strong for her.

"I'm sorry," he said, his voice low. "I don't know what else I can say, or how I can make it up to you. I love you, I always have, and if you don't want me to, I'll never leave you again."

She leaned away and wiped her face. She made a mess of it and sniffled a laugh when he handed her a handkerchief. It was just like him to carry a handkerchief, and if she looked, she bet she'd find his monogram embroidered into the corner.

His words seeped past her pain and joy sparked and crackled like fire eating freshly cut wood, but she knew Logan, maybe better than he knew himself. "Don't tell me that out of guilt."

"It isn't guilt." He paused. "Will you tell me about it? Joey's death?"

She stepped over the wooden planks, sliding in her flats. The soles had worn down so much they didn't have any tread. She slipped easily, spinning like a ballerina, her arms held out, Logan's handkerchief fluttering in the air.

What she wouldn't give to be five again, dancing, her hair flying around her, secure in her pretty house, in her parents' love, and not a care in the world.

She stopped and looked at Logan, lowering her arms, the handkerchief grazing her leg. He was waiting so patiently, though it was freezing and he must be so cold.

At five years old, Logan's dad smacked him around. He and his mother would hide in his closet and play Go Fish by flashlight. At five years old Logan didn't bring lunch to school and didn't bring his own school supplies to class. At five years old, with her mother's help, she'd taken care of him, and he'd let her. And even at five years old, she knew she'd grow up to love him, and she had.

More than anything, she'd wanted to somehow share

the security of her life with him, but the little things she'd been able to do hadn't been enough.

"They'd gone swimming, he and his friends. A couple of kids that don't live in town anymore. One of them tried to hang himself. He felt responsible for Joey's death, but only Joey was responsible for what happened on the lake that day."

"He was fourteen, right?"

"Yeah. They went out in his friends' parents' boat. Leo and Theo. Twins who lived down the street. I'll always remember them. Do you?"

He nodded.

"They didn't go to the funeral. But Joey . . . he'd been hurting, Logan. I didn't know. Maybe I was too busy working, at the time I was thinking about moving out. Or maybe I was trying not to miss you so much, maybe I was dating, trying to forget you, I don't know. I know about guilt, and I know it's hard to live with." She met his eyes. "And I know how you'd do anything to get rid of it."

"What happened, Ivy?"

"They'd taken the boat out, and Joey had it all planned. That's what his friends said, and the police didn't open an investigation. He wanted to play a game. See how easy it was to swim if they had something tied to their ankles. They tried a a bobber, a stick. Funny things. A bottle of suntan lotion. An empty Thermos. Leo and Theo were goofing off, but Joey wanted to push it further. He said he wanted to try the boat's anchor. The boys said no, it was too heavy, but Joey always got his way, didn't he? All freckles and smiles. One more cookie. One more hour past curfew. And he did that afternoon. He hooked himself to the anchor's chain and jumped overboard. By the time his friends thought to pull him up, it was too late. He was gone. The coroner said maybe if the boys had known CPR . . . but they hadn't, and Joey drowned. Alleged suicide."

"It could have been an accident. Boys playing games."

"Maybe. But then I look back and see the signs. Mom saw the signs, and that's why she drinks. Because she didn't get him the help he needed. I miss him. I miss him so much, and it was my fault, too." Tears dripped down her cheeks.

"Don't say that. You spent more time with him than any big sister spends with their little brother. He knew he could have reached out to you, and he didn't. Depression isn't anyone's fault."

"Sometimes I know that, but then I'm lying in bed at night, listening to Mom stumble around the apartment and I'm exhausted because I've been on my feet for fourteen hours and I get tired. I get so tired."

He stepped forward. "You're not thinking of doing anything, are you?"

She hunched her shoulders and started walking toward Logan's truck. Any more time out in the cold and they'd risk hypothermia. "No. I can't do that to Mom."

Grabbing her arm, he twirled her to face him, and he said, "No. You can't do that to me."

She yanked her arm out of his grasp. "I could have killed myself, or moved, or married, or gotten cancer and died, and you never would have known because you didn't bother to come back and say 'Hi, how are you?' You didn't bother to call or send a card. You didn't send flowers to the church when we had Joey's funeral, and you didn't know my mother's a drunk." She clutched at the handkerchief.

Moaning, he dropped to his knees, his arms hanging by his sides in defeat. "I've apologized, Ivy. I said I'm sorry. I went to see Rosie, and I . . . I'm sorry about Joey and I'm sorry I didn't come back. I'm sorry about your mom, and I'm sorry that I left without you. I told James I should have married you, but he said I made the right choice. I didn't. Somehow I should have taken you with me because you'll never forgive me. After all you did to help me, and I left you behind. Tell me what you want. I'll do anything if you'll forgive me for going to school without you."

"I have forgiven you for that."

"Ivy—"

"No. I have. It was the right thing to do. I know it was. It was the silence after you left that broke my heart, and I have to see if I can get past it. What kind of future will we have if I can? I'll always have to take care of my mother. If I quit my job at the resort and move to Decatur, she'll have to come with me and suddenly you're supporting two more people than you were before. I can't do that to you."

"Yes, you can." He stood, his breath streaming white in the frigid air. It was stupid to argue in the cold. "Rosie took care of me while I was in school just as much as you did. Things I needed didn't magically appear. She was there for me when I needed her, so I can be there for her now. We'll bring her to Decatur and dry her out. You can take more classes if you want, figure out what kind of work you want to do, not the kind of work you have to do because it's the only thing available. You have choices. I'm offering you choices. Just say yes."

She swallowed hard. She wanted to believe him. Even with the sincerity shining in his eyes brighter than the moon, a wiggle of doubt told her to take it slow, but she had to start somewhere. If she couldn't trust him, they would have nowhere to go.

She stepped into his embrace and wrapped her arms around his waist. "Okay."

Logan held her hand and didn't let go.

The scent of steak and salmon permeated the air in the truck and his stomach rumbled, but he wasn't hungry for food.

It had been an unspoken agreement she'd go to his cabin, and her hand trembled in his when he parked in the resort's parking lot.

Things would change between them tonight, for the better, because he couldn't take much worse, and neither could she. Living the life she'd been living since Joey's death wore her out, and he couldn't let her break down.

She said she'd let him help her, and all he could do was hope she meant it.

"Stay there," he said, opening the door and letting in a blast of frozen air.

"I can open my own door," she said, smiling faintly, a tired pull around her eyes.

"You've been taking care of yourself for a long time." Logan brought her hand to his lips. "Let me help you now."

"Okay."

He circled the back of the truck and opened her door. She hadn't unfastened her seatbelt, and he did that for her, leaning into her, inhaling a light, clean scent of hair product and outdoors.

Cuddling her to him, he mumbled, "I want this to work."

She twisted in the seat and cupped his face between her palms, her fingers rasping over his whiskers. "I do, too."

Chills traveled down his spine. How in the hell had he lived without this?

She kissed him, gently, slowly, and widened her legs. He stepped closer and her knees hugged his hips.

He prodded her lips open, tasting her, the time lost sour on his tongue.

A gust of wind interrupted them and pushed through his jacket. He tensed and broke the kiss. "Let's go to the cabin. Will Rosie be okay alone?"

"She won't even know I'm gone."

She didn't say it with bitterness, just a fact of life, and he skimmed his fingers over her cheek, brushing her hair away from her eyes. "I'm sorry."

"If you want us to move forward, you're going to have to stop apologizing. And I'm going to have to stop asking you to do it."

She might have a point, but he'd never stop trying to make up for the past eighteen years. "You're right. I'm sorry." It made her smile, and that's all Logan wanted to do with the rest of his life. Be the reason she smiled.

"Come on, we've spent enough time outside," he said, lifting her out of the truck. He remembered their to-go boxes the waitress put in a crinkly plastic bag, and a squirrel ran up one of the trees that bordered the parking lot, the loud noise startling it.

He held her hand as they walked down the path, snow the blizzard dumped on them pushed to the side creating a deep walkway.

They reached the porch and he helped her up the steps. She crowded him as he unlocked and opened the door.

Cold, or she didn't want to be away from him? He wanted it to be the latter, but judging by how she shivered, he guessed the former had a lot to do with it.

"I'm hurrying," he said, chuckling. "You're the one who wanted to fight outside."

"We weren't fighting, exactly," she said, edging around him into the cabin. "I needed space. The restaurant was too crowded."

He moved to flick on the lights, but she stopped him. "Keep it dark, okay?"

"Okay." He dropped his hand.

He helped her take her jacket off and hung his next to hers on the hooks near the door.

Moonlight sparkled through the picture window and shined off the stones on Ivy's dress. It was surreal to see the woman she was now. Whenever he'd think about her, he pictured the young girl standing on her parents' porch as he said goodbye. That's all he *could* picture, because living in Decatur, he hadn't seen a recent photo of her. He could still see her, lipgloss and wavy hair, but she'd faded under grief and years gone by.

"I never told you how pretty you look tonight," he said, stepping closer.

"You did, but thank you."

He wrapped her arms around his neck. His glasses were fogged up, and through the lenses, she looked like a hazy goddess. "Dance with me. Do you remember?"

"Prom?" she asked.

"Yeah."

"I remember realizing you were taller than me."

He laughed. "I've been taller than you since we were twelve."

"I know, but I think that was the first time it felt like you were older than me. Even though we were the same age, you felt older, acted older. That was the night I realized deep in my bones I was going to lose you. We hadn't really talked about it, you going to school, but we danced to "It Must Have Been Love" by Roxette, and that's when I truly understood you were going to leave me."

He'd known it too, and that night at prom had been the first of their many goodbyes.

"Why didn't you say anything?"

They circled the small kitchen, the song weaving around them though it wasn't playing. Shifting back and forth on their feet, the way people dance when they don't know how. He rested his hands on her hips, keeping her close.

She was too short to lay her head on his shoulder, but she pressed her cheek against his chest and her lips brushed his shirt when she spoke.

"I couldn't. You worked so hard to get into the university. I suppose looking back I should have known that had been your plan all along. No one wanted more tutoring than you. I thought you wanted to spend time with me, but you wanted the As."

"I wanted both."

"And you got it. God, I was so sick of Calculus by the end of senior year. You worked hard, and under the sadness, I was proud of you. So proud of all you accomplished despite what you were living with at home. I never would have asked you to give that up for me. I wasn't worth it."

"Ivy—"

"No, I'm not saying that as some pathetic pity party. Our high school love wasn't worth you giving up your future, your career. You made the right choice. I just wish we would have stayed in touch somehow, but even that would have been too much, wouldn't it have?"

"I don't know, Ivy, and that's the truth. I missed you, but I didn't miss anything else. It was a strange limbo, straddling the fence, and I did what I had to do just to get through the day. I'm sorry. I'll try to make it up to you." His glasses cleared, and he could see her now, her sad and tired eyes.

"No. When we were trapped during the storm, what you said was right. I should have written. I should have sent you birthday cards. I should have—" She sighed. "When Joey died I should have asked you to come home, but as the years went by I felt you slipping away, and I was too scared to do anything about it."

"Time and distance will do that to anyone, sweetheart, not just us."

"And it happened, to the point where I didn't feel like I could ask you to give me anything."

He opened his mouth to deny it, to tell her he always would have helped her, even if he didn't know what he would have done had she asked, but she spoke before he could get the words out.

"I know that's wrong. I know it now. I know our love would have made it through anything. When we were at Evergreen Hill, you told me you loved me, but I was too scared to say it back. Now I feel like I'm too scared to *not* say it because no matter what happens, I need you to know. I love you, Logan, and I have since I was five years old."

"Come here, baby," he said, picking her up. That's what he'd been waiting for. Not the sharing of guilt letting their friendship crumble, though that helped. No, he wanted to hear she loved him, still loved him, after everything.

He carried her to the bed and let her slide down his body, his hardened cock rubbing against her.

As he unzipped her dress, she shivered, his fingers brushing her skin. Beneath her dress she wore a black strapless bra and black panties and tights.

The dress pooled at her feet.

"You are still perfect," he said, steadying her as she stepped free of the lace.

"Thanks. I guess that's stress. You look good, too."

He didn't comment, only tugged her tights over her hips, down her butt, and over her slim thighs.

She kicked them out of the way and pushed him to the bed. Standing between his knees, she said, "I've always loved how you look when you dress up. Your tux at prom made me crazy." She loosened his tie, letting the ends hang down his chest, and undid his shirt buttons one by one, her fingertips grazing his skin.

The first time they made love had been quick. He'd been starving, and he consumed her like a dying man. This time he would take care of her and let her have what she needed first.

She rubbed her lips over his neck. "You smell the same."

He took comfort in that. That after all this time, some things were still the same. "You do, too. Sweet. There's a scent on your skin that drives me nuts. I dated in Decatur because I missed you and I was lonely, but I could never find a woman who made my body respond like it does when I'm with you." He caressed her breasts through her bra, and she sucked in a breath. "If I touched you now, would you be wet?"

Making love to her as teenagers had been thrilling, exciting. Knowing they had limited time to show each other how they felt, how deep their love ran for each other. Loving her as an adult was different. They'd matured. He knew more of what would please a woman, and he could go slow and show her how much he adored her.

"Do you want to find out?" she asked, leaning into him, her breath tickling his ear.

She widened her legs, and he moved her panties aside,

his fingertips finding her slick and hot. He pushed his finger inside her and she gasped, tightening her hold on him.

"I don't want to wait," he said, stroking her sensitive skin.

She trembled. "What do you mean?"

He meant a lot of things. He meant he didn't want to wait to be inside her, but other things, too. He didn't want to wait to start their lives together. He didn't want to wait to start making things better for her. He wanted to start right now, not after the wedding. Right this second. Because he'd let too much time go by, and she'd lived through too much hell already.

His cock throbbed, jerking him out of the future. For now, they would wrap themselves around each other and revel in the fact that they'd found one another again.

"To be inside you," he said, answering her question with the most urgent answer. He unhooked her bra and tossed it on top of her tights and dress.

He unbuckled his belt and loosened his pants. He fumbled around in the side drawer, looking for the condoms he purchased, hoping he and Ivy would reconcile. More than hoped. He prayed like he'd never prayed before in his life.

Sitting on the mattress, he tore the packet open and sheathed himself. "Come here," he said, holding out his arms.

"You still have your shirt on." She wrapped the ends of his tie around her hands. "I like it."

She straddled him, and he guided her onto his cock.

"How did I live without you?" he asked, burying himself deep inside her.

"You didn't," she said, adjusting to take him in as far as she could.

"You don't know how true that is. God, Ivy. I love you so much." He found her clit, smoothing his fingertips over the engorged nub. "Come for me, just like this."

She cried out as he rubbed her clit, grinding into his lap, her face pressed into his neck.

"Let go, baby, I've got you." He wrapped an arm around her back to keep her in place. "You're almost there, I can feel it. Your pussy's hugging my dick. It's so good, baby."

She whimpered, and moving against his hand, she came, her muscles tightening as the orgasm rolled through her.

He twisted his hands in her hair and hushed her, his lips to her cheek. "Shh, shh, it's okay."

With his cock still painfully hard inside her, he picked her up and laid her on the crisp bedspread. He braced himself on his knees, his forearms on either side of her head to relieve her of some of his weight.

His heart slammed against his ribs, his mouth dry.

Tears glistened in her eyes.

He stared at her, their bodies joined, and he knew if he ever had to leave her again, it would kill him.

"Marry me, Ivy. Marry me so we never have to be apart another second."

Tears ran down her temples and dripped into her hair.

"All I need is for you to say yes," he said, her silence filling him with dread.

"Logan—"

He began to move, and she tilted her hips, gripping his dress shirt.

"Just say it. Make me the happiest man on earth. We'll figure out the rest, I promise. Our future starts with just one tiny little word. What do you say?"

CHAPTER SEVEN

Ivy clutched his shirt in her hands as Logan rammed into her, a look in his eyes she'd be hard-pressed to describe later. Intense, full of love, but dark, shadowed with broken dreams and a hard past. She had just as much to take on as he did.

He acted like he was okay, building a career, building a life in Decatur, but she was part of his horrid past. A past he'd had no trouble walking away from.

But nothing could be harder than the eighteen years she'd struggled to live without him, and she'd rather face the next eighteen battling his demons than another eighteen the way she'd lived them.

If he didn't leave her.

He came inside her, letting out a growl as he held her, as close as two people could physically be, and she breathed her answer in his ear.

His growl turned into a hoot, and he hugged her, laughing, his hand under her butt. "You won't regret it, I promise."

She believed him, and her heart wanted to believe

him, too.

She wrapped her legs around his thighs and giggled, peppering kisses all over his face, the tip of her nose smudging the lenses of his glasses he hadn't taken off.

They didn't need to figure this out tonight, or tomorrow, or even next week. They had time to puzzle out the practical things, like her lease, her job, and what they'd do with Rosie.

They had time to decide where they would live, and where she would work. Logan already offered to let her go back to school, and she loved him for that alone.

Together, they would work out his past. He needed to stop running, and she would help him.

He started to move again, his hard cock gliding in and out, lazy at first, then more urgently, and she held on, her fingertips digging into her shoulders. He was showing her he loved her, and she clung to it as if her life depended on it.

He came, though weaker this time, and when his shudders subsided, he let himself slip out of her. Lying in his arms, she let out a ragged breath.

"Say it again," he mumbled into her hair.

"Yes, I'll marry you," she said softly, and she wondered if that's how all women felt when they said yes, if Marnie had felt it when James asked her, that sliver of doubt that could do so much damage. That little sliver of apprehension she was doing the right thing.

"Thank you."

His arm grew heavy draped over her stomach, and she roused him out of his doze. "Get cleaned up before you fall asleep."

He stumbled to the bathroom and Ivy wiped between her legs using a tissue off the nightstand. Tender, she patted gently, then crawled into bed to wait for her fiancé.

She stretched between the cool sheets, the weight of the past lingering like a mist evaporating in the rising sun.

Logan would help her.

No, scratch that. They would help each other.

That's what couples did.

The mattress dipped as he climbed into bed, and he spooned her, an arm under her pillow.

"As soon as possible," he whispered. "At the courthouse. While I'm still in Rocky Point. After it's legal, we'll work on the rest."

"Can we get it done that fast?" she asked, happy they didn't have to wait. If he went back to Decatur without a ring on his finger, he would forget about her.

"I can pull a few strings and push our application through. It helps that Minnesota doesn't require a blood test."

"We'll have a Christmas wedding," she said, thinking red ornaments, red bows, red lights, red flags.

"My best Christmas present ever." His voice faded and his breathing deepened and evened out.

She laid awake long after he fell asleep.

When she laced their fingers, his tightened around hers.

She took that as a good omen. Took it as a good sign he wanted her and this time would do anything to keep her.

"How did it go last night? Saw your car in the parking lot this morning. Did you stay with Logan?"

Mitch hitched his butt onto a stool as she counted the cash in the register.

After spending the night with Logan, and another

lovely round of sex as the sun came up, she went home to check on Rosie. He'd wanted to go with her, but he looked so sweet lying in bed, his hair ruffled, squinting at her without his glasses, she hadn't had the heart to take him up on his offer. She kissed him and left him dozing in bed. He hadn't stirred when she let herself out of the cabin.

Rosie had fallen asleep in front of the TV, as usual, her pajamas the same as what she asked her to change into a couple of days before.

She didn't have time to wake her and insist on a shower. Rosie would have to sober up and shower alone or she'd have to wait. Her mother would have her own decisions to make in the coming weeks.

Nothing would happen overnight, and for now, she still needed to work, be paid to do that work, and pay her bills.

She poured Mitch a cup of coffee she put on the moment she arrived at the lounge. She liked the warm, earthy brew, too, and today the caffeine sizzled along nerves that were already dancing.

"Yeah, we didn't eat dinner, though." They hadn't eaten it when they got back to his cabin, either. "We started arguing about whose fault it was we didn't stay in touch. Mitch," she said, unable to keep the news to herself, "last night Logan asked me to marry him."

He didn't grin or come around the bar to hug her. He frowned, and her stomach sank.

"Are you sure that's a good idea?"

No, she wasn't sure. That was the whole problem, but didn't she say last night that she'd rather fight Logan's ghosts than be alone?

She slammed the register shut. "I love him. Why can you be happy, but I can't?"

"That's not what I mean. I want you happy. You don't

know how much I want this for you. You've been my friend for a long time and never once did you make me feel guilty about the accident or blame me. All you did was stand by my side, and you might not believe it, but I was really worried about what you'd do after I moved to Decatur. If I could trust Logan to take care of you—"

She bristled. "I don't need him to take care of me. I've been doing fine on my own since he left."

He wrapped his hands around the white mug that had the Rocky Point Resort logo stamped on the front. "I know you have, and that's the point. If you can depend on Logan, you won't have to be fine on your own anymore. But you know more about what he grew up with than I do. Has he put that away? Has he, I don't know, gone to a therapist? You don't shake off eighteen years of abuse."

"You're one to talk," she snapped, resenting Mitch and his caution. She wanted him to be happy for her, not echo the doubts lurking inside her heart. "You never went to therapy after the accident. You ran and hid from what happened, from how the people in town treated you. You said Callie saved you. Why can't I save Logan?"

"You can, but Callie and I aren't perfect. I haven't met her family yet, and they might not like me. She doesn't have a job, and I won't either, after my time here." He paused. "Does he know about your mom?"

She started slicing lemons and limes to keep her hands busy. "Yeah. He stopped by to see her. We haven't talked about what we're going to do. We can't force her to dry out, but I'm tired of taking care of her. Am I wrong not to want to do that anymore?" Tears sprang to eyes. Guilt and exhaustion. No matter where she turned, she couldn't get away from either one.

"No, you're not, but will Logan support you?"

"He loves me. There's no reason why he wouldn't."

There were plenty of reasons, one of which stared her smack in the face. If he could run out on her once, he could do it again.

"But why get married? Why not hang out? Talk? Date. He's practically a stranger. Callie and I aren't rushing into anything."

"No, he's not. We have a history, and it feels like we've already spent our entire lives together. That counts, Mitch. It counts a lot. You and Callie just met a few days ago, but you're already talking about marriage and how many babies you'll have. Logan and I don't want kids. We don't want to deal with that, ever. He had a shitty childhood and I'm tired of taking care of someone. The last thing we're going to do is pop out a helpless baby. We need the time alone, and I want to live for myself for a while."

"Then you guys are on the same page, at least?"

"Yeah. He said I could go to school and stop working a job that I have to because there's nothing else. That means a lot to me, that he sees me as more than a bartender. I know it's wrong to let someone else take care of you. Mom does that to me, and it hurts, but I need him to hold me up, just a little."

"And Logan? How can you help him if you can't help yourself?"

She rubbed tears off her cheeks. "I don't know, Mitch! Can't you just be happy for me? He wants to marry me, and I love him. Can't that be good enough?"

"It's not me it has to be good enough for," he said, his voice low. "I didn't mean to make you cry. If you're happy, that's all that matters."

She sniffled. "Thank you."

"When are you getting married? In the spring? This

summer? Please tell me you're going to do the long-distance thing for a few months."

She couldn't tell him she was afraid that if Logan went back to Decatur without her, he'd fall back into his old life and forget about her. Insecurity wasn't a great way to start a marriage. "He wants to before he goes back to Decatur and he's putting a rush on our license. I want this, Mitch. I need it."

Frowning, he thrummed his fingers on the bar. "Okay. If you need anything, tell me. If you want me to pound his face in, I will."

"No! Don't you think he's gone through enough? Violence isn't funny. Ever."

His cheeks reddened. "I'm sorry. I didn't mean that. I'd never hit Logan, but I know how much he hurt you and I hated seeing it. Don't let him do it again."

"I didn't let him hurt me. I let him get on with his life and *that* hurt me. If he would have stayed here, if I would have asked that, I would have been an anchor around his neck. I would have dragged him down." *And he would have drowned, just like Joey.*

He tilted his head. "And you think you won't this time?"

"No. We're both adults now. Things are different."

"Then I wish you nothing but the best."

She swiped the pile of lemon slices into a container built into the bar that would keep them chilled. "Thank you. You know I feel the same for you and Callie."

"I know." His cell phone chimed, and he pulled it out of his pocket and glanced at the text. "I better get to work. Let me know about the ceremony. If you need witnesses, Callie and I will stand up with you guys."

"Thanks. That means a lot to me. It really does."

"After the years of friendship you've given me, when no

one else would even look at me, it's the least I can do. Talk to you later."

Talking to Mitch didn't wipe away her doubts, in fact, it had accentuated them. But a shaky relationship with Logan was better than not having a relationship with him at all.

Living without him for the past eighteen years, she believed that with all her heart.

Logan searched for Ivy while he woke, his hand sliding over her empty side of the bed, but of course, she wasn't there. She left early to check on her mother and get ready to go to work. He fumbled with his cell phone on the nightstand to check the time. Already noon. He'd finally been able to sleep.

He couldn't help but smile. She said yes. After everything, she had faith in him and trusted him to take care of her.

He wouldn't let her down.

After he showered, ate a piece of toast slathered in peanut butter, and drank half a pot of coffee, he called his mother. She'd probably have a heart attack hearing from him twice in the same week, when before he'd gone a month or more without speaking to her.

Another thing he could thank Ivy for.

"Logan, is everything all right?" Elora answered, sounding worried and confused.

"Morning, Mom. Things are fine. How are you?"

"Good. Surprised. How are things? You're still in Rocky Point?"

He'd always thought his mother sounded like an actress

on *Downton Abbey*, full of kindness and grace. His father hadn't beaten it out of her.

"Yeah, I am. Things are good. Excellent, in fact. I saw Ivy last night, and we talked. I . . . asked her to marry me, and she said yes."

She gasped. "Oh, darling, I'm so happy for you. I'm so happy you two found your way back to each other. Tell me how she is? How's her mother? Did you go see her?"

He sank into a kitchen chair and propped his elbow on the table. "Ivy's had it hard since Joey died. Her dad took off, and Rosie . . . she's not good, Mom. She tries to drink away Joey's death. Ivy's been taking care of her since the funeral and they live in a crappy little apartment because it's all she can afford."

"I'm so sorry. Word hasn't gotten to me about any of that, but this tells me one thing. You were meant to go back to Rocky Point. You were meant to see Ivy again. I believe all things happen for a reason, and Marnie and James getting married there was for this exact reason. And she said yes. I'm thrilled for you."

Elora's excitement was contagious, and an idea popped into his head. "Thanks. I'm going to bring her ring shopping tonight, after she's done with work. There's a little strip mall that stays open until nine on the weekdays. I want to marry her soon, before I go back to Decatur. There are a few things we have to sort out, and I don't want to leave without my ring on her finger and papers signed. She'll feel better. I know she's nervous about me leaving her again, but until we get things settled, we're going to have to spend a little time apart."

"She feels like you abandoned her, and you're going to have to give her time. Trust takes a lot of work to earn back. Buy her something pretty, something meaningful."

He huffed a laugh. "You mean a diamond isn't good enough anymore?"

"Diamonds are lovely, but Ivy . . . she's not going to care what's on her finger. Your love means more than what stone you choose, but this is your promise to her. Make it count."

"We had dinner last night, where we went before prom. It was weird, seeing it again."

"You played with the idea then, of asking her to marry you. I was worried you'd come home and tell me you were engaged. I didn't want that path for you. I wanted you to graduate and get out of that godforsaken town. I almost cried when I asked how it went and you only said you had a nice time. What changed your mind that night?"

"I . . . wasn't thinking that, exactly. I was torn between staying with her and completely cutting her off. I made my choice, and now I wish the past eighteen years had gone differently, that I had found a compromise between staying and not looking back."

"If you had, you wouldn't be the people you are, either. Ivy's a strong woman, and I'm beyond happy you have a woman like that in your life. I saw a little of that, when she drove me to the airport. That spine of steel. Taking care of her mother after her brother's death made her indestructible. There's nothing you won't be able to face together."

"She's amazing. But she's tired, too."

"Yet she still soldiers on." She paused. "Logan, there's one thing you need to do before you say your vows."

Apprehension slithered down his spine. He knew what she was going to say, and already the words formed a pit of fear in his stomach.

"What?" he rasped.

"You need to go see your father. Show him he didn't break you. You need to do that, not only for yourself, but for

Ivy. You ran away from her to get away from him. Show her that he's no longer a threat. That nothing is going to come between you. She's always going to have that fear in the back of her mind if you don't."

"I don't want to see him, Mom."

"You can't let him win, Logan, or he'll be a dark cloud over your marriage. I know you hate him, but I know you love her. Show her which is stronger."

Panic rushed in his ears, anxiety writhing in his chest. He told his mother he loved her and disconnected the call. He didn't wait for her to say goodbye.

He crawled into bed and pressed a pillow over his head. His phone chimed, his mother calling back.

The urge to run overtook him, just like that afternoon he said goodbye to Ivy, James waiting, his only escape.

Ivy.

His little girl.

He couldn't leave her again.

He couldn't let his dad win.

Not again.

Sweat cooling on his forehead, he pulled himself together.

He couldn't let fear distract him. His mother was right, and he couldn't let the emotions that slithered to the surface whenever he thought about his dad be stronger than the emotions that swamped his heart whenever he thought of Ivy. He texted her and asked if she'd taken extra hours that day. She replied she hadn't and her shift would end at eight. It seemed silly to text when he could walk to the resort and ask her in person, but after his conversation with Elora, he needed room to breathe. He told her he wanted to take her shopping and he'd meet her in the lounge.

She didn't ask what they'd be looking for and ended their messages with a smiley face. He was glad if not a little disappointed. He wanted ring shopping to be a surprise, but it would have been fun to tease her a little.

He did walk over to the resort, though, and he knocked on James's door.

James answered in a cloud of steam, a white towel wrapped around his waist, shaving cream covering half his face.

"Did I come at a bad time?" he asked, leaning against the doorframe.

"Nope. Just getting cleaned up. Marnie and the girls are scouting bachelorette party locations. We're getting down to the wire. Crunch time. We need tux fittings soon, but Jared's working today. This afternoon Marnie and I are going to the church to look around and take some notes about flowers and stuff. Do you want to come?"

Happiness gleamed in James's eyes and he knew how it felt to be getting married to the woman he loved more than anything on this earth.

"Don't stand in the hall. Come in. There's still some coffee left if you want, but there's only plain creamer," he said, grinning, and ducked into the bathroom. "What are you up to?"

He cleared his throat, and his hand shook as he poured a mug of coffee from the room service cart. "I took Ivy out last night," he said, sitting in the desk chair.

Rumpled sheets and bedspread covered the king bed, and he felt strange somehow, sitting in the room where only hours before his best friend and his fiancée had probably made love.

James peered around the bathroom's doorframe. "How did that go?"

"We cleared the air about a few things. Not all of it, but some. We went back to my cabin and I asked her to marry me."

The more he said it, the more surreal it sounded, but even then the words sounded right.

James came out of the bathroom wiping his face with a hand towel. "Oh, yeah? I'm assuming she said yes because you're not a quivering sack of jelly crying on the floor. That's great. I'm happy for you."

"Thanks. She did say yes, and I'm buying her an engagement ring tonight. This is all moving so fast, but I don't want her to think it was a token proposal. I love her, it's real, and I need to prove that to her. So . . . that's why I'm here. What are you doing tomorrow?"

James dug through a dresser drawer near him and pulled out a pair of jeans and a shirt. "Tomorrow night's the bachelor party. Jared sent out a massive e-invite. The wedding's only a few days away, and it's time to rock 'n' roll. Why?"

"I need a favor, and I hate asking because of all you've done already."

James tugged a pair of briefs on under the towel then threw it aside in a wet heap by the closet door. They'd been friends for so long he didn't think anything of it, but he looked at the ceiling and rubbed his face.

"Don't talk like that. We keep going over this, and it's time to cut the bullshit. We're friends, we're always going to be friends, and we don't keep score. So tell me what you need, and I'll do it."

"Okay. I talked to my mom this morning, and she told

me the only way I can move forward with Ivy is to go see my dad."

James yanked a grey University of Decatur t-shirt over his head. His pecs bulged under the short sleeves.

"When did you get so ripped?" he asked.

James scoffed. "When I asked Marnie to marry me? You're always at the office. Not all of us live there. Don't change the subject. She wants you to see your dad?"

"She said I need to prove to Ivy that I love her more than I hate him, and I guess she has a point. She can't shake the fact I left her to get away from him."

"Your dad's a fucking asshole who liked to pound on you when he was drunk. You would have been stupid if you hadn't left when you had the chance. You have to stop thinking it was a bad thing, and anyone making you feel like it was is wrong. You were eighteen and had a full ride to good school and you took the out. I wondered if coming back to Rocky Point was going to fuck with your head."

"It hasn't."

"Then seeing Ivy has. Don't let her make you feel selfish because you were looking out for yourself." James frowned.

"I should have went to Joey's funeral."

"Why? So you could have felt like this twelve years ago? What would you have done then? We were getting our firm off the ground, and I needed you in Decatur. You can only help Ivy now because of the money we bring in. And Rosie's a lush? Did I hear the gossip right? Drying her out won't be cheap. You're going to have to buy a house, you know that, don't you? You can't move Ivy and her mom into your condo. You'd be tripping all over each other and you'd be miserable in five seconds. How could you have done that twelve years ago? Things work out how they're supposed to work out."

"That's what my mom said."

"Then listen to her. What's your favor?"

"I want to go see my dad. Confront him. Show him I made something of myself."

"And you don't want to go alone?"

"I don't need you in there with me. I haven't been working out like you have, but I'm not a scared kid anymore. If he wants to dish anything out, I can take it."

"Fucking don't be in my wedding with a black eye. You'd ruin the pictures and Marnie would be pissed," James said, but he was smiling, and he nudged his shoulder as he said it. "I'll be your driver, but be careful in there. Tomorrow, huh?"

"Yeah." He blew out a breath.

"We'll celebrate at the bachelor party tomorrow night." He picked up a mug of coffee and raised it in the air. "To putting old times to rest and looking forward to new beginnings."

He lifted his half-empty mug, and James clinked the Rocky Point Resort coffee cups together.

"It's going to be okay, you know," James said, lowering his mug. "You've wanted this since Kindergarten."

"Ivy?"

James laughed. "No, Mrs. Schmidtbower. Of course I mean Ivy. September sixth, 1988. Nine, six, eighty-eight."

"How do you know my password to—"

"Everything in your life? You're not that dense, are you? September sixth, 1988 was the day you met Ivy. The first day of Kindergarten. Your life started that day."

"I never realized." He hasn't, and the fact James had scratched at his heart.

"She's always been your other half. Now the time's right and you can build a life together. Like Marnie and me. Timing's everything, and from where I can see, this is good timing for you. Let's go get some food."

He followed James to the dining room. Usually, he agreed with James on almost everything, but this time, he thought James was off the mark. Timing *was* everything, but in this case, he might have waited too long to take what he wanted, and he hoped like hell that he was wrong.

Logan was going to leave Ivy alone and let her work, but in the end, he couldn't help himself and caught her leaning against the bar watching CNN.

He'd never noticed the TV in the lounge, and he said as much as he slid onto a stool, surprising her.

"I usually don't have it on, but I felt like watching the news today. Sorry I had to take off this morning," she said, her cheeks pinking.

"That's okay. How's your mom?"

"I made her something to eat, and I left her sitting on the couch as usual. Logan, I . . . she's going to need a lot of help. And that's only if she's willing to take it."

"I know." He kissed the top of her hand. Her skin smelled citrusy, like lemons. He nibbled on one of her fingers and she laughed. "But you don't have to take care of her by yourself anymore, right? I'll help you now."

"I'm going to need time to get used to . . . not being alone."

"I'll be more than happy to help you get used to it."

He leaned forward and she obliged, rising on her toes

and brushing her lips over his.

"Shopping tonight, maybe grab some food somewhere?" he asked.

"Sure. What are you going shopping for?"

He tapped her nose. "That's for me to know and for you to find out."

"Ah-huh. You're lucky I trust you."

"Do you? Do you trust me?" He hadn't earned it. He hadn't fought for it, and he sure as hell didn't expect her to throw it into his lap like he deserved it.

"I'm trying."

"That's all I can ask."

"Oh, the mechanic called and said my car was done."

He frowned. "The Outback's giving you trouble already? Why didn't you tell me?"

She shook her head and poured him a short beer. "If you're going to chit chat, you might as well sip on something."

"God, it's early for this," he said, turning the glass, the light beer foaming.

"Not so early, and you're on vacation. After the wedding, James and Marnie's, I mean, it's going to take a lot of work. Mom and I are going to be a lot of trouble."

"It's not work if you enjoy what you're doing." He sipped the pale ale she poured him and the apple notes teased his taste buds. "I'd do anything for you. You—" He was going to say, "You know that," but no, she didn't. "We'll go day by day. What was wrong with your car?"

"Not the one you bought me. That one's perfect. My old Camry. I didn't think I'd keep the Outback, and I gave my mechanic the okay to fix it. Six hundred dollars to replace the alternator and battery."

They needed joint banking accounts. He didn't want

her worried about money anymore. "I'll pay for that."

"I already did, over the phone. He said he'd put the keys on the visor if I want to pick it up later. Can you drop me off after shopping, and I'll drive it home?"

"I wish you'd stay at the cabin with me."

"I can't. I have laundry to do, and Mom isn't so good doing dishes. I can't neglect her because you're in town."

"After James and Marnie's wedding, we'll look at houses in Decatur. We're going to need something bigger than my condo. James clued me in this morning when I told him."

Her eyes widened. "You told James?"

"Is that a problem?"

"No. I thought . . ."

"You thought I wouldn't tell people in case I wanted to back out. Ivy, I love you. I want to get married. I'm not taking it back."

Tears filled her eyes. "It feels too good to be true."

Reaching across the bar, he caressed her cheek. "I know, it felt like that to me too, when I was talking to James. But it's going to happen, sweetheart. You make me happy, and I want to make you happy, too."

"You do."

"Good. I'm going to get a few things done at the cabin while you finish up your shift. I'll come by around eight when you're done, okay?"

"Okay."

He looked around the empty lounge and met her behind the bar. Cuddling her against his chest, he covered her mouth with his. He'd never get used to the fact he'd be able to do this for the rest of his life. That she would once again welcome his kiss, that she would kiss him back, her heart in her eyes. "Have I told you how adorable you look in your uniform?"

"No. This crappy thing?" She brushed a hand down her vest.

"Yep. Maybe you could wear it for me one night?"

Desire darkened her eyes. "Maybe, but then every time I wore it I'd think about sex."

"And that's bad how?" He winked.

Her giggles followed him as he walked out of the lounge.

He allowed himself to smile and breathe a deep sigh.

Life was good.

All he had to do was keep it that way.

Ivy finished her shift and had energy to spare.

It was amazing what love could do. It was amazing how someone finally on her side could make her feel. Logan would help her. She hadn't had help in twelve years, and the weight he'd help her carry meant more than possibly anything else he could give her.

"Where are we going?" she asked as he held her hand and led her through the lobby.

People watched them walk through the airy space, a huge Christmas tree sparkling near the fireplace, and she tried not to compare their appearances, but she couldn't help it. She wore her uniform and comfortable, worn out, shoes. Her dirty jacket needed a wash, but she never remembered when she did the laundry to throw it in there too, and grime smeared the sleeves. She hadn't anticipated going anywhere today and wore her hair in the simple pony-tail she usually did at work, but after her haircut, at least that looked better. She rarely wore makeup, and today was no exception.

Logan looked dapper wearing his black wool jacket, jeans and black shoes. His gloves probably cost as much as one of her entire paychecks, and it was difficult to think she had a right to be by his side.

He could have any woman in Rocky Point, probably any woman in Decatur, too, but he was opening his truck door for her, helping *her* into the leather seat.

All because, why? They had a history together.

She was deathly afraid that a crumbled history wouldn't support a solid future.

He climbed behind the wheel and she forced a smile. "Where are we going?"

"Be patient," he said, starting the truck. "You'll see soon enough. Where can we go to have dinner afterward? Or will we have to make do ordering room service at the resort?"

She laughed. "You'd like that. The diner downtown will still be open. Maybe we can stop and see Leah at the Supply Company. She'll just be closing up at nine. Did James tell you she bought it? Helen and her husband, Glen, ran it back when you still lived here."

"Yeah, he did. Jared looks happy. They're a nice couple. Leah's making a really big change moving here for him."

"It's not just for Jared," she said as he drove down the steep hill away from the resort. "She hates her life in New York and she's moving for herself just as much as to be with him."

He glanced at her. "Did you want to stay here?"

She shivered, and her mouth dried. Was he already looking for an excuse not to marry her? "While you live in Decatur?"

"No. Do you want me to relocate here?"

The town slid by as he drove through the heart of Rocky Point. Christmas lights and garland decorated Main Street, and the lights shined brightly in the dark that had descended hours ago.

"I . . . never thought that was a choice. You hate it here."

"I hate that my father's here. There's a difference. But I would move back if you liked it well enough you don't want to leave."

"Could you work with James long distance?"

"No. I'd open my own firm. People die here, too, but I wouldn't get the caseload James and I have in Decatur. We have to turn families down, and that's not a bad problem to have."

"No, I guess it's not, but I wouldn't ask you to do that. You and James worked so hard, and now you have a business you can be proud of. I won't let you throw that away."

He parked in the pothole-ridden lot of a small strip mall. She'd never had a reason to shop at the rundown plaza. The only stores that occupied the space were a Chinese restaurant she heard wasn't very good, the only daycare center in town that accepted the government childcare voucher, a small hobby shop, and a jewelry store. She had no idea what Logan needed and why he wanted her along.

"I wouldn't be throwing anything away to be here. You're my everything now, and I need you to start believing that."

Awkwardly, she crawled into his lap. There was barely enough space between his chest and the steering wheel. She pulled off her mittens and framed his face in her hands. His eyes twinkled behind the lenses of his glasses. "Sometimes I love you so much it scares me," she whispered. "You feel like you could disappear any second."

Logan skimmed a hand up her leg, and his palm warmed her through the thin material of her pants. "I feel like that too," he said, his breath fanning her cheeks. "That makes it real."

She pressed her lips to his, lightly at first, then harder, wrapping her arms around his neck.

He wedged his hand between her thighs. "Ah, you're warm."

"And curious. Why are we here? Are you buying James and Marnie a gift in the hobby shop? That's an odd wedding present."

"No. I'll show you if you stop trying to seduce me in the truck."

She laughed. "With nowhere to go, that's all we used to do."

"When was your favorite?"

He opened his door and pushed out of his truck holding her in his arms. He set her on the sidewalk and locked the vehicle using his key fob.

"I'm not sure. Maybe that time before prom when we drove out of town and parked at that abandoned hunting shack. Do you remember that? I probably couldn't find it again now."

"Yeah, I do remember. It was the first time we had sex while you were in my lap." He leaned over and murmured in her ear, "Like last night."

His gravelly voice dampened her panties. "I think it's becoming one of my favorite positions."

"Speaking of positions, who exactly were you dating to try to forget about me, anyway?" He held the jewelry store's door open. Maybe James had asked him to pick something up.

She quirked her lips. "Not that I slept with him, but do you remember Kevin Johnson?"

They entered the small shop and he frowned. "No."

"I'm not surprised. He was a wallflower in high school. Got good grades, but he was never in any extracurriculars. I think he might have dated Autumn. Anyway, right after graduation he got a job at the mill, and he bought a pretty house on the lake just a couple years out of school."

"How did he manage that? Get into the paper mill?"

"It's all he thought he'd ever be able to do and he put his name on the waitlist in ninth grade."

He laughed. "What the hell."

"I thought it was pretty smart."

"No kidding."

A saleswoman set her phone aside and greeted them. "My name's Dee. What can I help you with tonight?"

He stepped to the counter and leaned against it. "Good evening, Dee. I'm Logan, and this is Ivy. I asked her to marry me last night, but I was a bad boy and didn't have a ring. She said yes anyway because she loves me, but I need a ring on her finger, ASAP."

She gaped. "That's why we're here?"

"Why did you think we came in here?"

"I thought maybe James asked you to pick something up."

"James can take care of his own woman. I'm taking care of mine. Let's find something nice, okay? I want you wearing this thing for the rest of your life, so I need you to like it. Don't choose anything because of the price. Honestly, pick out what you're going to want to look at forever."

Tears filled her eyes, and embarrassed, she stepped into Logan's arms and pressed her face against his jacket.

Dee sighed. "Sometimes I really love my job. Let's look for something brilliant."

Her fingers were slim and several of the rings she liked would have to be resized if she set her heart on one. Dee told them it would only be a matter of days, but somehow she knew he wanted her to leave wearing a ring that night. She took her time looking at only rings that fit, and she finally chose one Dee dug out of a dusty and forgotten side display in a dark corner of the small store.

Two heart-shaped diamonds butted against each other in a silver setting on a thin, delicate band. Sold with a matching wedding ring, the set cost what she made in a month. No matter if Logan said it wasn't an issue, money always would be to her, and it pleased her she was able to find something she loved that wouldn't take a big chunk out of his bank account.

"Are you sure this is what you want?" he asked, tilting her hand and studying the ring. The stones sparkled in the dreary lights.

"It suits her hand," Dee said, leaning against her side of the counter. "Ivy's fingers are delicate, and a bigger ring would look clunky. It's perfect, really. I couldn't recommend anything better."

"Can you engrave something on the inside?" he asked, wiggling the ring off her finger. She was sorry to let it go so soon.

Dee squinted at the band, considering. "Yes, but barely. The script will be very small."

"That's okay. We'll know it's there." He looked at her. "Are you sure?"

She didn't hesitate. There were two hearts, like there were two of them. "Yes, I'm positive, but will you be able to have a matching ring?"

"Plain silver will be just fine," Dee said, moving down the counter. "We have several men's wedding bands to choose from." She laid a velvet display on the glass.

He asked her, "Will you choose mine?"

"Really?"

"Yeah."

He wrapped his arm around her shoulders while she perused the choices. She wanted something that matched hers, but Dee was right, all the plain silver wedding rings would work. "I like this one, what do you think?" she asked, sliding one that had two diamonds out of the slot. She wanted him to wear them as a couple, too.

Trying it on, he agreed, his voice wobbly. "It's perfect, Ivy."

She smiled, liking how it looked on his finger. "It is, isn't it?"

"You're easy customers," Dee said, amused, walking into the back to engrave her ring. "I'll be just a moment."

They sat while they waited, and she took her jacket off. "Thank you for doing this."

She leaned into him, reveling in his solid presence, and he kissed her cheek. "I want to do everything I can to convince you I'm never going to leave you. You'll never be on your own again. I promise."

Twenty minutes later Dee walked out of the back room holding her ring. "It turned out very nice, even with the small script."

He skimmed his fingers over the stones and the engraving inside.

Impatiently, she waited. She wanted to stare at her hand like the newly engaged women she read about. She wanted to be included because she never thought she would be.

She was beginning to think he'd found a flaw in the one of the stones or the engraving, but he finally turned to her, tears in his eyes. "You probably want to know what I had engraved inside."

She nodded, her throat scratchy, but she hadn't thought to question it. Something sentimental, but something, well, she didn't know. What could have lived in his heart for eighteen years? What could have been so important he never forgot it?

"I had September sixth, 1988 etched into your band. I wanted that date because it was the first day of the rest of my life. I hadn't known the date had stayed with me all this time until James mentioned it this morning. Do you know what date that is, Ivy?"

"No," she whispered.

"That was the first day of Kindergarten at Rocky Point Elementary. It was the first day you sat next to me in the cafeteria and offered to share your lunch because I didn't have one. But you did more than share your sandwich and a bag of cookies. From that day on, you shared your life with me, up until the day I left. Even though I was an asshole for the past eighteen years, I'm asking, no, I'm begging you, to share the rest of your life with me. I need you, Ivy, and I don't want to live without you anymore." His voice broke and he dropped to his knees. "Ivy Graves, please say you'll be my wife and let me put this ring on your finger. Please say you'll never take it off. Please say you'll love me forever."

"Oh, God." She wiped her cheeks and held out her hand. "I promise, Logan. I will."

The ring weighed almost nothing, and when he pushed it onto her finger, she could barely feel it. That would be Logan's love. She wouldn't need to feel the weight of it to know it was there.

"Thank you, baby."

She sank to her knees rested her head on his shoulder.

Dee blew her nose and she jerked out of his embrace. She forgot Dee was there.

"That was so beautiful," Dee said.

He helped her to her feet. "We appreciate your time, very much," he said, pulling his wallet out of his pocket.

He paid, tucking the receipt into to his wallet and zipping their wedding bands into an inside pocket of his jacket. He shook Dee's hand and she wished them goodnight.

Tangling their fingers, he walked with her out of the store. Dee flipped the sign to Closed and turned off the light.

Silently, he opened the truck's door and lifted her inside. He paused, resting his forehead against hers, and she rubbed her thumb over his damp cheek. "I love you so much," she whispered.

"I love you, too." He sniffled. "I guess we better get going. It's cold out here, and it's too late to eat dinner now."

She watched the town go by as he drove to the auto shop where her car had been repaired.

"Are you okay? You haven't said anything. Did I do something wrong?"

She squeezed his hand, the feeling of the ring on her finger unfamiliar. "I'm more than okay, and you didn't do anything wrong. This was perfect. Thank you."

"You're welcome." He idled near her old car. "I have a few things I need to do tomorrow, and James's bachelor party is tomorrow night. Their wedding's coming fast now, and there're going to be times I can't see you. Are you going to be okay?"

She leaned over and kissed him, grateful he thought to

warn her about his schedule. She would have been worried if all of a sudden he was busy all the time, certain he regretted his proposal. "I'll be fine. Have a good time."

"Will you come to the wedding with me? I can tell Marnie, and she'll make space at the reception. Mitch will probably be there so you won't have to sit by yourself."

She blinked. "Do you really want me there?"

"You're my fiancée. Of course I do."

"Sure, I'll go, then. I might have to borrow another dress from Callie, but it will be fun. I'll see you later. Drive safely back to the resort."

"I will. Text me when you're home, will you?" he asked, shifting his truck into Reverse.

She opened her door. "Yeah."

"Thanks. Goodnight, Ivy. I love you."

"I love you, too. Night."

She slammed the door shut, and he backed out of the small lot attached to the mechanic's shop. She sat in the cold car and found the keys in the cupholder. Squealing and groaning, the engine turned over. She'd gotten used to the Outback and driving her little Camry to her apartment was like being splashed with cold water after a hot shower.

She didn't mind.

She smiled at the pretty diamonds on the ring finger of her left hand all the way home.

Logan's stomach twisted in a big ball of knots. He sat in the passenger seat of James's truck as James navigated through town toward the old residential neighborhood where his father still lived.

Before leaving his cabin, he searched his father's name on his laptop, double-checking his current address. He wasn't surprised his father still lived in the old house he grew up in. After the mill closed, his father was one of the lucky few who got a job on the railroad. He made decent money maintaining the tracks and there wasn't any reason the old house wasn't paid off by now.

"It won't be so bad. You're not a little kid anymore," James kept reminding him. Huge mounds of snow hugged the sides of the street. Had the blizzard been only just a few days ago? Things had moved quickly, and the days felt more like weeks, or even months.

"I know, but the past eighteen years have built him up into a monster in my mind."

"Then it's good you're doing this. You're an adult now and you'll see him through adult eyes. He won't be so scary anymore."

James's words didn't ease the sick roll in his gut, and when James stopped across the street from the white one-story house, he felt like he could throw up in a snowbank.

"Don't take any shit. You don't have to."

That was easy for James to say, he'd be safe out here, but he said, "Right."

He stepped out of the truck, the snow on the side of the road burying his shoe. He leaned against the tailgate and took a deep breath of cold air. He didn't want to do this and he could turn around and get back into James's truck and tell his friend to drive him away, as fast as he could go.

No one was making him do this, but his mother had a point. He had to put his father behind him so he and Ivy could build a future. Tomorrow, if he could tell her that he'd faced his father and laid the past to rest, maybe it would take some of her pain away. Some, not all. He had a lot to make up for, but God, he loved her so much, he had to start somewhere.

He trudged through the deep snow to the side of the house. His father didn't use the mudroom's entryway, probably entering the house through the garage, but he knocked on the rotting wood. Heavy footfalls sounded behind the door, and his heart hammered and his hands shook.

Gunner Draper opened the door and stared at him through the ripped screen.

He didn't look any older, maybe more grey threaded through the man's hair, maybe there were more lines carved into his face, maybe his whiskers were more white than blond, but the look in his eyes was the same, and Gunner gripped a beer in the same meaty fist he'd used to keep his son in line.

But he could look the man straight in the eyes. His height had finally caught up to the man who'd sired him.

"You're back," Gunner said, stepping away from the door. "If you wanna do more than gawk, come in."

He forced his feet over the threshold and stepped into the mudroom. The same washer and dryer sat in the corner, now used as a dumping ground for dirty clothes that would never be washed.

The putrid odor of stale food permeated the air, and something had burnt, recently, if the acrid scent was anything to go by.

Gunner disappeared into the kitchen, apparently not caring if his son followed him or not. He paused and considered taking off his shoes, but dirt caked the floor and he wanted to be able to escape quickly. He left them on.

He walked into the kitchen, and Gunner opened the fridge and offered him a bottle of beer.

He shook his head.

"Too pussy to drink?" his dad asked, scoffing.

"No. I just don't want to drink with you."

"Then what the fuck you doing here in your fancy jacket and sissy glasses? You got some high-falutin' job now? You rich and came to rub it in?" Gunner's cold blue stare pinned him in place. "You remember where you came from."

He swallowed.

His father was exactly how he remembered. Mean as a snake.

"I just want to know why. Why did you need to put your hands on Mom? On me? What did we do to you? Did you marry Mom to have a live-in punching bag? Didn't you love her? Me? Even a little?"

"A husband's job is to keep his wife in line. Your mother needed a firm hand, and when you were born, you needed a whoopin' to remember who was boss. I put a roof over your head, food in your ungrateful belly. I worked my ass off in that paper mill for assholes who took home three times what I got."

"That's no excuse for the way you treated Mom. She cooked for you, cleaned for you, and you still slapped her around." Elora's cries echoed through his head. He could hear them bouncing off the walls in this room while he hid in his, terrified he would be next.

He always was.

"It was my right." Gunner's eyes zeroed in on the bare ring finger of his left hand. "And when you get married, it'll be yours. Keep a pretty little wife in line. Keep her ass in your bed and don't let her do whatever the hell she wants. Knock her up, keep her pregnant, and remind your brats you're the boss."

He stepped across the cracked linoleum. "I will never treat Ivy the way you treated Mom."

Gunner cackled. "Ivy? That little whore? Is that why you're back? You know she fucked her way through town after you left? You want crusty snatch like that in your bed? She's got more miles on her than my truck."

"Don't say that about her." He gritted his teeth and clenched his hands into fists by his sides.

Smirking, Gunner said, "What are you gonna do? Stop me? You're too weak. You can't take me." He set his bottle on a cluttered counter and flitted his fingers at him. "Come on. Ivy's a cute piece of ass. I'd bend her over a table. Would have to see a doctor, after. Probably give you the clap. You do her already? How was she? Tell your old man—"

He didn't give Gunner a chance to finish. He rushed at him and slammed him into the fridge. A box of cereal toppled to the floor.

He managed to land a weak right hook to the center of Gunner's belly, but he didn't know how to fight and the punch did little. Didn't know the first thing about taking down a man fifty pounds heavier and a hell of a lot meaner.

Unaffected, Gunner shoved him back, and he stumbled into a rickety kitchen table. He didn't see the punch coming, and Gunner's fist connected with his jaw. He fell to his knees, pain vibrating through his head.

"Want more?" Gunner said, huffing. "I can fucking do this all day. Haven't been in a good fight in a long time. On your feet, you weak-assed pansy. Show your old man what you can do."

Stars flitted across his vision, and his jaw felt like it was on fire. It brought back horrible, dreadful memories. Five years old. Ten. Fifteen. Then, at eighteen, one last punch before James could stop him.

He staggered to his feet and wiped his mouth. Blood smeared over the back of his hand. "You son of a bitch."

Gunner sneered. "You got that right. My ma did the same thing. Liked to take a belt to me. Not a day went by she wasn't teaching me a lesson, same as me and you. I grew into a man who could earn a living, keep a roof over his family's head. You made something out of yourself. You have me to thank for that."

"Are you out of your fucking mind? I made something out of myself in spite of what you did, not because of it. I don't owe you a goddamn thing."

He thought they were done taking licks at each other and the backhanded slap that caught him unaware knocked his glasses off his face and banged him against the stove. A crusted frying pan slid into a sink full of dirty plates.

"Watch your fucking mouth when you talk to me. You grown up don't mean shit. I'm still your father. You're mine, and I raised you right. You'll be just like me when you have little fucking rugrats."

Gunner turned and walked into the living room.

He knew it shouldn't go any further, but he tackled the man he'd feared his whole life, surprising the asshole. He'd never let the old man get the better of him again. They stumbled and crashed onto a coffee table covered in paper plates and beer bottles.

The table gave beneath their weight, wood splintering. Groaning, Gunner laid among the scattered bottles. He dragged himself to his knees and wiped at the sweat trickling into his stinging eyes.

He wobbled to his feet and swayed, lightheaded. He searched for his glasses and found them on the kitchen floor. Luckily, they weren't broken. He put them on and prodded his cheek, the left side of his face swelling.

"I will never be you." It hurt to talk. "Ever. You're pathetic, and weak, and you took that weakness out on the people you were supposed to love. I'm done, and you'll never see me or Mom again."

Gunner opened his eyes, his steely gaze full of satisfaction.

"My blood's your blood, don't you forget that, boy. You'll never be able to run from it. You marry your little whore, let her spread her used-up legs, and you take what you want. You think you're better'n me? Look at what you did. You take a good look at what you did to your pa and tell me you're better'n me."

Anger pulsed through his veins. He wouldn't waste any more time on this sack of shit.

Gunner moaned and sat up, what was left of the broken coffee table cracking.

"Hey, Logan."

He turned, startled. He couldn't remember when he'd ever heard his father say his name.

"Proud of you, boy."

Bile rose up in his throat and he gagged. He shuffled out of the mudroom, the old screen door slapping shut behind him, and staggered into the yard full of snow. Near the neighbor's fence, he threw up the breakfast he ate with James only a few hours before.

Using a handful of snow, he wiped his mouth, his stomach churning.

He held a snowball to his face and slogged around the side of the house where James waited to take him away from it, just like he had eighteen years ago.

CHAPTER EIGHT

Logan walked around the corner of the little house, the paint chipping.

James was leaning against his truck, hands shoved into the pockets of his jacket. Frowning, he stepped forward, his lips forming the word "fuck." He couldn't hear him, but the expletive coming out of his friend's mouth couldn't be mistaken.

Lurching across the street and holding the melting snow to his jaw, he waved James off.

"What the fuck?" James asked.

"He said some things about Ivy," he said, flinging the snow on the ground, some of it tinged pink. "I don't want to talk about it."

James nodded and without another word, slid behind the wheel.

He climbed into the passenger side, his head and heart throbbing.

He didn't deserve Ivy.

He shouldn't be messing up her life.

Gunner's blood pulsed through his veins, and no

amount of school or money would change where he came from.

Proud of you, boy.

He'd done the opposite of what he set out to do. He wanted to show his father that he was better than the old man who hadn't loved him. A better person, a better human being, but all he'd done was prove the apple didn't fall far from the tree.

"I don't like what you're thinking," James said, driving through town toward the resort.

"How the fuck do you know what I'm thinking?"

James didn't deserve the anger, but he let it slide.

"I don't have to know what you're thinking to know you're wrong. Do you want to tell me what happened?"

Proud of you, boy.

"No."

"Okay, but I'm around if you need to talk."

"Thanks."

"Still up for going out tonight?"

"Yeah. Might as well get shit-faced." He sighed. It's all he was good for.

"Are you sure you're okay?" James asked, parking in the resort's lot.

"Yeah, I'm fine. Do whatever you need to do. I'm gonna stay out here a minute and clear my head."

James lingered near the truck and kicked at a chunk of snow. He appreciated his friend's concern as much as he appreciated James knowing when he needed to let him be.

"Okay. See you tonight, then." Throwing a worried look over his shoulder, James left him in the parking lot, standing in the cold, a headache raging through his skull.

He leaned against James's truck, scrambling like hell to figure out what he would tell Ivy.

He couldn't be with her. Marrying her was out of the question. She needed to marry a man who could give her stability. A family.

What could he give her? He was a kid who grew up on the wrong side of the tracks who had a father who'd liked to beat him up and a mother who'd been too weak to stop him.

What had he been thinking?

That Gunner would apologize? Tell him he was sorry? Thank him for coming home so he could finally say the words he'd hoped for all his life? That Gunner loved him?

The man hadn't changed. He'd taken a swing the first chance he got.

Okay, so he'd been easy to manipulate, easy to taunt. Ivy was a hot button and Gunner slammed his fist on it the minute he walked in the door.

Logan had fallen right into the trap.

Ivy needed better in her life.

He thought money was all Ivy needed to feel secure, to have a better future.

She needed more, and he'd forgotten that. Or maybe he hadn't realized just how bad things had gotten since Joey's death. Maybe he hadn't wanted to know.

It was wrong to do this while she was working her shift, but he needed to get it out of the way, do it fast. He'd find out her bank information and wire her money. All he had. Help her make a fresh start.

She was so quick to forgive him, still so capable of loving him when he was nothing but rotten to the core.

He watched her lean against the bar in the empty lounge. She hadn't been on shift long, and her hair bounced around her shoulders. She was watching a wedding dress show on a lifestyles channel and happiness lit her face.

Shame burned in his throat.

He'd break her heart and she'd hate him for the rest of her life. She'd hate him, and that's how it should be. How it should have stayed.

"Ivy."

She faced him, and her smile faded. "What happened?"

"Nothing. I was on the wrong end of a fist."

"It was more than nothing and it looks horrible. Let me get you some ice."

He didn't sit on a stool, but he accepted the ice cubes she wrapped in a clean bar towel. Pressing it gingerly to his jaw, he said, "We need to talk."

"You need to tell me what happened." She walked around the bar and reached to hold his hand, but he jerked away.

Panic shot through her eyes and she stepped back.

No one could accuse her of being stupid. She knew what was coming, and he hadn't said a word.

"Is there someplace private we can talk?" Sweat slid down his back.

"In the storeroom. It's the best I can do because I can't leave the lounge."

In an elegant wedding boutique, a woman wearing a poufy wedding dress twirled on the TV. Her family and friends clapped, shimmering champagne flutes sitting on small, mirrored tables.

She clicked the TV off.

Tears burned his eyes.

He followed her into a small room full of bottles and cases of beer. Her old winter coat hung from a hook near the door and a hand truck was tucked into the corner near a box of whiskey.

"Ivy, you know what I grew up with," he started.

She nodded and chewed on her bottom lip.

"I've always been the kid who didn't have enough. Clothes, food, school supplies. Never had money because I didn't want to work and leave Mom alone, and the time I spent with you was too much as it was. Never had a car to get a job, anyway."

"None of that mattered to me," she whispered, twisting her engagement ring around her finger.

She'd hadn't worn it twenty-four hours, and he was going to tell her the promise he made last night meant jack shit.

"I know, but it mattered to me. For the past eighteen years I've tried to be better. Get good grades, build a career to make enough money to buy the best. But the problem is, I'll never be the best. I can't be the best because I don't have it in me."

"Where is this coming from? Who hurt you?"

"How many guys did you really date?" he asked, his raspy voice the only sound in the small storage room.

"What? I don't understand."

"I got into a fight this morning defending you. How many guys did you fuck after I left?"

She blanched. "I dated a little. I didn't sleep with everyone I went out with. I was lonely."

"And that gave you the right to spread your legs for whoever?"

"That's a terrible thing to say." A tear trickled down her cheek and it tore his heart in half. But if he could do enough damage, he could leave without worrying that one day she'd try to find him. She could do so much better than what a piece of shit he'd become.

No. That he'd always been.

"What's this about?"

Finish it.

"This is about me not wanting to marry a whore."

The blood drained from her face, but instead of running out of the room, she lifted her chin and narrowed her eyes.

"You're lying. You forgot that I know you. That eighteen years apart hasn't changed that. I told you I dated, and you dated, too. Be a fucking man, okay? You decided I'm too much work. My lush of a mother is going to be too much work. I'm a mess inside my head because Joey's gone and my mom doesn't love me, and rather than admit it, she drinks to hide it. Tell me the real fucking reason you changed your mind."

He leaned against the doorjamb and held the makeshift icepack to his jaw. He needed to put distance between himself and her words, and because if he hadn't, he would have fallen on his ass.

He hadn't expected her to take the blame, twist his lies into something that had more credibility, even if it wasn't true. No one was more fucked up than he was.

"You're right," he snarled, forcing a hard look into his eyes. "Rosie would be too much time, too much money. Do you think I want the responsibility of drying her out? Fuck that. I've worked my ass off and it's time to have some fun. Starting tonight at James's bachelor party."

"While you're celebrating James's wedding, you can celebrate the marriage you managed to escape." She yanked the ring off her finger and tried to hand it to him. "The date engraved inside didn't mean anything at all, did it?"

He shrank away. If he took the ring back, he'd sever any ties holding them together, no matter how tenuous, how fragile. If she kept it . . . maybe . . . It didn't matter.

Everything was ruined.

"Keep it. Pawn it or whatever. I don't want it."

She slipped the small silver circle into the pocket of her vest. "You never said what happened."

He'd forgotten the physical aches and pains. "I said I was defending you. No one needs something like that said about them. Even if it's true."

She stared at her old worn tennis shoes and he slithered out of the stockroom like the slime he was. He'd been nasty enough she wouldn't look for him, either during the rest of his stay or after he went back to Decatur.

Walking to his cabin, Logan passed Mitch.

He tried to say something, but Logan ignored him. Couldn't have Mitch thinking they were one big happy family, could he? Though once the idea popped into his head, he couldn't shake the images of him and Ivy, Callie and Mitch, and Marnie and James getting together for pizza and game night, or he and Ivy playing aunt and uncle watching little munchkins while their friends went on dates and kid-free vacations.

A cozy life, Ivy by his side.

It wouldn't happen.

He couldn't miss what he never had. He'd spent the last eighteen years alone, and he'd spend the next eighteen alone, too.

Ivy was a strong woman. His mother was right about that.

He sat on a fallen tree trunk and a grey squirrel darted up a tree.

She'd find someone. Maybe even get married. If his mom could give her heart a second chance at love after all his dad put her through, so could Ivy.

No wonder he'd fallen in love with her. Ivy and Elora possessed the same strength. The same spirit.

She'd be okay.

Especially without him in her life.

The little squirrel blurred.

He needed a drink. Some ibuprofen.

Tonight would be a long night, and he'd promised himself he wouldn't let his personal drama interfere with James's celebration.

He owed James too much.

The wind biting his face, he plodded through the snow to his cabin.

He opened his door and a familiar, comforting scent met his nose.

Drowning in misery, a little boy who needed the security and safety of his mother, he croaked, "Mom."

Sadly, it didn't take Ivy long to forget she wasn't wearing the engagement ring Logan bought her the night before. She'd had so little time to wear it.

It's not as if she hadn't expected something like that. Too good to be true, that's what it had felt like, and that's what it'd turned out to be.

She couldn't blame him, either. Oh, maybe the way he went about it. She hated him for being a coward. Hated that she had to pry the truth out of him when he could have just said it. It's not like she didn't know. It's not like she didn't go home every night and find her mother on the couch yet again, another empty bottle of booze at her feet, her grip on the picture of Joey so tight it was amazing the frame didn't snap.

But knowing that didn't mean it still didn't hurt like hell.

Using a rag, she wiped the tears off her face.

"What happened to Logan?"

Mitch stood by the bar, his toolbox hanging from his hand.

She shrugged. "I don't know. Said he got into a fight. He didn't say much more than that." Calling her a whore. That should have hurt too, but strangely, it hadn't. He'd used it as an excuse to get what he wanted, and she wasn't a whore. Looking for someone to spend time with, someone who had common interests, someone she could laugh with . . . that didn't make her or any other woman who wanted companionship a whore.

"What's wrong? Are you okay?"

"Logan broke off our engagement. He said taking care of Rosie would be too much work."

Mitch dropped the toolbox on the floor and stepped back. "That son of a bitch. Let me talk to him."

Waving a hand, she said, "Leave him be. You were right. He's too weak to give me what I need. Better I find out now than after moving to Decatur. I'd have lost my job here, our apartment. It's better this way."

At least she knew her bartending position could pay the bills and she was able to set aside tip money, too. Logan never said anything about giving the car back, and she'd keep it. Out of spite, out of necessity. Out of payment for her broken heart.

"I'm sorry."

She tried to smile. "It's okay. I saw it coming. Are you going to the bachelor party tonight?"

"No. I need to stick around. Besides, I don't feel like I belong."

"You'll get used to it. Moving to Decatur with Callie, you'll probably double date with Marnie and James all the time. I heard Marnie's pregnant. If you knock Callie up, you guys could even raise your kids together."

"A little too soon to be talking like that, but I like the idea. Are you going to be okay?"

"Same shit, different pile, right?" She tossed the ice into the sink and threw the blood-smeared rag Logan used into the plastic bin of dirty towels and napkins.

"I was hoping better for you," Mitch said.

"I was hoping better for me, too, but, you know, I don't need Logan to make things better for myself."

"I wish I would have had that attitude a long time ago. I shouldn't have waited so long to make a change," he said, settling onto a stool.

She poured him a cup of coffee.

"Did Logan say who he fought with? He had a big fat lip when I saw him."

She dropped ice to a lowball glass and poured a small bottle of San Pellegrino over the cubes. She sipped, the cool water soothing her dry throat. "All he said was someone called me a whore, and he was defending me. I didn't believe it. It was the excuse he used to break up with me and I had to force him give me the real reason. He could have gotten into a fight with anyone, about anything."

Mitch met her eyes. "Ivy, the only person who'd ever hit Logan in this town is his dad."

She jerked in surprise and fizzy water sloshed over the rim of her glass. "You don't think he went to see Gunner, do you? Why would he do that?"

"To put the past behind him?"

"Then maybe he succeeded. Put Gunner in the past, put Rocky Point in the past, put me in the past. Didn't want to drag me and my problems into his sparkly future. I get it. It's fine. Like I said, better that I know now."

He squeezed her hand, his palm warm. "You'll meet someone who deserves you."

"Maybe I will, but Logan's right. Rosie's a drain. I love her, she's my mother and I always will, but she's had her time mourning. How long do I have to take care of her while she hides? When is it my turn to mourn?" She pushed back tears.

"Sober her up and talk to her. See if you can get through. Call your social worker. They have programs, even here. I tried to go counseling after the accident. It didn't stick, but they have addiction therapy through the clinic. All you have to do is ask."

"And try to force her to go."

He lifted the good corner of his mouth. "Time to play hardball, I guess."

"Yeah. Thanks for talking to me, Mitch. I'm really going to miss you when you're gone."

"You can't get rid of me that easily. I'll catch you later."

"Bye."

She emptied his mug and loaded it into the dirty dish bin.

She rubbed her finger over the empty space where her engagement ring used to be. Logan's support had felt good the few hours it lasted.

That was the worst part about all of it. He'd go back to the city, to his clients, his friends, his lovely condo, and she'd be here, alone.

She wouldn't think about how much she'd miss his love.

Thank God he hadn't given her time to get used to it.

But she could dream about the way he kissed, how good he felt making love to her in the middle of the night, how safe she felt in his arms.

It'd be enough for a little while.

She'd make sure it was.

Because it's all she had.

"What are you doing here?" Logan asked, stumbling into the cabin. "And how did you get in?"

Elora Draper sucked in a breath. "I think I should be asking the questions, young man. What happened to you?"

What happened? Where would he start? Letting his dad kick his ass, kicking ass in return, and trust him, that did *not* make him feel like he thought it would. Thinking about Gunner lying on the broken coffee table churned his stomach. Trading punches with the man who had emotionally and physically abused him and his mother for eighteen years didn't make him feel good. It made him feel ashamed he'd stooped to that level. It made him feel dirty.

"I went to see Dad. And let's just say . . . some things never change." Wincing, ge took his jacket off and hung it on the hook next to the door. He wiggled his feet out of his shoes and sank into a kitchen chair. Fighting made more than his face ache. The joints in his hands hurt, and his muscles knotted in pain. Gunner had gotten in a few accurate jabs. "Come here and give me a hug."

Elora wrapped her arms around him and he melted into the familiarity. It'd been a long time since he'd seen his mother. Too long.

"I'm sorry I haven't visited you," he whispered.

"You had careers to build, fortunes to make. A mother understands these things. I'll get you some painkiller. Why did he go at you? When I encouraged you to see him, I didn't think he'd take a swipe at you. Not now that you're an adult and can defend yourself."

"He didn't start it. Well, he said some shit." He grimaced. "Sorry. He was spoiling for a fight and he said some things about Ivy. Got my temper up, just like he knew it would. I should have walked away then, but I didn't." He rested his head in his hands. "I wanted to pay him back."

Elora placed four blue tablets and a tumbler containing three fingers of whiskey on the table. "I don't condone mixing drugs and alcohol, but you're going to feel like you got hit by a truck. This is only going to take the edge off, I'm afraid."

"It's fine. If I get too sore, I can sit in the hot tub."

She sat at the table and brushed her finger over his bruised jaw. He didn't want to know if he looked as bad as he felt.

"What did he say about Ivy?"

"He called her a whore. Accused her of sleeping around town after I left."

Elora scoffed. "That's completely untrue. She didn't do any more dating than any other girl that age. After you left, I kept an eye on her to make sure she was okay. She started dating a nice young man who worked at the paper mill and I'd see them around town. I almost thought . . . well. For some reason, it didn't work out between them." She knelt in front of him and held his hands in hers. "You didn't believe him, did you?"

He looked away.

"Oh, Logan. Please tell me you didn't do anything you'll regret."

He squeezed her hands. "I didn't believe him, but it made me understand that I can't be with her. There's too much of him inside me. I don't want to be around her knowing I'm capable of doing the terrible things he did to us. What if I got mad at her? What would I do? Smack her? Rant and scream and curse until there's nothing she can do to block out the noise? I broke off our engagement. Not because I believed what Dad said, but because I feel it was the right thing to do. She can do better. And she will."

Elora *tsked*. "How did she take it?"

"Like she expected it would come. That's what made it so bad, Mom. She knew it was coming. She didn't trust me, and I proved her right." He rubbed his eyes. "I'm so tired." The words came out as a sob.

"Then you should lie down and get some sleep."

"I can't. James's bachelor party's tonight. I need to be there."

"I'll wake you in time to go. You have time, and you and Ivy have time, too. You didn't say anything that can't be taken back."

But he had.

He let his mother tuck him into bed like he'd done a million times when he was small. A kiss to the forehead, a promise that things would be better tomorrow. He'd always believed her, had never once lost faith that one day he would wake up free of his father, free of the fear his father would hurt him.

That morning hadn't come until his first night in the dorms, James sleeping in the bunk bed above him.

But there hadn't been anything else, either.

No scent of the coffee his mother brewed bright and early. No squeak of the floorboards as she tiptoed around the house so as to not wake his father. There hadn't been a smile, even if despair shadowed her eyes. There hadn't been a full day with Ivy.

There hadn't been lazy days by the lake and long kisses.

What had he traded? What had he gained?

What had he traded this afternoon to free her of him?

Her trust. Her love.

In the morning, what would he wake to?

The snow, the sun, and a future without her beautiful face.

What he'd said to her he couldn't take back.

"I said terrible things, Mom. To make her say goodbye one last time."

Elora sat on the bed and carefully slid his glasses off his face. She fold them and put them on the nightstand. "Good-byes can be undone."

Tears of frustration and exhaustion dripped into his pillow, and he clutched at her hand, so relieved she'd come to see him. "How?"

She kissed his wet cheek. "Sometimes by saying nothing at all."

Ivy did something she hadn't done in the twelve years she'd worked at the resort. She called in sick. She was already working, but she called Desiree using the lounge telephone and asked if there was someone who could take her place for the rest of the day.

A dining room waitress relieved her, and in the storage room, she slipped on her coat and lifted her purse off the hook.

She gave the waitress a feeble smile goodbye and walked out of the lounge.

"Ivy."

She stiffened. She hadn't heard the wispy voice in fifteen years.

"Mrs. Draper. What are you doing here? In Rocky Point, I mean?"

Elora tugged a taupe knee-length wool coat around her torso. Her hair was pinned into a bun, but tendrils escaped and framed her face. After the kind of life she'd lived, Ivy thought the years would show, but Logan's mom had an ethereal quality, a kindness and grace unmarred by life's circumstances.

"I came to visit Logan. Ivy, is there a place we can talk?"

"I just told my boss I was sick and needed to go home. We'll need to find somewhere else to sit."

"I'm sorry. Are you unwell?" Elora asked, reaching a hand toward her.

"I'm tired."

"I won't take up much of your time."

She'd always liked Logan's mother and didn't mind talking to her, but she doubted she'd like anything the woman had to say. She'd defend Logan, and she wasn't up to the fight. She wanted to forget it all ever happened. "I can drive us to Starbucks, if that's okay."

Mrs. Draper touched her shoulder. "That's perfect."

At least she had a decent car and didn't need to be embarrassed driving Elora anywhere, but she felt the urge to confess as she drove through town.

"Logan bought me the car."

"It's very nice."

That's all she said until they ordered coffees and sat in a corner, a small table that had issues of a free local magazine scattered between them.

It was her first time in the café. It would be her last.

"Thank you for talking to me," Elora said, shrugging out of her coat.

"It's fine. I'm surprised to see you in town." She took off her coat as well and leaned into the chair's soft faux leather.

"I spoke to Logan yesterday, and after our conversation, I thought I should visit. It seems my mother's intuition wasn't wrong. He didn't look good when I saw him earlier, and it brought back a lot of heartbreaking memories."

"Logan has dredged up a lot of memories for me, too, since he came back. Not all of them pleasant."

"Being here has been difficult for him, and I hope you won't punish him for that." Elora sipped out of the disposable cup that looked foreign in her hand.

"I don't know what he's told you."

"Can I see the ring he gave you?"

"He told you he asked me to marry him?"

"Yes, and he told me he rescinded it."

She handed Elora the engagement ring that was tucked inside her vest pocket. "He did, but he told me to keep the ring. I don't want it. You should give it to him."

"If that's what you want." Elora briefly studied the diamonds and put it in her purse.

She wanted to cry. Their engagement was officially broken. She'd stupidly harbored hope that he'd come back, that he'd tell her it had all been a horrible mistake and things would be how they were before.

Silence hung between them.

"He went to see Gunner today," Elora said.

"I thought so. I'm sorry it went badly."

"I don't believe it went as badly as you think. Gunner took a few swings, but this time Logan fought back. He seemed to think it made him despicable, to finally defend himself. That it lowers him to Gunner's level of hatefulness.

I wish I would have told him standing up to Gunner made him strong, not evil."

"What do you mean, you wish you would have told him? Did he go back to Decatur?"

"No. He was tired, mentally and physically, and I left him sleeping. I wanted to speak with you because after thinking about it, I believe you should be the one to tell him. That you don't blame him for fighting back. Gunner has had it coming for a long time now, and in some twisted way, Logan probably earned Gunner's respect. But you need to tell him, Ivy, that he didn't become less in your eyes."

She shook her head. "Gunner doesn't have anything to do with why Logan broke up with me. He doesn't want to help me take care of my mom, and I understand, Mrs. Draper, I really do. Rosie's a lot of work, will be more if I try to get her into rehab. She lost a lot when Joey died. She lost her husband, her home. Her physical home, the house, not just the people who made it a home, if that makes sense."

Elora nodded.

"My mother lost her favorite child." She said it without bitterness. She'd accepted that a long time ago.

"And what Joey's death steal from you?" Elora asked.

She drained her cup, taking solace in the warm, chocolate coffee. "Do you honestly want to know? I didn't lose anything when Joey died. Yes, I miss him. He was my brother, and I loved him, but the day James drove Logan out of town was the day I lost it all. Logan was my everything, and he took it when he left." She wiped at the tears on her face. "I almost had it back. I was so close. A family. Support. A man who loved me. Eighteen years I've been alone because Logan disappeared." She sucked in a watery breath. "I can't do this anymore. I'll drive you back to the resort."

"Come here, Ivy. Please."

She sank onto the loveseat next to Logan's mother and let Elora wrap her arms around her. She hadn't thought of having Elora as a mother-in-law after she and Logan married, and now that was another thing that wouldn't be hers because Logan was a coward.

"I don't think this is over," Elora said, smoothing her hair. "Logan loves you."

She kissed Elora's cheek and stood. "That doesn't matter, Mrs. Draper. He loves his freedom more. Every day he was gone for the past eighteen years told me that."

She dropped Logan's mother off at the resort and drove toward her apartment.

Talking to Rosie was first on the list. After that, a nice long soak. She meant it when she told Mitch she didn't need Logan's help to change her life. She'd find some help. Something, anything. And damned if she'd feel bad about taking back her own life.

Logan could do what he wanted with his, and she would do the same.

It wasn't that late when Ivy parked her car at the apartment complex and kicked the snow off her shoes at the front door. Exhausted, her heart hurting, she plodded down the stained carpet to their corner unit.

Rosie was watching fuzzy reruns of an old sitcom, content, her hair fastened into a messy ponytail, the picture of Joey laying in her lap.

She hung up her jacket and started a pot of coffee even though she had her fill at Starbucks. She wondered what, if anything, Elora would say to Logan. What he would do when Elora gave him her ring. Probably nothing. Maybe after the wedding he'd leave it behind in a drawer in the cabin and one of the housekeepers would find it, or a couple using the resort as a weekend getaway. Maybe the woman would wear it and make up melancholy stories about the engagement that had gone wrong.

While the coffee brewed, she changed out of her uniform. She had to work tomorrow, unless she called in sick. It didn't sound like a bad idea, as tired as she was, but staying home while Rosie sat drunk on the couch had never been pleasant and it was always better to make money than waste her sick time in case she ever really did catch the flu. Being heartsick didn't count.

She cleared the bottles off the coffee table and poured her mother a cup of coffee. She set the mug on the table and sat, turning the TV off.

Rosie's eyes finally focused, and her hands trembled on the frame. "You have your serious face on."

She'd only given Rosie her serious face a few times. Once when she told Rosie her father left them and he wasn't coming back. Another when she had to tell her they were losing their house. One more time when they had an appointment at social services to fill out financial assistance paperwork because she couldn't support them on her own.

Maybe once or twice if money had gotten low, maybe once or twice more when the weather was bad or the car broke down.

Her whole life was serious, and it was a dismal fact that her mother could identify only a handful of times it had affected her when she lived it every day.

"I need to talk to you."

Rosie's mouth drooped into an unhappy frown and she reached for a bottle near her feet.

She snatched it away, tightened the cap, and set it behind her on the floor. "No. I need to talk to you, and you can't hide from it."

"I don't want to hear it."

"Well, you need to. Joey's been gone for twelve years."

"Don't you dare bring his name into this," Rosie snapped.

"Mom, I have no choice because he's what this is about. I can't keep doing this. You've drank for twelve years, maybe trying to kill yourself, I don't know, but for twelve years I've worked my fingers to the bone to support you, to support us, and I can't do it anymore."

Rosie narrowed her eyes. "I know what this is about. Logan's back, and you want to be with him."

"That's not it." If only it was.

"Yes, it is. He said he won't marry you if your mother's a drunk. He was a poor, sad boy. His daddy liked to beat him up. I bought him school supplies and packed him a lunch like he was my own child, but the first day he could leave, he did. That's how he thanked us, that's how he thanked *you* for being his friend."

"Logan doesn't have anything to do with this. He doesn't want me, doesn't want what we had. He left and never looked back. Just because he's here to be in a wedding doesn't change that."

"He came to see me, you know," Rosie said, leaning forward. "He came to see me and told me off for living this way. It's easy to be high and mighty when you have a little money, but I didn't fall for that. I told him he was just as cruel leaving you when you were so in love with him."

"Then you admit you've been using me all this time."

"I loved Joey. He was my sunshine, my little angel. You don't understand, do you? You don't understand why I loved him best."

She sucked in a shocked breath, her mind reeling. "There's a reason? What in the hell did I do to you that you would ever say such a thing to my face?"

"From the first day of Kindergarten it was Logan this and Logan that and as the years went on your whole life was that damaged boy. You think I didn't see what was going on? You think I didn't know he meant more to you than me? Than your father? You didn't care when Joey was born. There wasn't any love between you, there wasn't any sibling rivalry, there wasn't anything. You lived in our house and you ate our food, but your heart was always with Logan until the day he left."

Tears ran down her cheeks. "How dare you accuse me of not loving Joey! I loved him with all my heart. It's normal for brothers and sisters who have been born years apart not to be as close." A grief counselor told her that. Somewhere. Sometime. "But I have good memories, too. He hung out with Logan and me a lot. Goofing around, teasing us."

"You were so busy mooning over Logan and how he didn't give a shit about you anymore that you didn't see what Joey was going through. You didn't see the pain he was in. You could have stopped him from going on that boat, you could have stopped him from doing what he did that day. But all you could think about was yourself and how after six years Logan hadn't so much as sent you a fucking card."

"That's funny because that's what I think about you. You drink because you feel guiltier than hell for not getting Joey the help he needed. What were *you* doing, *Mom?* What were you doing that you didn't see his pain? If you loved him so much, why didn't *you* see it?"

Rosie gripped the frame and traced a finger down her dead son's cheek. "I didn't want to see it. I didn't want to think he needed anything more than me."

"Well, he did. And he needed more than me, too, so there's no point in trying to blame me for not getting him help. Maybe I was still heartbroken after Logan left. Maybe I was confused and I didn't know what I wanted to do with my life. Maybe I still couldn't see my future without Logan in it. But guess what? I can now, and it doesn't include a drunk for a mother who blames her son's death on me. Maybe we're all to blame, maybe nobody is, but the way we're living has to stop."

Her mother lifted her chin. "You can't tell me what to do."

"You're right. I can't. I can't make you do anything. But I can tell social services that I'm not going to work sixty-hour weeks anymore. I can tell social services that I want to move out and that you're going to need someone else to buy you toilet paper and cook your food because I won't do it anymore."

Static rushed in her ears. Rosie understood more than she thought. She'd belonged to Logan more than she'd ever belonged to her own family.

Shame burned her cheeks.

If taking care of her mother had been her way of paying for it, then she'd paid in full. She deserved her own life now. Logan wouldn't be around, but that was okay. He hadn't been around, and she'd been fine. As fine as she could be, and his visit had given her closure. They were different people who had different needs and different futures. She could finally say goodbye.

She didn't have to stay in town. She didn't have to go to Decatur, either. She could leave the state. Live somewhere warm. Somewhere the temperatures didn't drop below zero. Maybe then her heart could thaw out. She'd bartend on the beach, get a tan. She could take care of herself. She'd proven that.

And maybe, just maybe, she'd find someone who could love her.

"You do whatever you need to do," Rosie said, gripping the frame and staring over her shoulder, avoiding her eyes. "Keep being the selfish little girl you've always been. Ain't no worry to me."

"Christmas is in two weeks. After the new year I'll contact your social worker and take it from there. I'm tired, Mom, and I don't deserve this anymore."

"We all get what we deserve, make no mistake."

She left her mother staring into space, the living room dark without the usual blue flicker lighting up the room.

Her mother hid bottles around their apartment. Rosie didn't think she knew, but she did. In the small linen closet, she ran her hands under the thin towels and extra sets of sheets. She struck pay dirt, her fingers catching on an elegant bottle of champagne. Even drunk, her mother had good taste.

She started to peel the foil off the cork but stopped and lowered the bottle to her side. She couldn't do this. This was what her mother did. Drinking her problems away wasn't the answer, not for her, and it never would be. Drinking socially with her new friends was fine. Adding schnapps to her coffee on a cold winter's night was fine. Sipping on a glass of wine was fine. Deliberately searching for a bottle of booze in an attempt to make herself feel better was not fine. There were other ways.

She smoothed the foil back into place and shoved the bottle where she found it.

Instead, she poured a cup of coffee, adding butterscotch creamer she forgot she bought, and as she soaked, tried her best not to think about Logan. Her thoughts turned to him anyway. He'd be smart and avoid the lounge when she worked. James and Marnie would get married in a week and almost everyone would go home. Leah would stay, and Autumn would still be here.

People didn't think bartenders paid attention, but she'd heard more than a few things about Autumn and Cole. She wouldn't wish bad times on anyone, but sometimes it was nice to know her life wasn't the only one that sucked.

She soaked until her skin pruned and the water cooled, and reluctantly, she washed her hair and face. She rinsed off, let the water go, and wrapped a towel around her body. The TV was on, playing an informercial, but Rosie wasn't sitting on the couch. She must have gone to bed.

Good idea, she thought, gripping the towel closed with one hand and holding her half-empty coffee mug in the other. She was so tired, but no amount of sleep would help.

Her movements slow and sluggish, she dried her hair and tugged on her pajamas.

Stress and caffeine rolled in her stomach, and she crawled into bed where she laid in a heap of heartbreak and fatigue.

Logan hunched over a high-top in the sleazy bar and grill Jared and James chose to have the bachelor party. The bartender looked like he could kick Gunner's ass inside of a minute, and he'd bet his next paycheck he kept a baseball bat under the bar to teach anyone who decided to cause a little trouble a lesson.

God-awful country music warbled out of a jukebox that had probably taken one too many hits of its own, and the felt on the only pool table was so worn in places the balls couldn't roll across the table no matter how hard someone poked them.

But the beer was strong and had just the right amount of foam, and the wings and fries were just greasy enough to taste good without fearing he'd have a heart attack in the middle of the ceremony.

Elora had been sitting on the couch when he woke up, reading on a tablet she brought with her. His body ached like a son of a bitch, and against his mother's wishes he downed more painkiller and another few fingers of whiskey.

Dark bruises began to bloom up and down his ribs, and the bruise on his jaw blossomed into a purple and pink area the size of a golf ball. His split lip throbbed, crusted over with dried blood.

He hadn't had time to sit in the hot tub, and he'd made do taking the hottest shower he could stand.

He'd come out of the bathroom to a bowl of soup and a tall glass of water.

And Ivy's ring sparkling in the chandelier's too-bright light.

"When did you see her?"

"I went to the resort while you were sleeping. She didn't want to keep it and asked me to give it back to you."

"I told her to pawn it."

Elora hugged a mug of tea to her chest and shot him a look that said she was disappointed in him. "Do you think she would have done that? Turned your relationship into something so small she could have gotten rid of it at a pawnshop? If you think she's heartless enough to do that, you've forgotten who she is."

After that, he'd eaten his soup in silence because he hadn't wanted to admit that he hadn't forgotten who Ivy had been, that maybe he'd never known.

Had he loved her? Loved the person she'd been, or had he loved what she'd done for him and the moment he hadn't needed her anymore, he'd taken off?

No. That couldn't be true.

He was sure that's what she thought he'd done, but it wasn't true.

He'd known what made her laugh . . . what made her hurt. What made her come.

He'd known her, dammit.

He'd left with the ring in his pants pocket, jingling with some change left over from a purchase he couldn't remember.

And now he sat at a rickety high-top, the horrible music blaring and his friends chattering around him like they didn't have a care in the world.

Jared looked like he was sitting on cloud nine, and James looked the same, about to get married in a handful of days. Mitch wasn't there. James said he declined days ago because of work, but Cole hustled through the door at the last minute, half present as a friend and half present as the paper's photographer, a sleek camera hanging around his neck. He didn't know how Autumn could blog about this. There wasn't a woman in the place.

He scowled at Jared. "Stop grinning."

Jared laughed. "I can't." He raised a tall beer. "Life's too good."

"Then you and Leah are okay?"

"We're great. She loves Rocky Point. I can't get her off

the ice. All she wants to do is stare across the lake. It makes her feel . . . I don't know. At peace, somehow, like she can finally breathe."

"She's doing all right having Rita in town?"

"Yeah, knock on wood." He rapped his knuckles against the table. "Rita keeps busy and doesn't bother us much. She's been taking Briar's car to Marengo to shop, sometimes Decatur. She and Briar spend a lot of time together, but I can happily say I don't think she'll ever come back. She remembered how much she hates it here and she won't forget it again. She'll leave Leah and me alone, and I'm grateful."

James nodded. "That's good. The last thing anybody needs is an ex getting in the way." He tilted his head toward Cole. "Speaking of exes, I hear someone's been giving Autumn a hard time."

"The women mentioned it," Jared said. "Mitch has been checking to see if he turns up at the resort. One day the asshole was hanging around outside the newspaper's offices, and Callie told Cole. He's been making sure Autumn's okay."

"Cole's got some of his own problems and can't always be around. We'll all keep an eye out. How's your plane?" James asked.

"Back at the airport. Pain in the ass getting her out of the field, but luckily there doesn't seem to be too much damage. FAA's looking into it, but it'll be a while before I can get her up in the air again. At least, not until summer. Leah's going to need some help moving her grandma to an assisted living community in Marengo, and unfortunately, there's only so much cash to go around."

"That sucks. I told Marnie that after this wedding we're going to need to watch it, but selling her townhouse will help. When we buy a house, we'll have to make sure our eyes aren't bigger than our wallets. I'm going up to grab another round," James said, sliding off the stool.

Jared chewed on a mozzarella stick and said around a mouthful of cheese, "I heard you and Ivy are engaged. Congratulations."

"Not anymore. I had a fight with Gunner this afternoon and broke it off."

"Why? Decide she wasn't a good fit after all? It was pretty quick, but so were Leah and me. If you know, you know. Trust you instincts."

He scoffed. "I punched my old man. More than once. What kind of man does that make me?"

"Everyone knows what you grew up with. You're only human."

"No, I'm a giant prick. Gunner's in my blood. My mother saw something in him when she married him, but if there was any good, it faded fast. I'm not doing that to Ivy. Hell, I already showed her the kind of heartless son of a bitch I can be when I'm only thinking about myself. I thought I could get around it somehow, that if she forgave me it would be in the past. Nothing stays in the past."

He looked across the room. Some of James's family were throwing darts. He recognized a few of Marnie's family members sitting at a large table playing poker. Marnie's dad held James up at the bar and respect shined in Hugh's eyes. He admired the man his daughter was going to marry.

Rosie wouldn't give him that.

He didn't deserve it.

Jared leaned closer as if to tell him a secret and he didn't want the other party guests to hear. "Listen, Leah doesn't come from a very nice family. Her mother abandoned her and her grandmother took care of her. Della's old-fashioned and raised Leah to be a wife. Not a grand-daughter, not a person, just a wife to pop out an asshole's babies, and minus the kids part, that's what happened. Her ex emotionally abused her for years. But Leah managed to hang on to her strength and find something better without sacrificing what she wants out of her future. Does that make sense?"

He frowned. "No."

Jared sighed. "Leah's past didn't interfere with our future. She didn't let it, and Christ, she could have. I was scared and treated her like crap, and she could have cut me loose, accused me of being like her ex. Instead, she gave me a chance to explain, and every day that passes, I love her more. Ivy knows what you came from and she still wants you. She never said anything about being afraid of you, or thinking it might not work out because you'll turn into your dad."

He sipped his beer to wet his mouth. "No, she never mentioned it." Just the opposite. She'd always been careful not to hit him, even as a joke.

"Then why are you making it an issue?"

"What'd I miss?" James asked, approaching the table and holding three beers in his hands, foam flowing over his fingers.

"Logan broke it off with Ivy because of Gunner."

"Yeah, I know."

He scowled. "Fuck. How do you know?"

"Ivy talked to Mitch who told Callie, who told Marnie, who told me. Welcome to the network." James pushed a glass of beer across the table. "I shouldn't've had to hear it that way, either, but I didn't say anything because I haven't had the chance yet."

"Leave it alone."

"Can't. You're one of my best friends. You broke off your engagement to the only woman you've ever loved—"

He frowned.

"Lie all you want, but I've seen you every day for the past eighteen years and you've never met a woman you could tolerate for long periods of time, much less love. So blow me if you think I'm going to believe your shit. You broke off your engagement to the love of your life because your dad's an abusive asshole, but did you ever think that one day Ivy would turn into her mother?"

"Of course not." The idea hadn't even crossed his mind.

"You never once thought that since Rosie turns to booze to numb her pain, that if something tragic were to ever happen, Ivy wouldn't do that same?"

"No. She's stronger than that."

"Then why is it so wrong to believe she feels the same about you?"

"Hey, hey, you pussies, are you partying or gossiping like a bunch of hens?" Roy yelled across the bar to a chorus of catcalls and hooting.

James laughed. "We're talking life, Dad."

"Philosph— philosophical—" he stammered, "philosophicalize on your own time. Come over here and get in on the game. Real money. Hundred bucks buy-in."

Sliding off his stool, James said, "Jesus Christ. My mom's going to have a hissy fit if I bring him home like this."

Jared chuckled. "Like what? Happy his only son found a nice woman to settle down with?"

"No. Drunk and broke. Come on, let's play."

He didn't want to play. He wanted to find a dark corner, lick his wounds, and turn what Jared and James said around in his mind.

Ivy had never been scared of him, had never flinched

when he reached for her. She'd always been careful not to invade his personal space, asking his permission to touch him, hug him, and later, kiss him, every time.

She never feared him. Even when the homework that came so easily to her frustrated him.

She'd hang over his shoulder and patiently explain over and over again, saying his growl was sexy.

But she was never scared of him.

Why had he thought he was protecting her from himself when the only times he'd hurt her were when he pushed her away?

He opened his mouth to decline, but James's and Jared's phones chimed. Across the room, Hugh slid his cell phone out of a case attached to his belt. Cole fumbled for his cell that was in the back pocket of his jeans.

He hadn't taken his cell out of his jacket pocket, and his jacket hung on a coat tree by the door.

James opened the text.

"What's going on?" he asked, his blood turning to sludge. It was bad news.

"It's Marnie. She texted all of us in case we didn't hear our phones. Ivy was in an accident. Mitch's at the hospital with her."

He jumped off the stool, his jaw working in agitation. "What kind of accident?"

"Smashed her car downtown. That's all Marnie said. Come on, I'll drive you."

"I can go alone. I don't want you to—"

"You're not driving like this. Dad, I'm taking Logan to the hospital to see Ivy."

"It's getting late, anyway. We'll all head out. I want to be in town, too, in case someone needs something."

James nodded. "Thanks," he said, though it was evident

Roy wasn't in any condition to help anybody. "Can you catch a ride with Jared? I'll take Logan straight to the hospital."

"Sure thing," Roy said at the same time Jared said, "No problem."

He stood frozen throughout the exchange, tears burning his eyes. She couldn't die. He couldn't live without her.

Not again.

"Logan?" James asked, bringing him back to the bar with a sickening jolt.

Jared handed him his jacket. "We'll be thinking about her. Keep us in the loop if you can."

"Thanks. I will."

He went through the motions of pushing his arms into the sleeves, zipping his jacket, and letting James guide him through the door and into the bitter cold of the Minnesota night.

He settled in the seat and leaned his head against the backrest. They had a half an hour drive to Rocky Point. Ivy could be dead by the time he reached her.

"Did Marnie's text say anything else?" he asked, too tired, too full of despair, to look at his own phone.

"No. Only that word spread through the usual chain of command. Mitch told Callie. She was sleeping in his room at the resort and she ran to tell Marnie in ours. She doesn't have all of our cell phone numbers like Marnie does."

"How did Mitch hear?"

James jerked a shoulder. "Don't know. Is he her emergency contact? Could be the hospital called him. Maybe he heard while he was doing a job or something."

"This is my fault, but I didn't think she would do anything stupid."

James tore his eyes away from the empty two-lane highway. "You think she did this on purpose?"

"I think she wasn't being as careful as she could have been."

"Bullshit. Maybe she couldn't sleep and went for a drive to clear her head and took a corner too fast. Maybe she swerved to avoid hitting a dog running across the road. You don't know."

He took his glasses off and rubbed his face. "I'm such a jackass."

"Yeah, you are, but I was with Marnie, too. It's like a prerequisite that men fuck up to make sure their women can handle their stupidity. Ivy will be okay, and she'll forgive you. A couple of mistakes won't erase how she feels about you."

"I hope you're right."

God, he hoped James was right, or he'd lost the only good thing that had ever happened to him and he would be the only one to blame.

CHAPTER NINE

Ivy's phone vibrated beneath her pillow, and she tried to force her eyes open.

What time was it?

Suddenly, she sat up, her heart racing. She was late for work! She scrabbled for her phone and hit Accept before the call went to voicemail.

"Hello?" she said, panting. Desiree would be ticked off. She liked the resort running smoothly.

"Is this Ivy Graves?"

Her head pounding, she looked around her bedroom. Reality slowly returned.

Light wasn't trying to peek around the blinds and the male voice on the phone sounded like he smoked a pack of cigarettes a day. Desiree wasn't the one calling her.

She rubbed her eyes and moved the phone away from her ear to check the time. It was past midnight.

"Miss Graves?"

"Yes. I'm sorry. I'm a bit disoriented."

"This is Officer Davis from the RPPD. We have a Roseanne Graves at the Good Samaritan Hospital. An ambulance brought her to the ER about ten minutes ago. She was driving while intoxicated and the car looks to be a complete loss."

"Wait. Do you have the right person? My mom's here, sleeping."

"Are you sure about that, ma'am? The car's registered to an Ivy Jean Graves. The woman driving the car had in her possession a Minnesota state driver's license that expired ten years ago."

That sounded like her mother, but through her fog, she had a difficult time processing the officer's words.

"Let me go look. When I went to bed, my mom was here."

"I'll hold," the officer said.

She crawled out of bed and stumbled over her damp towel and work clothes. She kicked them out of the way and peered into the hallway.

The TV gave off its usual dull glow.

She didn't see Rosie, but that didn't mean she wasn't there. She checked the couch in case Rosie had fallen asleep, but it was empty. Though her mother rarely slept in her room, she poked her head into the small bedroom. The bed hadn't been slept in.

"Officer?" She didn't remember his last name.

"Yes, ma'am? Did you find your mother?"

She swallowed down the panic. "No. Can I ask what car my mother was driving when she crashed?"

"A 2002 Toyota Camry. Didn't hold up against the corner of a building downtown on Main."

"Oh, God. I'll be there as soon as I can."

"Thank you. Please check at the registration desk in the emergency room. They may have forms you need to fill out, and they'll give you more information from there."

"Thank you." She disconnected and raced to her room to put on some clothes.

She threw on a pair of sweatpants and a t-shirt, forgetting a bra in her hurry, and grabbed the Outback's key.

Wait. She didn't want to face what her mother had done alone. She called Mitch, sorry to wake him, but she had no one else.

"Hello?" he answered, his voice groggy with sleep . . . or sex.

She winced. "Mitch."

"Is everything okay?" Callie murmured in the background, and her grimaced deepened.

"Yeah. Go back to sleep, sweetheart."

Despite the dread making her chest ache, her heart warmed. He sounded so much in love.

"Ivy?" he asked, his voice clearer. "Are you okay? What's going on?"

"My mom got into a car accident, and I need to go to the hospital. I'm a little shaky—"

"I'll be there as soon as I can."

"Thanks. I'll wait downstairs."

"Stay inside."

She opened her mouth to agree, but her phone beeped. He disconnected.

He'd need fifteen to twenty minutes to dress and drive across town, and she used the time to go to the bathroom, brush her teeth, and apply some deodorant.

At the last minute, she tugged a comb through her hair that was still damp. That would have to be enough. Instead of standing in the stinky vestibule, she waited outside on the snow-covered sidewalk and sucked in deep breaths of the frozen air to clear her head.

Just as she started to shiver, Mitch stopped near the

curb. The neon pink rectangles covering up the nasty swear words still pissed her off.

He didn't care about anything except his parents, Callie, and getting the hell out of Rocky Point, and she shared the sentiment. Her time to leave would come, and maybe sooner than she thought.

"Thanks for the ride," she said, climbing into the truck.

"It's okay. Do you know what happened?"

"Rosie went for a joyride in the old Camry. We argued before I went to bed, and I told her I wasn't going to take care of her anymore." Tears dripped down her cheeks. "I made Logan sound more important than anything else."

He patted her knee. "She knew you didn't mean it."

She tried to smile. "The sad part is, I did."

"Maybe when you said it, but not inside. You were okay after he left to go to school and you'll be okay when he leaves after the wedding. You know that, right? He's never been your whole life. He only felt like it."

"I don't know. I'm so tired, Mitch."

"I know you are. Rosie did you a favor. Hate to say it, but she'll have to clean up now. Driving while intoxicated will land her a huge fine and maybe some jail time."

"She doesn't have a valid driver's license, either."

"Yeah."

They were silent until they reached the hospital and he let her out in front of the ER's automatic doors. "I'll park and come in. I don't want you to be alone now. Do you want me to call Logan?"

She scoffed. "What for? He's out partying and wouldn't care anyway."

He looked like he was about to object, but she slammed the door shut and waited for the ER's doors to slide open. Sluggish because of the freezing temperatures, they moved slowly, and she squeezed through the narrow crack, too impatient to wait.

They may have had their differences, but Rosie was still her mother and she loved her, no matter what words passed between them.

She followed the sign to the reception desk, and a tired woman who was wearing a blouse and cardigan looked in her direction and smiled. "How can I help you?"

"I'm here to see my mother, Roseanne Graves?"

"Just a moment, please." She paused, searching her computer screen. "She's in surgery. You can wait in the family lounge on the second floor outside recovery. Your mother will be brought there after surgery. Let them know you're here. The doctor will want to speak to you."

"Thank you." She sighed. "Do you know how badly my mom was injured?"

She tapped on the keyboard. "Her chart says she has some internal bleeding. The surgeon will tell you more, okay?"

"Thanks."

The phone rang and the woman didn't respond.

She rode the elevator to the second floor and checked in at the desk outside the recovery area. A kind nurse told her it could be a few hours and she'd let her know as soon as she had any information. She texted Mitch and told him to go back to the resort. There was nothing he could do and she didn't feel like talking, even if he could sit with her.

Three large chairs, two loveseats, several plants, and a coffee kiosk were crammed into the small waiting area, and she had to give the hospital credit for trying to make families comfortable while they waited for news . . . good or bad.

She tugged off her jacket and made a cup of hot chocolate using the hot water dispenser and two packets of cocoa mix. She sank heavily into a blue chair and dragged a parenting magazine that had a smiling, bright-eyed baby on the cover into her lap she never once flipped through.

Logan flung himself out of James's truck before it came to a full stop beneath the concrete canopy sheltering the main entrance.

"Jesus Christ, Logan."

James's angry growl barely registered as he slammed the truck's door shut and raced into the hospital. Or tried to.

The doors stopped gliding half way, and impatiently, he shoved them open.

He ran down the hallway to the emergency room and rounded on Mitch the moment he spotted him.

Ivy's friend sat in a black plastic chair, his elbows braced on his knees, his fingers worrying a stocking cap.

"Why the fuck aren't you with her?" he cried, his voice as squeaky and high-pitched as when he'd gone through puberty.

"I can't. It's family only. Besides, she's in surgery. All we can do is wait."

He ran a hand through his hair, his heart pounding a mile a minute, the hospital's warm air fogging up his goddamned glasses. "She's by herself. Why aren't you with her?"

Mitch reared to his feet, his cheeks red. "Why aren't *you* with her? Too busy partying to give a shit about the woman you say you love. Don't give me bullshit about not being with her. *I'm here.* Where in the hell were you?"

He went at him, slamming Mitch into the wall, aware

that he was treating him the exact way he was scared he'd treat anyone.

With anger.

With violence.

Down the hallway, a janitor stopped mopping and stared. "Do I need to call security?"

He ignored him and fixed his eyes on Mitch. "I didn't mean to hurt her. I was—"

"Looking out for yourself. We get it, Logan. It's always been about you and what you lived with. It's always been about you and what you want."

"I didn't want to be around her if I'm like my dad." At that, he loosened Mitch's shirt bunched in his fists.

Mitch shook off his grip and straightened his flannel shirt. "Maybe you are if you can't see how you're hurting her. All she ever did was love you, and all you did was treat her like shit."

"I know. I know, and now it might be too late." He staggered to the elevator and jabbed the Up button.

"You can't see her. It's family only."

He looked over his shoulder as the elevator doors glided open. "I am her family, and I'll spend the rest of my life making this up to her."

"She's going to need more than that. She's heard it from you before."

Tears welled in his eyes, and he yanked his glasses off and swiped at his face. "I need her. I can't lose her now."

"She's broken," Mitch said, walking across the hallway. "If you hurt her again, she won't live through it. She loves you too much to survive it."

"If Ivy makes it out of surgery, I'll do whatever it takes." He pushed the button for the second floor, and the elevator doors began to close.

Mitch's lips popped open. "What the hell do you—"

The doors closed, blocking out Mitch's wide eyes and gaping mouth.

He leaned against the wall and tried to breathe.

She'd be okay. She'd be okay.

She had to be.

The elevator doors opened and he quickly approached the nurses' station. "I need to see Ivy Graves. I need to be in there with her."

"Visiting hours are over. Are you a family member?" the nurse asked, frowning.

"I'm her fiancé."

"She didn't say anything about expecting someone." Her gaze flicked to a set of doors. A gold plaque in black lettering declared, *Family members only beyond this point.*

He headed toward the forbidden doors. "I love her, and I need to see her."

"Sir, this area's for family—"

He didn't listen. He shoved desperately through the doors and swept the waiting area, unsure of what he was looking for or what he would do now. He didn't expect to see Ivy. In some part of his brain he knew if she was in surgery he wouldn't have access to her.

The only thing he'd been trying to do since leaving James's bachelor party was find her and stay as close to her as possible.

His eyes slid over her and back again before it clicked in, truly sunk in, that she sat in the family lounge, her feet propped on the coffee table, her head back, her eyes closed.

"Ivy," he rasped.

Her eyes flew open, then narrowed, guarded.

He didn't care. He didn't care about anything except that she was okay.

He knelt at her feet, servant, worshipper, and buried his face in her belly, breathing in the scent of fabric softener.

Letting the tears come, he cried into her shirt, his shoulders shaking, his stomach knotted in relief and fear.

It would be a different kind of hell if she told him to go.

But she wrapped her arms around him and laced her fingers through his hair.

The ease of her acceptance broke him, and he howled, sobbing in pain and regret.

She pressed her lips to his head and let him cry.

She smoothed his hair, the soft strands slipping through her fingers. The frames of his glasses dug into her stomach, but she didn't wiggle away.

The last person she expected to see was Logan, and she had no idea why he was crying. Maybe he had too much to drink.

She wanted to nudge him away and ask why he was at the hospital, but someone cleared her throat.

An older woman wearing scrubs, her hair tied back, stood in the doorway of the waiting room. Over Logan's sniffling, she asked, "Are you Roseanne Graves's daughter?"

Trapped under Logan's weight, she couldn't stand like she wanted to and could only say, "Yes. How is she?"

The doctor walked into the little room and sat next to her. "She made it through surgery just fine. She had a ruptured spleen and some internal bleeding that we were able to stop. She'll be wheeled into recovery in a few minutes. She's sedated, and I suggest after you look in on her, you go home and get some rest." She tilted her head at Logan. "Is he going to be okay? Can I call someone?"

"No, ah, he heard some bad news. Thank you, for my mom, I mean. I appreciate it."

"You're welcome."

She left in a rustle of green scrubs, and Logan sat up, rubbing his hand under his nose. "That was embarrassing."

She turned away. It hurt to look at him. "Why are you here?"

Using the hem of his sweater, he cleaned his glasses. "I was at James's bachelor party when Marnie texted him. She said you were in a car accident. I was so scared. I thought you were dying."

"Right. Thanks for your concern, but I'm fine and you should go. I'm going to check on Mom then go home and get some sleep. It's been a long night."

"I was hoping we could talk."

"I don't think there's anything left to talk about. You made your feelings clear enough the last time. I have a lot to do and I'm tired."

He trapped her face between his hands and made her look at him. "Please let me say what I have to say, and if you can't forgive me, I'll leave you alone. I swear."

Tears wet his cheeks and his eyes were bloodshot. Scruff covered his jaw, but not enough to disguise the purple bruise that looked worse now than when he'd broken their engagement.

Had that only been yesterday?

She felt like she'd lived a hundred lifetimes of heartache in the past twelve hours.

"Okay. We'll talk, but my life hasn't changed since this afternoon. I'm still the same person who has the same baggage." She lightly skimmed her fingers over his jaw. "Does it hurt?"

"Not there." He pushed her hand over his heart. "Here. When Marnie said you were in the hospital, my whole world caved in."

"Miss Graves?" A nurse stood in the doorway holding a tablet. White and pink unicorns decorated her light blue scrubs. "Your mother's settled in a room if you'd like to see her."

"Yes, please. Thank you."

Logan stood.

The nurse cast a glance at him. "Recovery's family only."

She thought about telling the nurse they were engaged, or that they were married, but they were neither of those things and she didn't have the energy to pretend. "I'll see you in the lobby, okay?"

A hurt look flickered through his eyes, but she didn't let it tug at her heart.

The pain was too fresh.

"If that's what you want."

"Yeah."

He couldn't expect that she would fall into his arms like nothing happened.

She followed the nurse down a short hallway and through a set of heavy doors that opened into an area divided into four small rooms. Her mother, attached to several tubes and a heart monitor, laid on a bed opposite the nurses' long counter.

"She made it through surgery without any complications. According to her chart, her injuries were minor. She was lucky," the nurse said, her voice hard. She must know

Rosie had been driving drunk and that she was lucky in more ways than one. She could have killed someone.

She sat by her mother's bed and held her hand, an IV taped to her wrist. A bruise marred her cheek, and purple shadows rested under her eyes, her skin pale.

"Whatever we have to do," she told Rosie, "we'll do it together."

There was so much to consider. The car would be a loss no matter if Rosie totaled it or not. Her insurance was liability only and she couldn't afford repairs. And how much trouble her mother was in she couldn't begin to guess.

Her eyelids drooping, she sat until she started to fall asleep in the chair. She'd call a taxi and go home and get some real rest, but before she could succumb to the past twelve hours of exhaustion, she'd have to call Desiree and leave her a message, letting her know what happened. Stacy in HR would offer her FMLA, but she couldn't take time off without pay.

If her mother ended up going to jail, well, that was a different matter. She prayed Desiree wouldn't fire her over this. The resort's manager had little patience for these kinds of circumstances.

She kissed her mother's cheek and thanked the nurse as she walked into the hallway.

Logan leaned against the wall near the doors on the other side of the waiting room, the nurse sitting behind the desk glowering at him.

"Can we talk now?" he asked, following her down the hallway.

She sighed. "Can't it wait? I'm so tired, and all I want is to go home."

"I'll say what I need to say, and that will be the end of it."

"Fine. " It wasn't fine, but she didn't see any other option. He was determined to get something off his chest and it made her crabby he was wasting her time to do it.

All she wanted was a bed.

And a lawyer.

Oh.

Not this one.

For her mom.

"Where can we go?" she asked, standing in the middle of the second-floor hallway of the small, quiet hospital.

"Let's talk in the atrium."

She didn't know Good Samaritan had an atrium, but Logan, in his self-assured way, led her down an empty hallway that spat them out into an open area made of glass.

She sank into a chair similar to the one in the waiting room, and he paced in front of her, his boots squeaking against the tiles with every step.

"I went to see Gunner today." He frowned. "Yesterday, I guess."

"Your mother said." She wanted to be cold, she wanted to be angry, but the vulnerability and sadness in his eyes made it impossible. "Was it bad?"

He heaved a sigh. "Yeah. He antagonized me, and I let him. I wanted to prove to him that I turned out to be a decent person despite what he did to me. That I was a better person than he was. But all I did was show him that I'm just like him."

"What happened?"

"He knew I still had feelings for you. I don't know how, but he knew, and he used them against me. He accused you of some nasty things, and it pissed me off."

"He said I slept around."

"Yeah. I didn't believe him, Ivy, honestly, I didn't, but

the thought of another guy touching you . . . I was furious. He knew it and taunted me with it. Said you spread your legs for any man who looked at you and I snapped. I hit him. More than once."

She sat on the edge of her chair. She wanted to go to him, but she had to let him finish.

"I got a couple good licks in, but so did he. He never lost any of the mean, and he'll always be bigger than me. We crashed onto a coffee table and the cheap thing broke. That was when I knew I'd gone too far. Gunner though, the son of a bitch, he just laughed."

He tipped his head back, his Adam's apple bobbing as he tried to hold back his tears.

"What else, Logan?" she asked.

Tension stiffened his body, and his hands shook.

"You know me so well," he said, his voice cracking. "How did I ever think I could live without you?"

She shook her head. "What else did he say?"

"He said that he was proud of me. He was proud of me for kicking the shit out of him."

"Maybe he was."

He scoffed. "Proud I'd turned into a son of a bitch like him?"

"Proud that you could defend yourself. Proud that you did."

He unbuttoned his jacket, pulled it off, and dropped it onto a chair near her. "I don't think that's what he meant. He was proud I have bad blood running through me like him."

"That might be true, but why think that when you don't know? Logan, you stood up for yourself, you stood up for me. When you were a kid you couldn't do that. You're an adult now, and you filled out."

He tilted his head in question and she tamped down a smile. "What? You think I didn't notice when I had you in bed? You can defend yourself now when the younger you couldn't. Isn't that the real reason you went to see Gunner? You said he provoked you, but be honest. It didn't take much, did it?"

"It didn't, and that's what scares me, Ivy. I have his blood in me. I have that hate."

She slipped off the chair. It was time to go to him now. "No, you don't. You are the kindest man I know. You'd do anything for anybody if they asked. You did well in school and started a business helping people who need you in their time of grief." She wrapped her arms around him and rested her cheek against the soft material of his sweater. "That you'll defend someone, stand up for someone who needs help, how can you twist that into something bad?"

He brushed his hand over her hair. "You've never been scared of me."

She smiled sadly. "Not in the way you mean."

"You've been scared of me? Why didn't you say anything?"

She stepped away and studied a flower blooming in a large taupe planter. "Because I've always been afraid you'd break my heart, and you did. There're different kinds of pain, Logan. I was scared you'd hurt me, and it was inevitable. You went to school. You broke off our engagement. I'm not good enough for you, and that hurts me, too." She traced her fingers over the orange petals. So fragile. "Fear comes in different forms. I've never been afraid you'd hit me, but I'll always be afraid I'm not good enough and that you'll find someone better. I'm nobody but a woman who has an alcoholic for a mother, who uses food stamps to buy groceries and a rent credit to pay for a place to live. You think I don't look at you and know that? Your dad liked to beat you up, but you still did something with your life, and I'm proud of you. It cost me a huge chunk of my heart, but I'm so proud of you." Her voice wavered, and she sucked in a breath. "Let's leave it at that, okay? I can't keep doing this. I'm so tired, and now Rosie's in a load of shit that I'll have to clean up. I need to go." She looked one last time at the man who would never be hers. "Be happy, Logan. Marry someone who isn't so fucked up, huh? You deserve it."

Her legs were so heavy she didn't think she could move, but she picked up her dirty old jacket and scuffed purse and trudged to the entrance of the atrium.

His voice stopped her.

"I can't."

He couldn't let her walk out that door. He had to convince her that they belonged together despite the lies he told her.

She turned, her motions dragging.

"I can't marry anyone else. No one would make me as happy as you do. When Marnie's text came through and James told me you were in a car crash, I couldn't think about anything except getting to you. My entire world collapsed in that one moment. I pictured you bloody and broken, bleeding out on the operating table, believing the lies I told you because I was too weak to tell you the truth."

She stared.

"All this time you've been saying I'm too good for you, but it's the other way around. You've always been too good for me. How smart you are. Why aren't you the attorney who has her own firm? How kind you are. Why aren't you a mother taking care of your kids instead of working your fingers to the bone supporting Rosie? Because you're compassionate, and you didn't abandon her when she needed you. I left and never talked to you again. When I came back to Rocky Point, you should've spit in my face and told me to fuck off. What kind of man am I to do that to the woman he claimed to love? I don't deserve you, Ivy. I know that. Especially after yesterday and what I said. Rosie isn't the problem. *I* am. When I look in the mirror, I see Gunner and all his hate, and I wonder how I'm supposed to believe you love me. But I learned something at James's bachelor party tonight. I learned we aren't our parents. I'm not Gunner, and I won't be like him. I'm not like him now. And you aren't Rosie. Since I've been in Rocky Point and saw what Rosie has turned into since Joey's death, I never once thought that if we were to ever go through a tragedy that you would try to hide in a bottle of Jack. That's not who you are. The way you handled me leaving you and the way you've stepped up and taken care of Rosie all this time proved that. We aren't who we came from. We're our own people, and I didn't see that until tonight with Jared's and James's help." He wiped his palms on his jeans. "I need you to tell me I didn't realize it too late. I know you don't trust me, but I promise I'll make it up to you. Rings don't matter, promises don't matter. Me staying here will be the only way to show you. After the wedding, I won't go back to Decatur. I know we talked about living apart until things were settled, but I ruined that option. I can't be there, and you be here, ever again. I did that, and I'll fix it." The words rushed out of him and he hoped against hope that they were enough to keep her in his life. "I'll stay with James's parents until you can move to Decatur or . . . our marriage license came through. We can get married today—"

She opened her mouth, but he stopped her from speaking.

"I'll stay with you. I don't know what's going to happen to Rosie, but I'll be by your side through every second. It's the only way you'll believe me, but I don't care because I can't be away from you again. I can't." Tears stopped him, and he swallowed back a sob. "I thought you were dying, and I can't. You're my whole life, and I don't want to live without you anymore."

He didn't have anything left to say. He felt like he'd just given a speech that could cure world hunger or stop the next world war, so important was her answer.

He'd given her nothing, and he was asking her to give him all she had. It wasn't fair and he knew it, but if she agreed, he'd try to give her everything she could ever want.

And if that only happened to be him, so much the better. He had plenty of love to give her.

"Please, Ivy?"

"Our marriage license came?"

A seed of hope bloomed. As bright as the lush flowers around them.

"Yes. We can get married anytime. Today, if you want."

"And you won't leave?"

Tentatively, he step forward. "No. We'll never be apart again. Unless one of us has to go to the bathroom. We'll have to negotiate an Open Door policy before we say our marriage vows."

He said the last to make her smile, and it worked, a small one turning up her lips.

"Tell me."

He didn't have to ask what she wanted to hear. She knew him, but he knew her, too.

"I love you, Ivy Graves, and I'll never leave you again."

She dropped her jacket and purse and ran to him.

He picked her up and she wrapped her legs around his waist. He buried his face in her hair, and she clung to his shoulders laughing and crying at the same time.

Gunner tried to take the one thing that meant anything to him, but the bastard failed.

Maybe his father *was* proud of him, but he didn't need Gunner's approval to be a good man. He needed Ivy's love, respect, and trust.

Without those, he was what he feared he'd become—a broken son of a bitch who had no future.

But his future whispered "I love you" into his ear, and he knew things would be all right.

CHAPTER TEN

I vy held Logan's hand as they walked to the hospital's lobby.

James sat in one of the chairs scrolling on his phone, and when he saw them, he shoved it into his jacket pocket and stood. "Thank God you're okay. How's your mom? Why was she out driving so late?"

She squeezed Logan's fingers, and he squeezed back. It was the best feeling in the world. "We argued earlier, and I don't know if she was upset or if she was trying to pay me back for the things I said. She's out of surgery, but I wasn't able to talk to her."

James hugged her, and she stiffened in surprise. "I'm sorry."

She briefly returned his hug and leaned away, uncomfortable. It'd been a long time since someone had cared enough to bother. "Thank you, and thanks for driving Logan to school all those years ago. For being his friend."

"You don't need to thank me for that. That's what friends are for. You should know."

She smiled. "Yeah." For thirteen years Logan had been her best friend. Now he was more.

"Come on, the truck's running. I sent Mitch home. He said Marnie got Callie's message mixed up. I think when I get back to the resort I need to give her a spanking." James leered and laughed.

She blushed, and chuckling, Logan bent and whispered in her ear, "I think we need to have a little alone time too, don't you think?"

They followed James out of the hospital and into cold.

"That sounds good, but I need a few things from the apartment."

"Let's sleep there."

"Are you sure?"

"You don't have to hide anything from me, okay? I understand. Besides, after the wedding, if it's okay with you, I'd like to stay there. Please." He glanced at James. "I'm going to have to talk to you about that."

"I figured something like that would go down. Don't worry about it now. We have plenty of time to hash it out," James said, and he turned to Ivy. "You'll have to give me directions."

Embarrassed, heat stained her cheeks.

James scoffed. "What? You think I didn't hear you two making a sex date? I'm happy you got it worked out. Logan looked like a kicked puppy through my whole party." He winced. "Sorry, I didn't mean that literally."

Logan held the trucks' door open, and she climbed into the cab, sliding across the bench to sit in the middle.

"You don't have to apologize, it's true. But I gave as good as I got. At least I can say that," Logan said, sitting next to her and shutting the door.

James settled behind the wheel. "We should have a redo, anyway. What do you think?"

"I think I need to get some sleep before we plan any more parties."

"Sleep, ah-huh. Right."

She rested her head on Logan's shoulder, and he hugged her to him the entire way to her apartment complex.

"You need a ride later?" James asked her, rolling to a stop in front of her building.

Logan opened the door and stepped into a snowbank.

"No, thanks. I appreciate the offer, though."

James looked between her and Logan. "No problem. You be good to him, huh?"

"Yeah. We've hurt each other enough."

"Agreed. Goodnight."

"Goodnight."

With an arm around her waist, Logan helped her out of the truck and shut the door. He lifted a hand to James in goodbye, and James nodded, shifted into Drive, and slowly drove away, his taillights bright red in the dark.

She led Logan up the short sidewalk that was still covered in snow. "I try to keep it clean . . ."

"I've already been inside, remember? Come here." He tugged her to him and kissed her, his lips warm against hers. "You never have to hide who you are from me, do you understand? We're too close for that."

"I know, but I'm going to need time to get used to this." She unlocked the security door, and out of habit, she kicked the snow off her boots on the stairs.

"That's my fault. I'll give you all the time you need. Just promise me, if you're unhappy, you'll tell me. Give me a chance to fix it before you walk away."

She stood on the first step wanting to look into his eyes. His glasses were foggy and fatigue and worry pinched his mouth. "I'd never do that," she said, skimming her fingers over his bruised jaw. "I know how it feels. I'm not saying it to rub it in or jab at you. I know we need to leave the past behind us, and I'm ready to do that. More than ready. I'm saying it because it's true. I know how it feels, and I would never do that to you. I'll always tell you if I'm unhappy, and you need to tell me, too. I'm in this for as long as you want me."

"Then I guess we're in it forever. I meant what I said at the hospital, Ivy. I can't live without you."

"Yes, you can. We both did, but now we don't have to."

"And I'm going to thank God for it every day. Let's go upstairs."

"Okay."

They reached her apartment's door and he backed her into it, trapping her. He kissed her again, and she melted in his arms. "Mmmmm," she sighed. "I missed you."

"I missed you, too. Hurry up."

"I'm trying," she teased. "But someone can't keep their hands off me." She looked at him. "Don't ever stop."

He brushed her hair out of her face, his gaze softening. "You don't have to worry about that."

She unlocked the door and he followed her inside. She moved to turn the lights on, but he said, "Don't. Let's stay in the dark."

"All right."

He gave her enough time to only kick her boots off.

"Are you hungry, or thirsty?" she asked as he tugged on her hand. "Coffee?"

"Yes, but not for food. We'll make coffee later. Take your jacket off."

"No, you do it." She couldn't get enough of him. Love

shined pure and true in his eyes, and the fierce emotion made her heart stop.

He slowly unzipped her jacket, the sound hissing through the room. Heat filled her, and his desire consumed her. No one had ever looked at her the way Logan stared at her now.

He pushed the jacket off her shoulders and she parted her lips to apologize for her worn-out clothing. "Shh. Don't say anything," he whispered. "Don't say anything." He covered her mouth with his, and she hungrily opened for him. It'd been too long since he kissed her like this. He lifted his head. "You always did know how to kiss."

She unbuttoned his jacket and he took it off and tossed it onto the floor near hers. "You were the only boy I ever kissed until you went to school. Do you remember our first one?"

"I was so scared you wouldn't talk to me anymore if you didn't feel the same. I tried to keep you as just a friend."

Shoving her hands under his sweater, she said, "We've always been friends."

"Friends don't make each other hard." He tugged his sweater over his head revealing a plain black t-shirt.

"I didn't get hard for you."

He slipped his hands into her sweatpants, the elastic easily giving away her secrets. "I hope I make you wet. I hope I make you dripping wet." He nudged her thighs apart. "Like now. God, Ivy."

She sucked in a breath, his touch lighting her on fire. "I can't help it. It's what you do to me. It's what you've always done to me." She unbuttoned his jeans. "We were at the lake."

"You were wading in the water. We should have been

doing homework, but I think you were getting tired of trying to explain geometry to me."

He took his t-shirt off and kicked his jeans across the floor. "You're wearing more clothes than I am now."

His cock strained his briefs and she skimmed a finger up and down his length.

"What are you gonna do about it?"

"Sassy. When did that start?" He yanked her t-shirt over her head and threw it on the floor. Gently, he trailed his fingers down her neck, over her collarbone, and to her breast. His thumb grazed her nipple.

She shivered. "Logan."

"I know. I feel it too."

He pushed her sweatpants down her legs and she kicked them and her panties off while he did away with his briefs. In seconds, they were a tangled heap of limbs on top of her messy bed, their tongues swirling together.

His cock nudged between the legs, and she widened her thighs, urging him on top of her, desperately needing him. "Please, Logan, now. I need you now," she murmured.

"Wait. I don't have any condoms." He leaned away.

"I don't have anything here," she said, brushing her hand up and down his arm. "We should have gone back to your cabin after all."

He kissed her, lazy strokes with his tongue. "This is fine. Besides, my mom's at the cabin, remember? We wouldn't be doing this," he said, nibbling her jaw, "and I really want to be doing this. Ivy, we need to talk about babies."

"I know how they're made," she said, tilting her head and giving him access to the sensitive skin between her ear and her shoulder. She loved it when he kissed her there.

"I know you do, and I need to know if you want children, sweetheart."

"Because if I do you'll call off our engagement again?" She sat up and yanked at her comforter. It didn't budge under his weight and she used a pillow to cover herself instead.

"No. I made a promise at the hospital, and I won't break it." He rested his head on her other pillow and laid his hand on her thigh. "I love you, and nothing could happen that would make me leave you ever again. But if you really want kids, we have to work it out because it's going to take a lot for me to accept it and give them to you."

"But you would?"

"I told you I'd give you whatever you wanted if you forgave me," he said, his voice low and sad.

"That's no way to start a family."

"I know, but I'd be lost without their mother."

It sounded romantic, but she knew the truth. After a few years of taking care of someone he didn't want to take care of, it would turn his heart and one day she'd wake up and he'd be gone.

"I don't want our children to be a burden, and that's what someone is if you don't want them. If you really don't want kids, then I can give that to you. I've spent twelve years taking care of Rosie and I know how being trapped feels. You'd turn bitter and possibly into the person you're afraid of becoming. It wouldn't matter how much you love me."

He blew out a breath, and she could hear the relief in it. "Are you sure? It's not a decision you can make in a few seconds."

"I'm sure. I've thought about it longer than you think. I'm tired and Rosie's still going to take up a lot of my time, and you said I could go to school . . ."

He kissed her palm. "You can definitely go to school."

She wiggled onto her side and nuzzled his jaw, the stubble stinging her lips. "And maybe . . . instead of a baby, we can get a dog?"

Laughing, he kissed his way from her neck down to her breasts that were still covered under her pillow. Pushing it aside to lick her nipple, he said, "We can get a dog. Two of them if you want."

"That sounds perfect."

His fingers found her clit and as he nibbled her breast, he swirled the sensitive nub. "We can still play without protection," he said, kissing lower. "Spread your legs, sweetheart."

"Will you kiss me?"

"You don't have to ask." He slid to the end of the bed.

"No, I mean, I want you to kiss me while I come."

"That's the sweetest thing I think I've ever heard you say," he said, lying next to her and propping onto his elbow.

He kissed her long and deep, and in his arms, she fell to pieces.

Ivy cracked her eyes open.

She had to go to the bathroom and her aching bladder made it an urgent matter. She didn't know how long they'd been sleeping—long enough the sun blazed around the edges of the cheap blinds—and as she pushed the comforter away, her ring finger on her left hand glittered.

Sometime while she was sleeping, Logan put her engagement ring back on her hand.

They showered together, to conserve water, he said playfully, and afterward, she drove him to the resort. He wanted to check on Rosie with her, but she told him to let Elora know what was going on and to try to get some more sleep. She idled in the staff parking lot while he tried to argue his case.

"But I told you—"

She pushed a finger to his lips. "I know what you told me, but it isn't practical to go everywhere together. We've had a bumpy start and we both still feel it, but you sticking like glue to my side isn't going to help. Always feeling guilty isn't going to help."

"I can't help it. I *am* going to feel guilty. Maybe for a long time. I could have really fucked us up and I'm damned lucky you listened to me last night. Christ." He shuddered. "Are you sure you don't want me to go to the hospital, at least?"

"I'm sure. I said some nasty things to her, and she said some nasty things back. We need to clear the air, in private, and see where things go. She told me Joey was her favorite because I'd always belonged to you. Maybe that's true . . . maybe I cared more about you than I cared about my own family, but I've taken care of her when I could have said 'Screw it' and walked out. I don't know if that means anything to her. She may want to be on her own." She sagged in her seat. She hadn't gotten enough sleep, and though working things out with Logan made her happy, her mother would always be a rough patch on her heart.

"That would be good for her, sweetheart. If she lived on

her own and learned to take care of herself again, that doesn't mean she still wouldn't be part of your life."

"I know. But . . ."

"But you'd be happier being with me if you were on good terms with her."

"Does that make me a bad person?" She reached for his hand.

He squeezed her fingers. "No. It makes you human. I love that my mom's here. I haven't seen her in a long time and I'll miss her when she goes back to Denver. Ivy, if there's a way to keep Rosie in your life, do it, okay? You're my family now, and that makes her my family, too. I'll give you whatever you need."

She unlatched her seatbelt, leaned over the storage console, and kissed him. "I love you."

"I know, and God knows, I struggle to feel like I deserve it. I love you, too." He paused. "Your mom's wrong. You didn't love me more than you loved your family. The booze and pain over the years have confused her. You can't love someone more than somebody else. Love doesn't work like that. It doesn't run out."

She blinked. "That's beautiful."

He kissed her, his warm hand to the back of her head. "And true. Marry me tonight?"

His eyes blazed bright, his hair tousled. He hadn't shaved and scruff covered his jaw. He wasn't the boy who left Rocky Point eighteen years ago. A man had returned in his place, but the vulnerability was still there, and a shadow, however brief, flickered across his face.

"I'd love to."

He smiled and brushed his fingers over her cheek. "Good. I'll see you later, Mrs. Draper."

"Yeah," she said softly.

"Bye." Reluctantly, he opened the door and stepped out of the car.

"Bye." Leaning her head against the steering wheel, she watched him walk down the path toward his cabin.

He turned and lifted his hand, and she shifted into Drive and slowly drove away.

His words rolled around her head as she drove to the hospital. Love didn't run out. There was plenty to go around.

She parked in the visitor parking lot and asked at the reception desk if her mother was still in recovery. Rosie's doctor released her into her own room, and the receptionist told her the room number.

Her heart thrummed with nerves. It'd be hard on her if Rosie decided to go her own way. It may be for the best like Logan suggested, but her father hadn't contacted them in several years, Joey was gone, and if her mother left too, well, she loved Logan, but he wasn't a replacement for her mom, no matter what Rosie believed.

Hesitantly, she stepped into Rosie's small room, and her mother turned her head away from the window.

"Ivy."

"Hi, Mom." She stood awkwardly, shifting on her feet, the scents of bleach, regret, and guilt swirling around the white, sterile room. The silence made her uncomfortable, and she asked, "If you don't feel like talking . . ."

"No. Please, stay."

"Okay." She put her jacket and purse on one chair and sat in the other, inching it closer so she could hold her mother's hand.

"I'm sorry for what happened," Rosie said, rubbing her thumb over her knuckles, "and for what I did to the car. That made a big mess, didn't it?"

"I'm not worried about the car, I'm worried about you. What did you think you were doing?"

"I hated that we fought, and I hated what I said to you. I hated you were right. I tried to run away, I guess. Tried to block it out. I think I managed that part."

Rosie's dull blonde hair scratched against the crisp pillowcase and lines of strain and exhaustion hugged her eyes, but for the first time in many years, they were clear.

"You're in deep shit, you managed that part, too. Driving while intoxicated, without a valid driver's license. The car's totaled and insurance won't cover it because you're not listed as a driver and I don't have full coverage. No one's told me if there's any damage to the building you crashed into downtown. I haven't spoken to an attorney, but you're looking at going to rehab, if not jail. You're damned lucky you didn't kill someone, or yourself." Tears pooled in her eyes.

Rosie swallowed. "I know, and it doesn't make it better, but I think . . . I think I needed some help, kiddo, and you weren't around to ask for it."

"Why do you think that is?" Fury sparked in her blood. "Do you know how hard I work to keep a roof over our heads and food in the fridge? You spent your checks on booze and I couldn't stop you. I pay for rent, electricity, my car, and every other stupid little thing that comes up, and you blame me for not being around when you needed to talk. That's bullshit." Her voice cracked.

"Ivy, please don't. That's not how I meant it. You think I'm a pathetic drunk, and maybe I am, but under the booze, I knew what you were doing for me. For us. I didn't mean you were too busy to talk to me. I meant that I didn't know how to ask. You were already doing so much and I couldn't ask you to do more."

"That would have been easier than doing this, you know that, right?"

"Yeah, I know, but I have no choice now and maybe that's a good thing."

She rubbed her eyes. "Maybe it is. I'm sorry we argued. I'm sorry that we used that time to swipe at each other instead of talk. Logan has never meant more to me than you or Dad or Joey, but he was, and will be, a big part of my life."

"I know. I was jealous of that. We never had mother/daughter lunches or went to get our nails done. We never went out of town to go shopping because you were always with Logan and wearing cheap jeans and shirts didn't bother you. You never . . . it was all Logan, and it shouldn't have upset me, but it did."

"Why didn't you ever tell me that?"

"What am I going to say to a ten-year old girl who liked to hang out with the kid down the street? I'd sound crazy. I didn't have Joey to replace you, but when he came along, he gave me something to do, someone to take care of. You were always Logan's little mommy. Little mommy bringing him lunch, kissing away his owies. You never needed me, and taking care of Joey, that felt good. I latched on to him. Maybe too much. Maybe if I would have given him space, encouraged him to be more independent . . ."

"He was. He was always flying around the neighborhood on his bike. You didn't smother him. You were a good mother, to both of us."

"I want to believe that, but I'll always wonder if I had done something differently, if Joey would still be alive."

"There's no point in wondering about things like that. We can't change the past, we can only try to do better, be better, in the future. Things are going to have to change. I can't do this anymore, and Logan won't let me. He asked me to marry him, and I said yes."

"You two made up? The last I remember, you said he didn't want you."

"Someone told him I was the one in the car accident and it changed how he thought about a few things. He went to see Gunner and . . . closed out that part of his life. It's been a long time. Eighteen years since Logan left town, twelve years since Joey's passed on. We can take this chance to look forward or we can keep wallowing in the past. I want to move forward. Logan loves me, and I love him, too. We're getting married, and I'm moving to Decatur. Not right away, things take time, but I want you to know that's what the plan is and if you want to move too, then you're more than welcome. Logan will help you find an attorney, and we can ask for rehab and community service instead of jail time. You didn't hurt anybody but yourself."

"That's not true. I hurt you."

"Yeah, you did. I've never not loved you, Mom."

"I know, and I'm sorry I ever thought it. Come here."

She leaned over and rested her head on her mother's stomach.

Rosie brushed her hair from her face, an IV taped to her wrist hindering her movements. It was the first time her mother had shown her any affection since Joey passed away.

She sat up and wiped her eyes.

"When are you getting married? In the summer?" Rosie asked, wiping her eyes, too. "A wedding by the lake would be beautiful."

Shaking her head, she said, "No. Logan doesn't want to wait. We're getting married tonight at the courthouse."

Rosie's face fell. "I know I don't deserve to be there . . . I haven't been a mother to you for a long time. You and Logan are a good match and always have been. After I clean up, I hope you'll let me be a part of your lives."

"I would like that, but Logan and James have a law firm in Decatur. He said he would move back to Rocky Point if I wanted to stay, but I don't want to live here anymore."

"Decatur's a nice city." Rosie smiled tentatively.

"Joey's grave is here. Would you be okay moving?"

Rosie scratched at the tape keeping her IV in place. "I think I could compromise . . . if you're open to that."

"What kind of compromise?" she asked cautiously.

"I'd like to buy a plot near him in the cemetery, if I can. When I die, I want to be with him. I don't want him to be alone."

She squeezed Rosie's hand. "I have some money saved, and we can arrange that . . . well, you need an attorney. We're going to try to keep you out of jail, but after you're discharged, that's probably where you'll go until you see a judge and we can pay your bail. Logan will get that part worked out. He knows more, okay?"

"I'm not worried about it, Ivy. I'll take the punishment I deserve and we'll go from there. Thank you. For coming to see me. For not giving up on me."

"You're my mom and we're family, but you said some nasty things about Logan and none of them were true. He did what he thought was best, and that's all anyone can do. I've let it go, and you'll have to, too."

"He loves you, and tonight he'll promise to take care of you forever. That means more than anything else."

"Thank you."

"Take pictures for me, please?"

"Sure, Mom."

"And one more favor."

"What is it?"

"My dress. I still have it. In the back of my closet in a plastic tote. Your dad and I didn't make it, but . . . it's a simple style. Nothing fancy. If it fits you, I'd be happy if you wore it."

"I didn't know you saved it." She could have sworn she knew every item in their apartment. She moved everything they were allowed to keep herself.

"I knew what was happening and that it was my fault, but I couldn't do anything to stop it. My heart had shut down and I'd given up. I hid a few things to remember happier times. One day I'll try to find your dad. He left because of me and I'll apologize and tell him I don't blame him."

"I'll look. Do you want me to bring you back anything? Magazines? A book?"

"No, baby, but thanks. It will do me a bit of good to spend some time inside my head and work out a few things."

"Okay. Get some rest. We have a lot to do." She kissed her mother's cheek.

Pushing back tears, she stepped into the quiet hallway. No more crying. No more unhappiness. Today would start the rest of her life, and she'd hold on with both hands and not let go.

But first, she had an idea. She didn't want to get married without her mom, and if anyone could make that happen, it would be Logan.

In the dim room lit only by flickering candles and the light seeping underneath the door, he and Ivy stood at the foot of

Rosie's bed, his hands shaky and sweaty as he held on to her steady ones.

The hospital's chaplain quoted the scripture that was spoken at every wedding. Love is patient, love is kind. Truer words had never been spoken.

Ivy was the epitome of patience and kindness. Not only since he'd been back in Rocky Point, but always. When she looked out for him all those years, making sure he had something to eat, helping him do his schoolwork, being someone he could depend on. She'd been showing him love, even when back then neither of them would have called it that.

She looked beautiful wearing a simple white dress she said belonged to Rosie, her hair pinned into a messy bun, holding a bouquet of white roses Marnie reminded him at the last minute to buy at the flower shop.

His future mother-in-law had burst into tears when they told her that instead of the courthouse, they would be married in her hospital room.

Elora sat by Rosie's bed, holding her hand.

The evening nurses stood off to the side. One of them asked if they could watch, and he agreed because nothing mattered except he was marrying the little girl he'd fallen in love with.

The chaplain pulled him out of his haze.

"Do you, Logan, take Ivy to be your wife from this day forward, to join with her and share all that is to come, and to be faithful until death parts you?"

He cleared his throat. What a fool he'd look like if he couldn't answer because he was crying. "I do."

Ivy pushed the ring she'd chosen for him onto his finger.

A nurse sniffled.

The chaplain turned to Ivy. "And do you, Ivy, take Logan to be your husband from this day forward, to join with him and share all that is to come, and to be faithful until death parts you?"

"I do," she whispered.

His hands trembling, he gently slid the silver ring onto her finger.

"Then with the power vested in me by God and the state of Minnesota, I now pronounce you husband and wife. You may kiss your bride, Mr. Draper."

His bride.

He liked the sound of that, but as he cuddled her against his chest and pressed his lips to hers, he knew she was more than just his bride. From this evening on, he would do whatever he needed to protect her and keep her safe. She was his everything.

The same promise sparkled in her eyes.

After years of being apart, he found his way back to her, where he'd always been meant to be, and Ivy, with all her grace, accepted him like she always had.

It humbled him.

He swore, as she wrapped her arms around him, he would never take it for granted.

Ivy stood on the small porch of Logan's cabin, shivering in her pajamas and jacket, wearing her boots without socks.

She kept running the simple ceremony through her mind, how wonderful it had been, how her mother cried knowing she'd be able to watch her say her vows.

The evening had been perfect.

"Ivy?" Logan said behind her. He hugged her, wrapping

his arms around her. "Are you okay?" he asked, sounding concerned.

She hadn't meant to worry him. "Yeah. Just getting some air."

He turned her to face him. "Are you sure? You don't regret tonight, do you?" Moonlight glinted off his glasses.

She rubbed her thumb over his cheek. "No. I was thinking about how lovely it was."

"Good. Come to bed. I want to make love to my wife."

Amused, she smiled. "Again?"

"You mean twice is enough?"

"It will never be enough." She laughed. "Tell me you love me."

"God, Ivy. I don't think I'll ever be able to tell you how much, or show you how much." He lifted her onto the railing and stepped between her legs.

She rested her arms on his shoulders and linked her fingers. Taking a deep breath, she said, "Logan, I couldn't sleep because I want you to know I don't blame you for breaking our engagement. You *do* know that, right?" She'd laid next to him, his breathing slow and deep in sleep, but her mind kept churning over what he said before, the meanings behind the words. "You don't have to make it up to me because there's nothing to make up for. We were married tonight and the past is gone. We put rings on each other's fingers and promised our lives to each other. Don't ruin what we have because you're trying to apologize for something that doesn't need it. We're equals now."

He scoffed. "Ivy, I broke your trust. How can you say I don't need to repair that?"

"Because the vows you told me tonight did that. Your promises did that. The way you love me, it does that. And that's all I need."

He cried into her hair, and the last remnants of the past faded into the frozen air.

"I hope those are happy tears."

He chuckled. "Yeah, they are."

"Good. Are you sure Elora's okay spending the night in my mom's room? I know she said she and Rosie have a lot to talk about, but it won't be comfortable sleeping there. We should go pick her up."

"My mom wanted to stay with her. She didn't want Rosie to be alone, *and* she wanted us to have the cabin to ourselves. We can move into your apartment tomorrow. I don't know how long Mom's going to stay in Rocky Point, but for now, let's go back to sleep. We can play musical beds tomorrow."

"If you're sure," she said, shivering.

"I am. I learned a long time ago not to argue with my mother. You're cold. Let me warm you up."

He carried her to bed and after more promises in the dark, she dozed, secure in her husband's arms, his ring on her finger, his love in her heart.

And right before sleep claimed her, Joey's laughter rang throughout the room, and she smiled.

Cole and Autumn's story is now available! *Her Frozen Promises* is available on Kindle, in Kindle Unlimited, and Paperback.

Do you like billionaire romance? Sign up for my newsletter and receive a free standalone novel, an ugly-duckling billionaire romance, *My Biggest Mistake*. There you'll be the first to know of sales, new releases, and what I'm working on. Don't miss out! Go to www.vmrheault.com/subscribe.

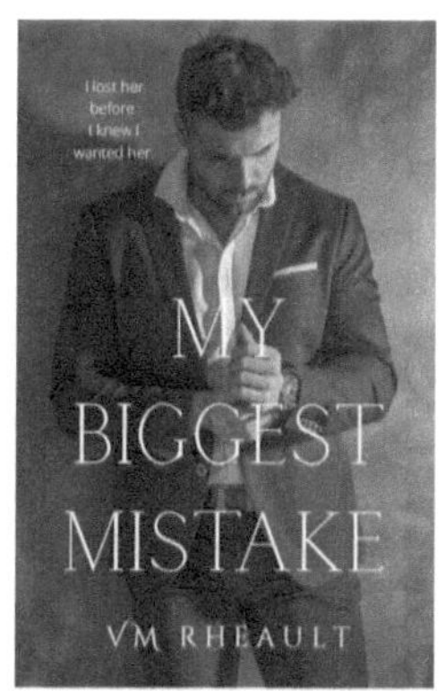

ALSO BY VANIA RHEAULT

Don't Run Away

(Tower City Romance Trilogy Book One)

Chasing You

(Tower City Romance Trilogy Book Two)

Running Scared

(Tower City Romance Trilogy Book Three)

The Finish Line

(Tower City Romance Trilogy Book Four,

Bonus Novella)

Wherever He Goes

(A Steamy Forced Proximity Standalone)

The Years Between Us

(A Steamy Age-Gap Standalone)

All of Nothing

(A Steamy Enemies to Lovers Standalone)

His Frozen Heart

(A Rocky Point Wedding Book One)

His Frozen Dreams

(A Rocky Point Wedding Book Two)

Her Frozen Memories

(A Rocky Point Wedding Book Three)

Her Frozen Promises

(A Rocky Point Wedding Book Four)

As VM Rheault

Captivated by Her (Cedar Hill Duet Book One)

Addicted to Her (Cedar Hill Duet Book Two)

Rescue Me

Give & Take (The Lost & Found Trilogy Book One)

Lost & Found (The Lost & Found Trilogy Book Two)

Safe & Sound (The Lost & Found Trilogy Book Three)

Faking Forever

Twisted Alibis (Ghost Town Trilogy Book One)

Twisted Lullabies (Ghost Town Trilogy Book Two)

Twisted Lies (Ghost Town Trilogy Book Three)

A Heartache for Christmas

Cruel Fate (King's Crossing Book One)

Cruel Hearts (King's Crossing Book Two)

Cruel Dreams (King's Crossing Book Three)

Shattered Fate (King's Crossing Book Four)

Shattered Hearts (King's Crossing Book Five)

Shattered Dreams (King's Crossing Book Six)

ABOUT THE AUTHOR

Vania Rheault has lived in Minnesota all her life. In 2003,
she graduated with a BA in English with a concentration in
creative writing from Minnesota State University,
Moorhead. When she's not writing, she's sleeping, working
her day job, or going to movie night with her sister.
Find her at vmrheault.com